BALLENGER

MATT BANNISTER WESTERN 8

KEN PRATT

Published in the United States by Wolfpack Publishing, Las Vegas

CKN Christian Publishing
An Imprint of Wolfpack Publishing
6032 Wheat Penny Avenue
Las Vegas, NV 89122

christiankindlenews.com

Paperback ISBN: 978-1-64734-038-4
eBook ISBN: 978-1-64734-037-7
Library of Congress Control Number: 2020938990

BALLENGER

Dedication

On a personal note, two women that are very important in my life were in abusive marriages. One was my mother, and the other was my wife before I met her. My wife and I raised three daughters and our fear was they would date and fall in love with abusive men. There were "red flags" that we were quite aware of and tried to teach our girls to watch out for. This story is a cautionary tale.

This book is dedicated to those who are in an abusive relationship. It's scary to make a significant change, but something's got to change. If you or someone you know is in an abusive relationship, make the call.

National Domestic Violence Hotline 1-800-799-7233

Acknowledgments

As always, I want to offer my appreciation to my wife, Cathy, for always listening and getting her feedback to my questions and, at times, direction. My son, Keith, for his brutal honesty, which I appreciate a lot. I need to thank my daughter Katie for her technical suggestions and help. Having a large family where every one of them are both supportive and encouraging is a blessing that I can not express enough appreciation for.

I also want to express my gratitude for the people who make this book possible, the staff of CKN Christian Publishing. A special thank you to Mike Bray, Lauren Bridges, Rachel Del Grosso, and Tracey Govender too.

1

Matt Bannister had spent a good portion of the day settling a property line dispute between neighbors about seven miles from Branson. He had to get a copy of the county plat map and measure to the property line, which was fenced correctly, but one troublemaking neighbor insisted he was being robbed of a fifty-foot swath of fifty acres. The farmer apologized to his neighbor for being wrong and his false allegations. In all, it felt like a waste of a sunny but cold early December day. It had snowed a few days before, and a few inches remained on the ground. The property dispute made for a long day of hammering stakes in the field and measuring, but the deed was finally done.

Matt wore his buffalo skin coat to keep him warm, and a brown Stetson hat to keep the sun's glare off the snow out of his eyes. His long dark hair was in a ponytail hidden beneath his coat, and his beard was nicely groomed on his strong-featured handsome face. Although his brown eyes appeared to be a bit bored as he rode back into town. He passed Rose Street and began to hear some screaming from the next block over, by the sound of it. It wasn't a scream like someone being startled or seeing some horrifying sight; it was the scream of a child that was in a great deal of pain. Matt kicked his horse to a gallop and turned up Dogwood Street and then onto Second Street to the source of the screams.

The Dogwood Shacks was a single level housing complex with twenty small apartments. It was shaped like a horseshoe with six apartments on one side leading back away from Second Street with eight apartments stretching across the center, and six more leading back to Second Street. The design left a small space in the center that some folks called a courtyard with a single willow tree at its center. Initially, it was an unusual design with benches under the tree and a beautiful little place to live for the hardworking people of Branson. But, over the past twenty years, it had become a cockroach-infested, rat filled, nearly debilitated complex for the poorest citizens, prostitutes, and those barely able to keep a roof over their heads. The property was owned by Big John Pederson, the owner of Ugly John's Saloon, and as long as he got his ten dollar's rent per apartment a month, he couldn't care less what happened there. Maybe that was one reason why none of the people standing outside watching had interfered with the screaming Matt heard.

A man had a little girl, no older than six years

old bending over a bench that was pulled over near the door of their apartment, with her dress pulled up over her head, exposing her bare skin while he whipped her with a three-foot-long willow switch. The back of her legs and her naked buttocks were red with welts that were clearly visible as the man beat her upper legs again. She screamed in agony as her wailing was uncontrollable.

The man shouted at the little girl, "Rrr...really! Say it right, damn it! Now say it!"

Through her sobs, she cried out, "Wheely. I keep saying it," she sobbed desperately.

"Not wheely, really! With an R!" He yelled and began whipping her again brutally as he shouted, "Now say the damn word right!"

Matt jumped off his horse, flicked off his hat, and handed the reins to a lady standing near them, and walked quickly to the man and caught his hand before he could strike the child again. He yanked the switch out of the man's hand and pushed him away from the girl.

The man turned around and seen Matt's enraged expression. He held up his hands defensively. "Marshal..."

Matt glared at the man fiercely. He shouted, "You're beating a child for not saying a word correctly?" He didn't wait for an answer; he swung the willow switch and struck the man across the cheek.

The man grabbed his face and cried out in pain. He turned his back to Matt and was struck again across the back of his thigh. When the man reached down to protect his stinging leg, he was struck across the ear, then his across leg again. The man tried to speak but collapsed to the ground hoping for a moment of mercy. Matt struck him again and again, whipping him across his body from his head to his ankles repeatedly. Whatever was unprotected by the man's arms was open for a full-force swing by a powerful and angry man with a downward swing. The level of pain increased until the man curled up in a ball on the ground and began sobbing himself.

Matt stopped and breathing hard, said, "Say wheely!"

Through his painful sobs, the man said, "Really."

Matt began lashing him with the switch again until he cried out loudly. Matt stopped. "That's not what I said! Say it wrong. Wheely."

"Wheely." The man sobbed, holding onto his thigh, where the last strike hit.

Matt knelt in front of him. "It doesn't hurt so much to pronounce it wrong after all, does it? She's just a little girl. Leave her be!" He glanced up at the mother who was holding the crying child in her arms. The mother was crying too. Matt stood up and stepped nearer to her. "Don't ever let your husband beat on her like that again! Good heavens, what is wrong with you? You see the welts on her, right? Isn't that enough? Over a mispronounced word, you stood there and let him beat your daughter? And keep beating her expecting her to say it right when she has trouble with her R's obviously!" he shouted. "Do you think hitting her is going to help that? If you love your daughter, get that piece of trash out of here. If I ever catch her father doing that again, I will throw him jail and forget he's in there. And he might come out with trouble pronouncing his R's too!"

"He's not her father, Joe Thorn is," she said softly.

"I'm sorry to hear that," Matt said, knowing the character of Joe Thorn.

"It wasn't by choice, Marshal." She was a fragile woman in her late twenties with a thin face and uncared for brown hair that fell lazily to her shoulders. She wasn't overly attractive nor too appealing, but her eyes revealed the sorrow that had taken over her young life. She explained, "My family disowned me when I got pregnant, and my stepfather didn't believe me when I told him what had happened."

"And who is this?" He pointed at the man sitting up against the building, wiping his eyes dry. He was an older man in his forties. He had a balding head of light brown hair and a round face to match his short, stout and round body. He had a pointed nose and two red welts across his clean-shaven face. He didn't appear to be dressed as impoverished as the young mother was.

"Roger Stevens. The new schoolteacher. He was helping Bonnie with her reading and the way she talks."

Matt grimaced. "You have to be kidding me." He stepped back to Roger Stevens. "You're the new schoolteacher?"

He nodded silently.

"There is no way I will permit you to teach our children like this. I'll be taking this to the city council today. You're gone, or every parent in this community will know the kind of man you are. Quit your job and get out of town." He turned back to the young mother. "What's your name?"

"Viola Goddard. This, is my daughter, Bonnie." She turned Bonnie around to face Matt.

"Take care of her, Viola. Can I speak with your parents and let them know the kind of man Joe is? Maybe they'll change their minds and help you out some. Maybe?" he asked.

She smirked sadly and shook her head. "I'm dead to them, and you can't resurrect a relationship with them. Thanks anyway. I'm taking her inside; it's too cold for her out here."

"Nice to meet you, Miss Goddard." He watched her take her crying girl inside and close the door behind her. Matt walked past a few onlookers and reached for his reins and thanked the young lady who held them.

A young man stepped quickly towards Matt. "You're Matt Bannister? The Marshal?" he asked with a grin.

"I am."

"Nice to meet you. Wow, we've never met anyone famous before. We just moved here a couple of weeks ago, and not so sure about the people around here. I didn't want to stop that man because I don't know if I'd get shot or not. By the way, I'm Martin Ballenger, and that's my little sister that you handed your reins to. And that over there is my mother, Sylvia. We just moved here from a town over by Salem. A small little farm town you probably never heard of. I worked at the silver mine for a few days but realized I prefer above ground work. I heard you might be in the market for a deputy? I heard one of your men was hurt pretty bad. Are you hiring?"

Matt shook the man's hand and nodded at his mother and sister. He shook his head. "No, I'm not hiring. Welcome to town. It's nice meeting you, folks." He swung up in the saddle and said, "Thank you," as Sylvia Ballenger handed him his hat.

"Thank you, Marshal, for stopping that man. I hate to see anyone being hurt, especially a child. I'm Sylvia Ballenger; this is my son, Martin, and my daughter Barbra. My husband left us a long time ago, so it's just us three." Sylvia was in her early forties with thick brown hair that fell to her shoulders, with a hair comb holding her bangs out of her eyes. She had an oblong face with round lively brown eyes and had a flirtatious expression on her face.

"It was my pleasure. It was nice to meet you, folks."

Martin Ballenger sputtered before Matt could ride away, "Hey, do you know where else I could look for work? I may not know much outside of farming, but I can learn anything quick." He was shorter than an average-sized man in his mid to late twenties. He had straight short light brown hair that was uncombed and fell flat against his head. He was clean-shaven except for a light brown goatee that was shaped into a point an inch below his chin. He had a thin body and a narrow face, but he was a handsome and respectable looking young man with large blue eyes that were his most prominent feature. He didn't look very robust, but he seemed persistent if nothing else.

"You could try the sawmill, any of the stores, grist mill, or if you want to go out there, there's the granite quarry about two miles north of here. Or if you want to be a lawman, there's always the sheriff you could try. I took his best man not long ago."

"Hey, I'll go see him right now!"

Sylvia tapped Matt's knee to get his attention. "Marshal, I have some soup on the stove and some fresh buttermilk or hot coffee if you'd like to come inside and warm up for a spell."

He smiled uneasily. "No, thank you, Miss Ballenger. I must be going."

"I wanted to offer it anyway. We don't know anyone around here yet, and just settling in. I don't want to come across as too forward, but I notice you're not wearing a ring. Are you not married? Because if not, I could change that for you." She raised her eyebrows up and down twice before smiling.

She was an attractive lady for being in her mid-forties, and Matt couldn't help but smile. "I do have a lady friend that I'm pretty well stuck on. Nice to meet you folks, though," he said with a slight chuckle as he rode away.

Sylvia Ballenger looked at her twenty-seven-year-old son. "You should go speak with the sheriff and say whatever you must to get him to hire you on. We need money, or we're going to starve. Barbra, you're old enough to help bring money in. Tomorrow morning, I want you to find a real job."

"I have one, Mama." Fifteen-year-old Barbra Ballenger said softly.

"Watching that baby across the way is not a job. Fifty cents a week is not going to get us out of this cesspool and into a house."

Barbra rolled her eyes. She watched Bonnie Goddard while her mother, Viola, worked in Ugly John's Saloon.

"Yeah, I'll go see the sheriff right now," Martin said with a determined look in his eyes.

2

"What's going on?" Bella asked several of her dancers who were lined up in the dance hall front entry looking outside through the door window.

A red-haired dancer named Rose Blanchard answered with a devious smirk on her cute freckled face, "Edith and her beloved Paul are arguing. And it looks like a big one."

Bella frowned and peered out the window. Out on the street in front of the dance hall, Edith Williams spoke heatedly to Paul Johnson, who seemed to be taking a verbal beating with his head down and then replying heatedly himself when he reacted to her words with strong emotions. "Can you hear what they're saying?" Bella asked anyone who would answer.

"No!" Rose said with disappointment in her humored expression. "I've been trying to hear, but these girls won't quit rambling on in here."

Helen Monroe answered sadly from her seat on

the staircase that led to the ladies' rooms upstairs, "I think he's ending their courtship."

Bella turned to her. "Why?"

Helen raised her eyebrows with a full eye roll. "Paul doesn't want to marry an ex-whore. He's always kind of been slow to move their relationship forward anyway."

Bella groaned. "And she was the one afraid to commit to him originally. I could wring his neck if he breaks her heart. It seems like all she's ever known is heartbreak, and if this man throws her away like a dirty dishrag, I'll never let him in here again." Bella was the owner of Bella's Dance Hall. She was a sixty-one-year-old graying brown-haired lady, who was a bit rough occasionally but had a heart of gold for her girls. She wore beautiful expensive dresses and kept her hair in an elaborately weaved bun.

Helen sighed. "I know. He was so eager to court her at first, and she was so scared to open up and let him get to know her, and now that she has, he doesn't want her," Helen said with a sad frown. "Sam and I have both tried to talk to Paul, and although he hasn't said it, I think that's why he wants to end it with her." Helen Monroe was Edith's best friend and was being courted by Sam Troyer, Paul's best friend. The four of them had become good friends in the six months that they've known each other.

"Is there another woman?" Bella asked bluntly.

Helen shrugged. "I don't think so. I just think it's the fact that she has a whoring past and he can't forget about it. It's not like he's the pope or all too wholesome himself either."

"And what about Sam? Is he going to let you go too?" Bella asked pointedly with a touch of irritation in her voice.

There was a fear in every one of the dance hall ladies that their appeal to the men would cease, and their earnings would become less until they were let go, and a younger and prettier girl was hired to replace them. It was a real fear because their income and their home were dependent upon Bella and the number of dances and drinks the ladies could sell on a nightly basis. For Helen, the fear of being replaced was elevated because she knew she wasn't as pretty as any of the other girls, and her last dance auction bids were consistently lower than any of the other ladies. Being the lowest earner on a consistent nightly basis was a good indication that sooner than later, she would be replaced. For most women who were released from the dance hall, if they hadn't found a man to marry, they lost their income and their home and were forced into prostitution to survive. Luckily, Helen had met Sam Troyer, and he had fallen in love with her. Sam and Paul were best friends and lived together in a small house across town. Sam had proposed to Helen not long before, and they were engaged to be married; but hadn't set a wedding date as of yet. Helen wanted an outside wedding, and they were waiting for better weather. To answer Bella's question, she held up her left hand with the palm down to show her bare fingers to Bella. "No, I don't have a ring yet, but we're still engaged."

A blonde named Angela sighed, "I want to be engaged."

Rose Blanchard scoffed. "It's overrated, Angela. Dance as long as you can, I'm telling you."

Bella smiled comfortingly at Helen. She feared Helen would have no place to go when she was released from the dance hall. Bella loved all her girls and wished them all the best, but the dance hall was a business, and there was the heartache of letting the lowest producers go if she couldn't get them married off first. Helen Monroe had her days in the sun, but those days were dwindling quickly. "Good," Bella said pointedly. "I don't need two heartbroken women here."

Outside, Edith slapped Paul's face and screamed a few words before turning away from him and storming towards the door.

"Geez!" Rose laughed.

"Get back, ladies, let her through," Bella ordered.

The door opened, and Edith saw the women lined up by the stairs wanting to pry into her and Paul's private business. "Excuse me, maybe next time I can take my private conversations to your rooms!" Edith's pretty blue eyes were red with tears. "Excuse me," she said as she made her way to the stairs and ran up them quickly, beginning to sob under her breath. A moment later came the sound of a door slamming shut.

Rose sighed purposely. "And there, Angela, is love in a nutshell," she quipped.

Bella walked to the stairs and tapped Helen's shoulder. "Come with me. You all get busy with your chores today."

Bella knocked on Edith's door and opened it slowly. "Sweetheart, Helen and I are coming in, okay?"

Edith was lying on her bed with her face buried in her pillow, crying when they entered. Bella sat on the edge of the bed softly and laid a tender hand on Edith's back as Helen closed the door behind her. "What happened, Sweetheart?"

"It's over..." she mumbled from inside the pillow.

"Why?"

Edith looked up from the pillow with reddened eyes as another tear slipped out of her eyes. "He doesn't think he can love me like he's supposed to. He wants to be free. He wants to be free like a raven in the sky."

"A scavenger, huh?" Bella asked, disappointed. "Well, Sweetheart, you're too beautiful to be dead meat. We need to find you a sparrow for you to build your nest with, not a scavenger. Did I ever tell you about the birds and the bees?"

"Yes," she moaned and buried her head back into the pillow.

"Well, let me tell you again. Bees fly around until they find a pretty flower and land on it for a bit to get some nectar and leave some pollen. Then it goes to tell its friends about the flower and the friends come flying by to see what nectar they can find before they move on to the next pretty flower. Their motive is always the same; to get some nectar and leave some pollen. You see, all the bees want from the pretty blossom is its nectar. Nothing more. When the nectar is used up, the flower is forgotten about; it's of no more use. Bees never settle down; they just pollinate until they die. You can't trust a bee, you never know precisely when they're going to sting you, and that sting can hurt. You're a beautiful flower, but like I always warn you girls, don't give your nectar away without a wedding ring first.

"Birds on the other hand and I'm talking about sparrows, look for a safe place to build their nest and every day they're out there laboring for a stick, a blade of straw or grass, whatever they can find to build a nest for their home. They meet another sparrow, and together they labor to make the nest safe, warm, and cozy for the future eggs they will raise together. The mother and father share the duties and labor daily to feed each other and their babies too. Sparrows stay together for life, just like we're supposed to when we get married. They strive to make a good safe home and live a good life. Sparrows are committed to the love they have for their future and their family. And that's the difference between the birds and the bees. One wants nectar and the chance to pollinate every pretty flower they see. The other wants love, commitment, and a family. It's up to you to decide which one you are. A pretty blossom that fades a little more with every bee she let's fertilize it, or a sparrow working to make a long-lasting home with a life long commitment of love. My dear ladies, a handsome hard-working sparrow, has no use for a used up and wilting flower. Be a sparrow."

"I feel like a fool, is what I feel like."

Bella said softly, "Edith, you're a sparrow, that's

what you are. You need to find another sparrow to love you for the rest of your life. And you will. Take tonight off and rest up. It'll be okay."

Edith glanced up at Bella with her reddened wet eyes. "I love him, Bella."

Bella smiled empathetically. "I know. And I'm proud of you for allowing yourself to fall in love again. I know it wasn't easy for you to do that as bad as you've been treated in the past..."

"What's wrong with me?" Edith asked suddenly. "Why does every man I love...How come I can't keep them? What's wrong with me? Helen has Sam and Christine has Matt, all my friends find love, why can't I?" she wept.

Helen spoke bluntly, "I think Paul's a jackass for losing you! You are so much better than he'll ever find."

Bella nodded. "That's true. Sweetheart, there's nothing wrong with you. You are amazing and so beautiful. One of these days, some Prince Charming will come in here and sweep you off your feet like Matt did Christine. And you know, I remember her and I had a talk very similar to this one right before she met Matt. Keep your head held high and don't frown too long over Paul. If he's stupid enough to let you go, then move on to someone smarter and let him sit in his foolishness. Don't waste time looking back; it gains nothing for tomorrow."

3

Matt Banister walked into the Marshal's Office and rested his hands on the three-foot partition that separated the entry from the main office. He looked at his deputies Truet Davis, Nate Robertson, and Jed Clark. Matt didn't look pleased. "Three things I need to tell you all. First, Deputy Marshal Phillip will be returning to work in two weeks. We want the scar on his cheek to be completely healed, and Phillip used to talking again before he comes back here. From this point on, Phillip will be confined to doing the office work and not participating in anymore outside deputy duties."

Nate frowned. "So, he really is a secretary?" Nate had made it a constant joke to poke fun at Phillip for doing woman's work. It was no longer funny to him now that Phillip was injured, while Nate was out of town for Thanksgiving.

"Basically. Don't tease him about it anymore. Secondly," Matt paused and shook his head with disgust.

"What?" Truet asked, already having a good idea of what it was.

Matt continued, "Our District Attorney has dismissed all charges against all seven of the mine employees for busting up our office and the murders of Chee Yik, Kot-Kho-Not, and the scourging of Ah See. They said I had no evidence since Leroy's whip was taken out of my office when they busted this place up. The only man that was punished was Oscar Belding, and the Slater Mining Company's Attorney plea-bargained that down to a fine and compensation to Phillip. The Slater's will pay for both it appears, to keep their name in the good graces of the city. So, there you have it. Leroy Haywood, Oscar Belding, and Roger Lavigne are getting away with murder, and there's not a thing we can do about it. If you have a chance to arrest them for any reason, do not hesitate to do so."

Jed Clark said scornfully, "There's no justice here if you're Chinese, that's for sure."

Truet leaned back in his chair with his boots on his desk and looked over at Jed. "It's good to be rich enough; you can purchase a murder and the courts, right?"

"Yeah. It must be nice not to fear anyone or anything. By the way, what's the third thing, Boss?"

Matt sighed. "When William and I went to Prairieville, we ended up shooting the Sheriff Chuck Dielschneider in the back. A letter came in today, saying he died of an infection due to his wounds. That probably doesn't mean too much to you, but the Dielschneider family seemed pretty close-knit, and now three of them are dead, and a fourth lost his hand. They have a sister that doesn't like me much and quite a few friends. I doubt any will come looking for trouble, but another family was good friends with them. The Crowe Brothers, who happen to be the cousins of either the Sperry's or the Helms' or maybe both, I'm not sure which. They're bad news at any rate. If any of you hear anything about them coming into town, let me know. I don't want any of you facing them alone, are we clear?"

"Sure," Nate said, looking at Matt with a concerned expression. "Are you worried about them coming here?"

Matt shook his head. "I'm not worried, but I am cautious. William and I shattered the hub of their criminal monopoly of that rural part of Oregon. The only thing that does scare me a bit is if they move over here and join up with their cousins. The Sperry-Helms Gang has gotten away with too much around here and are dangerous enough without joining up with the Crowe Brothers. I'll put it to you all this way, if they do show up, keep your guns oiled."

Jed answered, "I always do."

Truet asked, "So, is this getting away with a murder going to happen every time we arrest a mine employee?"

Matt shook his head. "Leroy's wife told me that Josh Slater himself told him to pick two men and go meet those Chinese men out at the quarry. She said he would pay them for their missing a day of work. I'm assuming it'll happen like this anytime

Josh or anyone else in their corporate office sets it up. To answer your question, I don't know. Josh played stupid when I asked him about it. He plays stupid a lot."

"It's not an act," Truet said simply.

Matt smiled slightly. "I know."

"So, Leroy Haywood, Oscar Belding, and Roger Lavigne are getting away with torture and murder, huh?" Truet asked no one in particular. "That's a shame."

Matt stood up straight. "Listen fella's; it's kind of a laid-back day, so let's close the office and get some lunch. I'll even pay today."

They walked down Main Street towards Regory's Italian Restaurant on the way they were met on the boardwalk by the Branson Sheriff, Tim Wright. He was with a young man wearing a Branson Deputy Sheriff's badge on his dingy brown coat. He was a thin young man with a narrow face with big blue eyes and goatee that came to a sharp point an inch under his chin. He wasn't a bad looking young man but was slight in physical stature.

"Gentlemen," Tim said with importance. "I'd like to introduce you to my new deputy, Martin Ballenger. Martin, this is the famous Matt Bannister, and his deputies, Truet Davis, Nate Robertson and Jed, the judas, Clark. I think Martin's going to fit into our community well," Tim said with a friendly smile to Matt.

"Judas?" Jed repeated with a laugh. "You're a joke." Jed was a former deputy of Tim's until he recently began working for Matt in the Marshal's Office.

Martin smiled and offered his hand to shake as

he said, "Marshal, it's good to see you again. Thank you for recommending me to the Sheriff's Office. I'm excited to work with you all."

"Yes, thank you for recommending him," Tim said appreciatively.

Matt nodded. "You're welcome." He added while Martin shook hands with the other men, "Congratulations on finding a job so quickly, Martin. I hope you honor your badge and what it stands for and not use it for your personal gain."

"Of course. I've always wanted to be a lawman, and now I am. Today we're just out meeting the folks around town, but I'll be making arrests in no time. I believe in the law and will enforce it for sure. And if I need help, I've got the sheriff to back me up, and if that isn't enough, I now know you fellas. I look forward to working with you all."

Tim spoke, "Let's go meet some other folks, Martin. The Marshal and his boys are busy."

Nate spoke as Tim and Martin walked away, "Well, Jed, there's your replacement. You shouldn't have been such a judas in the first place. Let it be known; lord Tim replaced you, Judas."

Jed smirked. "Matt, I just want to say thank you for hiring me. Because I like you guys, especially this big dumb blonde kid." He backhanded Nate's stomach playfully.

"I kind of like him too," Matt said. "And I'm glad you're with us. I think we all are."

"Yep," Truet agreed. "I think we have a good bunch of strong men and not scrawny weak-willed boys like the sheriff hires."

Matt smiled. "I don't like to judge people really, but when Martin asked me if I was looking to hire a deputy, I looked him over and thought the guy couldn't fight his way out of a newspaper suit, let alone arrest someone like Leroy Haywood. And we don't always need to use our guns to make an arrest. I have a feeling Martin's in over his head, and dog-paddling against the current just isn't going to do it for him. In other words, I wouldn't hire him even if I was hiring for a deputy."

Nate spoke, "I get it because that's what I thought when I first saw Jed." Nate was over six feet tall and was a big man with broad shoulders and muscular. He weighed close to two hundred pounds with short blonde hair and blue eyes on a clean-shaven face that revealed his youth. He was twenty-six years old and already showing his grit when it came to being new to the life of a lawman. Jed, on the other hand, was close to forty years old and weighed a hundred and sixty pounds at most. He was five foot ten inches tall and slim with short brown hair with a long mustache that went down to his chin. He was the smallest of the four men, but his hazel-green eyes revealed a toughness that not many others wanted to challenge.

Jed smiled and chuckled a bit at Nate's words. "Matt, if we ever get into a gunfight, stick me with this big blonde goof so I can watch him piss his pants, will ya?"

Nate laughed with the others. "You just want to use me for cover."

Jed laughed. "That too, yeah."

4

Henry Redlin was the owner of Redlin Meats, a butcher shop on the north end of town on First Street across the road from the livery stable. Henry and Old Pete O'Grady, who owned the stables, had an agreement where livestock could graze in a pasture or be kept penned in a barn beside the stables until they were butchered as needed. A continuous flow of livestock and poultry was housed next to the stables until they were slaughtered. Redlin Meats had the freshest and most delicate cuts of meat in town. It was a small butcher shop despite its reputation, and Henry lived in a small house beside the shop. He was a lifelong bachelor with a good reputation for being a friendly man and treating people well. Henry wasn't one to be seen around town much and stayed to himself, keeping busy in either his slaughterhouse behind the shop or in the backroom of his butcher shop cutting meat for the next day. He worked long hours and didn't seem to enjoy much more than his chosen career path. The busiest time of year was between Thanksgiving and Christmas when poultry was quickly his biggest seller. Turkey for those who could afford it, and chicken, duck, and quail for those who couldn't. Beef still ruled the typical dinner plates, along with pork, venison, elk, and when delivered fresh salmon, crab, and oysters as well. He was a busy man and seldom had time for idle chit-chat with his customers. He had two employees to help slaughter the product, whatever it was, and help prepare the meat. He had orders from most of the restaurants in town that wanted quality meat and many walk-in customers looking for a steak, pork chops, or whatever else they might want for dinner.

Henry was a large man at six feet and one inch tall and a bit obese at nearly two hundred and sixty pounds. He had short black hair and a full-faced beard on his round face. His beady brown eyes appeared too small under thick eyebrows, and having a large nose hadn't attracted too many women, but what he lacked in looks was made up by his friendly and caring reputation around town.

He was covering his baked homemade spicy meatballs with a lid when an attractive middle-aged lady he had never seen before stepped into the butcher shop. She was dressed in a black dress with a long purple coat over it. She didn't wear a hat, and her shoulder-length brown hair was brushed back and hung loosely with a hair comb holding her bangs out of her face. She smiled at him as Henry stood up from behind his counter. "Can I help you?" he asked, breathing through his thick lips.

She smiled shyly, lowering her head with a slight flirtatious glance upwards of her fluttering eyelashes. "Maybe you could help me. My name is Sylvia Ballenger. Maybe you've met my son, Martin? He's the new deputy sheriff here in town."

Henry shook his head. "No, Ma'am. I don't get out much."

She frowned. "Oh, well, that's too bad. I am new here and haven't met too many people myself. It would be nice to run into you on the street one of these days. Oh my gosh!" she exclaimed with an embarrassed smile. "I didn't mean it like that! I'm not a prostitute." She laughed with her face reddening slightly.

"No, Ma'am, I didn't take it like that at all." He chuckled.

"Oh, thank goodness. I only meant it would be nice to see a friendly face that I knew on the street. Oh boy! I'm nervous, and I don't even know why. It must be you. You're a very handsome man. What is your name?"

"Henry."

"Henry, what?"

"Redlin."

"Oh! You're the owner?"

"Yes, Ma'am."

She waved a hand at him. "Oh, stop calling me Ma'am, Henry. Call me Sylvia, like a friend would. By the way, what smells so good in here?"

"That would be my meatballs. Would you like to try one? I normally sell them for a nickel apiece, but I can give you one to try."

"You make them?"

"I do. It's a recipe my Granddad brought over from England."

"So, it's a family recipe?"

"Indeed, so. Here." He handed her a meatball on a small plate with a small fork. "Try one and tell me what you think."

"Alright." She cut the meatball in half and ate one piece. "That's very good." She ate the other half. "My goodness Henry, I'm going to have to marry you. Those are good!"

He took the small plate back with a smile and put another meatball on the plate and handed it back to her. "Have another."

"Oh, I probably shouldn't, but I will. I'm sure your wife wouldn't want you giving all of these delicious meatballs away."

"I'm not married, Ma'am."

"Sylvia...remember?" she asked as she ate another half of the meatball. "Delicious! I always thought I was a good cook, but these are far better than anything I make. I'd be afraid to invite you over for dinner now that I've tasted your cooking."

He smiled at the compliment as he took the plate back. "Thank you."

"And your polite too. You're not married? That surprises me. I'm not either. Hmm," she said thoughtfully. "Maybe we should get together and share recipes sometime."

He laughed nervously. "I don't have too many."

"See? There's something else we have in common; I don't either." She laughed. "Henry, I came in here to ask if you give credit? We just moved here, and I don't have any money at the moment. My son's the new sheriff's deputy and my daughter's watching the neighbor's baby, and I'm looking for work, but haven't found any yet. So, I came to see if I could get some credit for a roast?" she asked sincerely.

"Oh…" Henry said with a hesitant grimace. "No, I don't give credit to people. Most of my customers are the restaurants or folks who pay upfront. Now, there's another butcher shop up on Eleventh, and Ash Streets called Sam and Lee's Butcher Shop, and they give credit. They're a bit bigger than my store."

She smirked seductively. "But they're not as good as you, are they?"

He chuckled. "No. I'll tell you what, I'll let you take a roast and you can pay me later when you have the money, okay?"

"Henry, you're a lifesaver. I appreciate that so much. But I wonder, would it be okay if I worked it off cleaning up or working behind the counter? I could help you here and learn the business. I think I would enjoy working here and getting to know you and your customers more than doing anything else. If you'd be interested in something like that? I'm easy to get along with, and I don't bite. Maybe if I do good work, you could hire me for real. How's that sound?"

He looked at her thoughtfully. "We could try it. Can you start tomorrow morning?"

"Absolutely. I think we're going to get along very well, Henry."

He smiled shyly. "I hope so. Let's get you a good roast."

"Henry," she said, sincerely getting his attention. Her eyes widened just a bit with a touch of affection. "Thank you. You really are a lifesaver. I didn't know what I was going to feed my family."

5

Sheriff Tim Wright stepped into Bella's Dance Hall with his two youngest deputies; Mark Thiesen was twenty-five, and Martin Ballenger was twenty-seven. He wanted his two deputies to get to know each other, and where better to do it than a night out at the dance hall? The Sheriff was stopped at the door by the dance hall security guard, Phil Mears. Phil wasn't a tall man, but he was a stocky and strong man in his late forties with a serious demeanor and took his job to protect the ladies who had become his family, quite seriously. Phil was an average looking man with short, balding brown hair with a mustache and a face that hadn't shaved in a week or so. He was dressed in a suit and carried a small .38 revolver in a concealed shoulder holster if he ever needed it.

"Sorry, Sheriff, you'll have to get Miss Bella's permission to come in here. I can't just let you come in."

"Phil, what are you talking about?" he laughed slightly embarrassed to be stopped in front of his two young deputies. The truth is he had not come back to the dance hall since he had tried blackmailing Bella and Christine back in August. He knew why he wasn't being allowed inside, but had already invited Martin and Mark to join him for a night of dancing and drinking at Bella's. "Phil, this is nonsense. Where is she?" he asked, looking through the crowd inside of the main dance floor and bar. "There she is. I'm going to talk to Bella, you boys wait right here. I'll be right back," he said, leaving them in front of the stairway that went upstairs to the ladies' rooms. Phil stayed next to the stairs to make sure no men went up to them.

Tim walked to the far end of the bar, where he saw Bella glaring at him as he approached.

She spoke loud enough to be heard over the band, "Sheriff Wright, how did you slither your scaly ass past Phil? You're not welcome here, so you might as well slither your scaly skin back out of here."

"Can we speak more in private?"

"No. You can threaten me out here in front of everyone if you want," Bella answered shortly.

"Bella, please. I'm not going to threaten you."

"What do you want, Tim?" she asked. She despised him.

"I just want to bring my deputies in here and enjoy a few drinks and let them dance if they want to." He held up his hands in defense. "We won't cause any trouble, and I'm not here to harass you in any way."

She shook her head. "Fine. But I do not forgive you for what you tried to do to Christine and me. But Matt took care of that, didn't he?" she smiled slightly. "I like how the doctor straightened your nose, but the scar's still there, isn't it? Have fun, and don't try anything with my girls, or Matt will be knocking on your door." She took a sip of her wine.

He glared at her angrily for a moment. "Thank you," he said and walked away back towards his men.

Martin looked around as he waited by the stairs with excited anticipation in his eyes. The band played a foot-tapping polka, and he couldn't resist tapping his toe to the rhythm. His eyes watched the ladies dressed beautifully, dancing pleasantly with their partners. The atmosphere was euphoric, and he couldn't wait to go inside further and order a drink and meet one of the beautiful ladies he saw dancing. He glanced up the stairs as a slight movement caught his attention. His eyes widened when he saw a yellow wavy-haired lady stepping down the stairs. She wore a pink dress and had her hair weaved artistically into a loose braid that allowed her hair to fall over her ears but was swept up and tied in a knot before slipping down her back. Her hairstyle appeared to be far more complicated than any hitching knot Martin had ever tied before. She was beautiful and looked like an angel descending from the heavens coming for him. His jaw fell in wonder as he couldn't take his eyes off her. She was the most beautiful woman he had ever seen.

Phil spoke kindly, "Miss Williams, how are you feeling?"

She paused on the third step from the bottom and smiled sadly at him. "I'll be okay. He hasn't come in, has he?"

"No. And I won't let Paul come in unless you

want me to."

She shook her head slightly with a sad twist of her lips. Her eyes were slightly puffy from crying as she stepped down to the main floor. She made eye contact with Martin and smiled slightly before turning to go into the ballroom.

"Hi," Martin said quickly with a captivated grin.

She turned towards him. "Hello. Did you want to dance?" she asked with a flat monotone.

"Sure," he said with a growing smile.

"Do you have a ticket?"

"Ticket?" he asked, not knowing how the dance hall functioned.

She spoke shortly, "This dance is almost over anyway. Buy a ticket, and I'll save the next dance for you." She walked away without giving him a chance to respond.

"Where do you get a ticket?" Martin asked Mark Thiesen.

"You have to buy one from the bar. They're kind of spendy though. That's why I never come here."

Martin cast his eyes downward with disappointment. "I don't have any money."

Tim put a hand on both of their shoulders with three dance tickets in each hand for them. "Here, you boys go. Go find a lady to dance with, and I'll meet you over at that table in the back. I'll get your drinks too. As I said, the tab's on me tonight."

"Thanks," Martin said with a wide grin. "I already found the one I want." He took the three tickets and went to talk to the pretty blonde girl. He found her at the end of the bar, talking to an older woman dressed in a bright yellow dress with a white feather boa wrapped around her shoulders and a large decorated hat on her head. It was the same woman that Tim had been talking to.

"Excuse me, Miss, but I have a ticket now."

Edith was irritated to be interrupted as she spoke with Bella. "Very good, the next dance will be yours."

"My name's Martin. I'm the new Deputy Sheriff in town."

She showed no interest as she said, "Nice to meet you, Deputy. My name is Edith. Is this your first time here?"

"Yeah!" he answered with an excited smile that he found hard to contain. His eyes dilated as he stared at her.

Bella observed him and asked coldly. "You're here with Sheriff Wright?"

"I am. Yeah, he hired me yesterday. I just moved here a couple of weeks ago."

Bella was unimpressed. "Well, I hope you're an honest young man because the Sheriff is a snake," she said bitterly.

"I am Ma'am. I wouldn't want to be a lawman if I wasn't."

Bella nodded. "Just so you know, it's customary for the gentleman to buy the dancer a glass of champagne after the dance."

Martin's face turned downward with a touch of humiliation. He answered Bella, "Miss, I'm afraid I just started working and haven't been paid yet. I'm trying to support my mother and little sister, and in truth, if the Sheriff hadn't bought these tickets, I wouldn't be able to even ask for a dance. So, I can't afford to do that. I would love to, though, if I could. I think this lady here is the most beautiful lady I have ever seen. And I mean that with everything I am."

His sincerity touched Bella's heart, and the corners of her lips turned upwards as she watched Edith's response to his words. Edith stared at him, stunned by his words. "You're supporting your mother and sister?" Bella asked.

"Yes, Ma'am. Right now, we're living in a terrible place down the road, but I hope to get us into a nicer place."

"What's your last name, Martin?"

"Ballenger."

"Where'd you move here from?"

"Western Oregon. We lived in a small town outside of Salem a few miles."

"Why did you move here?"

"We wanted to get away from the constant rain. It rains here too, but not like over there. It rains every day over there."

Bella nodded. "Well, this is Edith, and you enjoy a dance with her or three as I see your tickets. And I'll pick up the cost of her drinks; you just make sure she gets them okay?"

"Yes, Ma'am. And thank you."

She leaned next to Edith's ear and whispered so not to be overheard, "If you like him, let me know. We'll give him the auction dance for free and maybe invite him to stay late. But that's up to you. I like him so far, though."

Edith smiled slightly. "I'll let you know," she answered doubtfully.

Tim Wright grinned widely as Martin finally came to the table to sit with him and Mark. "About time you join us. I thought we were going to have to call in a posse to find you."

"I was dancing with Edith," he said with an excited smile. He had danced with Edith twice, and like so many other men in the hot room, he was sweating and a bit out of breath when he sat down.

"I see that. She's a beautiful woman, but watch out, because I think she's engaged to Paul Johnson still."

Martin's smile faded. "She didn't say anything about that."

Tim laughed. "Do they ever? You have to watch out for the ladies around here; they're all a bunch of snakes. They're just vipers that want your money and to steal your life before they wind up on the street selling themselves, which most of them did before they started working here."

Martin narrowed his brow. "Not Edith. She's far too beautiful to be a prostitute."

Tim chuckled slightly. "Not now, but she was. Now she's taken by Paul. Last I heard they were close to being engaged. And whatever you do, don't mess with that girl." He pointed at Christine Knapp as she walked to the bar with a logger by the rough looks of the man. He was buying her a glass of champagne.

Martin watched Christine and noticed how pretty she was, but the only one he could think about was Edith. "Why?" he asked.

"That's Matt Bannister's lady. And he's killed a

few people now for messing with her. Stay away from her."

"I will. So, Edith has a fiancé?" he asked, sounding troubled.

"I believe so."

Martin appeared to be annoyed. "She should probably tell me if she does."

Mark Thiesen shook his head in disagreement. "She dances for a living. Her private life isn't any business of ours."

Martin glared at him for a second with a hint of hostility in his eyes. It disappeared as quickly as it came. "Your right. But it would be nice to know before we waste our dance tickets on the taken ones, right?" he asked with a short chuckle.

"Exactly," Tim said, agreeing. "As I said, they're vipers. But of all the vipers, I like the redhead," he said as Rose walked past the bar.

Martin wasn't paying attention to him. "Dang, I liked Edith too. I liked her a lot."

Tim laughed as he took a drink. "Buddy, heartbreak's a way of life. You've never been married?"

Martin frowned, as a slightly troubled expression crossed his face. "No. I asked a lady one time, but she choked to death on a radish. That was a couple of years ago. But now I'm here learning that the most beautiful girl I've ever seen is engaged."

"That's some bad luck all around," Tim said as he watched Bella walking towards them with Edith holding her arm. "What's this?" Tim asked Bella.

Bella laid a red piece of paper down in front of Martin. "I don't ever do this, so be honored. But we would like to invite you to stay after closing time to visit with Edith a bit longer if you would like to. Also, since you are a new deputy in town, we're giving you the auction dance for free with Edith."

Martin's face brightened like a lantern's gas being turned up on high. "Fantastic! But I don't know what an auction dance is..." he chuckled good-humouredly.

Bella waved him off. "You'll figure it out later. Now go use your last ticket with Edith."

He smiled at Edith. "Sure."

Tim frowned skeptically. "I thought Edith was engaged to Paul?" he asked as Martin led Edith out to the dancefloor.

Bella glared at him scornfully. "Their relationship ended today. Edith is devastated, and Martin seems like a nice and respectful young man. Not to mention he seems to have taken a great interest in her."

"Edith's single now?"

"Yes. For now, anyway." She put her eyes on Mark Thiesen. "Are you new too?"

"No, Ma'am. I've just never been in here before."

"Are you not dancing?" Bella asked, raising her eyes brows questionably.

"No, Ma'am, I don't enjoy dancing too much."

Bella held her arm for Mark to take. "Well, come along, let's introduce to someone who will change your mind about that. I know just the girl. You're a shy boy, so you need a spirited lady, and I know just the one. You will love Rose."

Tim laughed. "Go get her, Mark!"

Bella said to Mark as she led him through the crowd. "You seem like too nice of a man to be working for such a snake. Please tell me you're not like the sheriff."

He chuckled uncomfortably. "I'm not."

"You should be working for the Marshal."

"I'd like to."

"I'll talk to him for you. What is your name?"

"Mark Thiesen, Ma'am."

She stopped and looked at him frankly. "I knew that. I know who you are. The Marshal told me you were one of the only good deputies in the sheriff's herd of misfits. Now tell me, how do you like Martin? Is there anything I need to know about him before I allow him to get to know any of my girls?"

He shrugged. "So far, he's okay. I just met him yesterday. I don't know anything about him except he's new here and lives in the Dogwood Flats."

"Okay. If any concerns ever come up, you let me know immediately. I'm allowing him to stay after, but for some reason, I'm having second thoughts about him. I don't know why. Will you do that for me?"

"I will."

"Thank you. Now, let's introduce you to Rose. I think you'll like her and I'll tell you, she's a wonderful lady. Mark, enjoy yourself." She glanced out on the dance floor and seen Martin talking to Edith while they waited for the next dance to begin. There were no obvious red flags, but for some reason, Bella was wondering if she had made a mistake to be so welcoming and charitable to Martin. There was something that bothered her about him, but she couldn't identify what it was. It was just a feeling in the pit of her stomach that wouldn't rest easy.

6

When the dance hall closed for the night, Tim Wright and Mark Thiesen left the dance hall with every other man, except for a few that were welcomed to stay after to spend another hour or two with the lady they were courting or seeking to know. To be invited to stay after took the interest of the lady and the permission of Bella. It was Bella who would formerly ask a gentleman to stay after to visit with one of her girls. The doors would be locked, and the security guard Phil Mears would remain in the main dance hall overseeing the visitors to verify that all of the rules were being followed.

Martin Ballenger was invited to stay after at Edith's request. He sat at a square table beside Edith with her best friend Helen Monroe and her fiancé Sam Troyer seated across the table from them. Martin was happy to meet Helen and took an immediate liking to Sam until he found out Sam was best friends with Paul Johnson, the man who broke Edith's heart earlier that day. Edith had told him of her six-month courtship with Paul and how it ended somewhat unexpectedly. Martin listened with care at first, but now he was getting tired of the conversation continually being brought back to Paul. Helen and Sam were both disappointed in Paul and his decision to end their relationship. Martin knew that because they had repeated it numerous times already.

Martin was feeling a bit self-conscious and out of place as the conversation between the three of them left him feeling like a stranger invading a private conversation. Edith was heartbroken, he understood, and being social with her friends was better than hiding alone in her room. But he wished she would pay some attention to him.

Sam was the one speaking, "Again, I think Paul made a grave mistake and will come to regret losing you, Edith." Sam had a similar body build as Martin, around five foot eight, and a bit stronger than Martin. Sam had blonde hair and a blonde beard about an inch long, with blue eyes on his oval face. He laughed a lot and seemed like a delightful man despite his sincere words.

Edith smirked kindly with her sadness showing in her dull eyes and long face. "I would have made him a good wife. As you know, it took me a while to trust again, and this is what I get for it." Her eyes watered painfully. She wiped her eyes.

Martin was tired of the conversation, and it wasn't helping him get to know her at all. He said, "If there's anything I can say about it, granted I don't know any of you well, but I think Edith is the most beautiful lady in the world. And if I was ever lucky enough to steal her heart, I'd never let her go."

Edith glanced at him, appreciatively. "Thank you," she said softly.

"It's the truth," he added sincerely.

Helen smiled. "That's so funny because that's the same kind of thing Sam says to me. It's so cute!" She held Sam's hand tightly and nudged his shoulder with hers, "Isn't that right?"

Sam's eyes widened in response. "I have no idea what he's talking about because I can't take my eyes off you."

Helen laughed. "See?"

Edith smiled sadly and spoke to Helen, "He's always been cross-eyed and crazy over you."

Martin looked at Edith and crossed his eyes, looking at the tip of his nose. "I know how he feels!"

Edith laughed lightly with her friend Helen. Sam faked a smile as he leaned back in his chair with his arm around Helen. "Maybe you should get to know her first before you let your eyes cross too much. You don't want to be too blinded, staring at your own nose when the right lady walks by. Angela is a very pretty blonde too."

Martin shot a quick menacing glance at Sam and then laughed it away lightly. "I intend to get to know Edith, thank you. If that's acceptable to her, that is." He spoke sincerely. "I know you just had your heart broken by a fool who made a big mistake in my opinion. I just met you tonight and haven't had too much time to get to know you, but everything I know about you so far is amazing. Absolutely amazing."

"Thank you," she answered softly.

Helen giggled. "How sweet."

Martin smiled. "I'm not just saying that either. I am very sincere."

Edith grinned slightly with the compliment. "Thank you." Her eyes went to the kitchen door that opened and watched Christine Knapp come out of the kitchen, loosening her hair. Her long dark auburn hair fell below her mid-back. "Christine, do you want to sit down and join us?"

She shook her head tiredly. "No. I'm going to go up and get some sleep."

"Are you okay? You seem sad," Edith asked.

"I'm just tired. Washing a hundred and some glasses, cups, and other dishes has a way of putting one to sleep. Goodnight, I'll see you in the morning."

Martin couldn't take his eyes off Christine. He asked, "So you're Matt Bannister's lady, huh?"

She smiled slightly. "I'm not his lady, but we are very good friends."

Edith spoke, "Christine, this is Martin Ballenger. He's the new town deputy. This, is Christine."

"Hello," he said.

She smiled slightly. "It's nice to meet you."

Helen added, "Christine and Matt are courting, but neither one of them knows it."

"No, we're not," she said with a smile. "You all have a good night."

Martin spoke as she began to walk away, "I met Matt. A neighbor was beating on a little girl pretty harshly; you might have heard about the teacher that was terminated today? It was him. I watched Matt take that man's switch he was using to beat that little girl and beat that man to tears with it. He worked that man over pretty good and then got the teacher fired." He chuckled while shaking his head at the memory. "He's the one that recommended me for this job. But it doesn't pay to hurt a child with him or me around, that's for sure."

Christine nodded. "No, it doesn't. Nice meeting you," she said and walked away towards the stairs to go to her room.

Helen nodded at Martin. "They are courting."

Later on, Martin had to say goodnight to Edith at the door and hoped he had impressed her enough to capture some interest. He lingered on the steps silently for a moment with his hand holding the door open. "I don't know if I'll be back tomorrow night or not, but if it's okay, I would like to call on you sometime."

She smiled tiredly. "I'd like that."

"Do you dance every night?"

"Every night except Sunday night."

"You have Sunday's off?"

"I do."

"Any chance we can spend some time together?"

"Maybe. Come back tomorrow night, and we'll talk about it."

He watched her close the door and walk towards the stairs while Phil locked the door and pulled the curtain closed.

Martin walked back to the Dogwood Flats with a euphoric sense of joy running through him. He found his apartment door locked; he knocked. It was opened by his mother, who appeared to have been sleeping. He swooped inside and grabbed her hand and danced her around in a circle with a laugh. "Mother, I've had an amazing night! Not only do I love my new job. I have met the most beautiful girl! We made the right choice moving here." He noticed her angry frown in the faint lamplight. "You look tired. Sorry to wake you, but I told you I needed a door key."

She walked away from him towards a corner of the room that held a cookstove, counter, and a few cabinets. "Martin, I haven't seen you all day. I start a new job in the morning, and I don't appreciate being woken up so late. We need money to buy wood to heat and cook with. Tomorrow I need you to find out where to get a cord of wood and have it stacked on the back porch. There are only a few pieces of wood left out back, and we're going to freeze to death before we starve to death thanks to my new boss. I need you to do whatever you can to get some wood in this house. We need ten dollars in two weeks to stay in this rat hole, or we'll be on the street in January, but until then, we have to stay warm and cook. Can you please take some time and do that for us? Maybe we can get a cord of wood on credit? Or maybe you can cut some fallen old tree or something. I need you to do whatever it takes to make sure we're taken care of."

"Mother, I am a deputy sheriff now. We'll be okay. Did you hear what I said, I met an amazing girl tonight."

Sylvia glared at him tiredly. "That's nice, Martin. But I don't really care. I care about keeping the house warm, so we don't freeze and having something to burn to cook the porridge on. We have enough wood for tomorrow, but tomorrow night we have nothing. Do you understand? Get it through your head; the girl doesn't matter, but staying alive does. Get us taken care of, please. Now, I must get some sleep. I work tomorrow."

"Where?" he asked curiously.

"The butcher shop."

"Oh. Well, bring home some steaks, and I'll have the wood taken care of and stacked up. Don't worry about it, Mother. But, the girl does matter. That she does."

7

To celebrate their pardon from the Marshal's charges, Leroy Haywood and friends, Oscar Belding, Roger Lavigne, and Tony Rosso, went into Branson to Ugly John's Saloon on Rose Street to celebrate their freedom. It was Friday night, and they didn't have to work over the weekend. It was late when they left Ugly John's with a bottle of whiskey to share on their walk back out to Slater's Mile two miles outside of town.

"Wait," Leroy laughed. He was a big man at over six feet tall, broad, and obese. He had long black hair that fell uncombed and uncared for down to his shoulders and had an unkempt long black beard. "Let's go through Chinatown and see if we can't catch a rat outside its box."

Oscar shook his head with a humored smile. "Didn't we just get in trouble for that?"

Leroy spat out a mouthful of whiskey he took from the bottle. "No," he laughed. "You did, for crippling a deputy marshal, but not us," he laughed. "Come on, let's go raise a little hell in Chinatown!" He pulled the corner of his eyes to make his eyes small slits. "If they look like this, knock them out."

They walked through Chinatown block after block yelling loudly and banging on doors as they went. Occasionally, they broke out windows and pushed over tables or whatever else they could find. One old Chinese man stepped outside, rattling on in his incoherent language. The Chinaman's anger over them busting his hand cart only humored the three drunk men.

"Oi, oi, oi. Oi ha!" Leroy shouted in the man's face and put his big hand on the man's face and pushed him down on the frozen ground. "This rat squeals a bit too much. Tony shut him up if he gets up again. I should've brought my whip."

The Chinese man stood up quickly and began speaking angrily, which was in his tone, but the man was knocked unconscious by an unexpected right cross from Tony Rosso.

"Nice hit!" Leroy shouted and then laughed.

They moved up the street, causing as much mayhem as they could in any way they could. Roger Lavigne kicked a door open and went inside, and a few moments later, dragged a young woman out into the snow-covered road wearing a loose white cotton shirt over her loose-fitting pants. The young woman couldn't have been over twenty-one or two. Her long hair was in a long queue, and she didn't resist as she was drug out into the street towards the group of drunk friends.

Roger spoke loudly, "Look, the beasts do have women! Ain't she pretty?"

"She ain't got much up top," Oscar noticed, looking at the Chinese figure hiding her eyes while she sat on the ground with her arms wrapped around her knees quietly.

"Let's see!" Tony said and ripped the shirt off the young woman. "It's a boy, Roger! I think living alone has finally gotten to you." He laughed. "Ain't he pretty! Huh, Roger?" he teased.

Roger glared at the young man with a hairless and youthful face without any manly features. "What the hell? Do they not have women? Maybe this is a woman, let's get those pants off and see what's under there."

The young man cried out harshly in Chinese, with fear filling his eyes of being outnumbered and humiliated in the middle of the street. It may not have been noticeable to the white men, but he knew everyone was watching from the darkness of their homes. He also knew better than to stand up and try to fight a group of Americans looking for trouble. It was best to stay down, quiet, and hope they would lose interest and leave. However, he refused to let the men pull his pants off. The young man rolled across the cold and icy ground and stood up and shook his head.

"Are you a man?" Roger asked perplexed as he stepped forward. "Or are you a woman? What are you?"

Oscar laughed. "He's a male, you idiot! I wouldn't call him a man, but a male anyway."

Roger turned to him. "How would you know?"

47

"I'm married! I know what a woman looks like!" He laughed.

Leroy and Tony both laughed loudly.

Roger was growing angry. He thought he had finally found a Chinese woman, and now his friends were making fun of him. "I know what a woman looks like. These Chinese men need to quit acting like women and cut their damn hair!" He turned around and faced the young man. He could see the young man was scared and was about to run away. Roger held up his hands in a peaceful manner and spoke in a friendly way. "I'm sorry. My mistake. Hey, let's shake hands and be friends." He held out a hand to shake.

The young man was weary but slowly like a skittish pup, allowed Roger to get closer. He could see the sincere expression of Roger's face.

"Here, for your shirt," Roger pulled a coin out of his pocket and tried to hand it to the young man. When he reached out to accept the coin, Roger grabbed his wrist and yanked him forward. Roger forced the young man face down in the snow and quickly straddled himself over the youth's back to hold him down. Roger pulled his six-inch-blade hunting knife out of its sheath on his belt and grabbed the man's queue. "You need to look more like a man!" He began cutting the man's hair at the base of the braided queue. The young Chinese man started screaming in agony.

"He's crying like a baby!" Leroy laughed. "He's crying more than my wife did."

"You could use that for firewood!" Tony laughed as Roger held up the thick queue of hair.

Roger put his knife away with a satisfied smile and spat on the wailing Chinese man. "Now, you look like a man."

A sudden fierce voice spoke something in Chinese from behind them. They all turned around and seen three men standing in the middle of the road. The one standing in the middle was older and stared at the men calmly. The two men at his side were looking at them fiercely.

"What's this, China's cavalry?" Tony Rosso asked with a bit of humor.

The Chinese man in the middle spoke calmly, "Gentlemen, people are trying to sleep. Please leave us tonight and come back tomorrow as my guests."

"What?" Tony laughed.

Leroy stared at the man to the left of Wu-Pen. It was the same man that had forced him to his knees in jail a week before. "I remember you," he said to the fierce-looking man whose eyes were on the weeping young man still on his knees.

Wu-Pen smiled. "As we remember you and your friends. We want no trouble. So please, come back tomorrow as my guests."

Leroy shouted angrily, "We ain't your guests! You're in our country; we're not in yours! I'm going to run all of you slits back on board some ship like a herd of rats and hope it sinks halfway back to China!"

"Slits?" Wu-Pen asked curiously.

"Yeah, you know, slits!" Leroy once again pulled the corner of his eyes outward to imitate their eyes.

Wu-Pen smiled and nodded. "I see. You'd still be ugly in Chinese."

Leroy swung a hard right at Wu-Pen's face, but Wu-Pen pulled his head back, and Leroy almost fell, losing his balance without hitting anything at all.

"Please don't," Wu-Pen said kindly. He spoke in Chinese to his two men, and they grimaced with displeasure and answered.

Tony Rosso tried to hit the nearest Chinese man to him like he had the older man a bit earlier, but the man's head moved out of the way, and a double-armed block stopped his strike in mid-air. The Chinese man Tony tried to hit was suddenly at his side and kicked the back of Tony's calf, which dropped Tony to the ground with the man holding Tony's hand in a wrist lock. The wrist lock was so painful Tony begged to be let go. He glanced up and saw no mercy in the man's eyes as they glared down at him. It took no effort on the Chinese man's part to hold him there.

Roger Lavigne pulled his knife and moved to stab Wu-Pen, but the man to Wu-Pen's left moved swiftly and ended up behind Roger with his hand bringing Roger's knife back towards his own abdomen. It stopped a half-inch from plummeting into Roger's gut. It had happened so fast Roger had no idea how he could be holding the knife blade, and the Chinese man's hands controlled it over his own. Roger could only stare at the knife and try to catch his breath. All he remembered was stepping forward with the knife and seeing a black blur, then feeling the force of the blade coming towards him out of his control. He was stunned.

Wu-Pen spoke in Chinese, and the man behind Roger took the knife out of Roger's hand and slammed it back into its sheath of Roger's side. He felt a knee push him forward, and then a driving kick to his back sent him quickly forward and down to the snow-covered street. He peered back and seen the fierce-looking man who had saved Wu-Pen's life.

Wu-Pen smiled slightly. He spoke to Leroy, "I recall you spat in my face at the jail. Bing Jue could have broken your wrist then, but I stopped him. He could have killed your friend with his own knife just now. Please no more. I'd prefer to be friends."

Leroy waited for both of his friends to stand back up. They were both were dazed by what had happened to them and how it could happen. Leroy breathed in through his nose and sucked up all the mucus he could gather and spat it out into Wu-Pen's face. It was a glob of thick yellowish slime that landed over Wu-Pen's nose and left cheek.

Both men began to step forward when Wu-Pen said a single word in Chinese, and the two men stopped and stepped backward obediently. Both of their eyes were enraged.

Leroy laughed. "I ain't friends with no slit-eyed rats! Next time we won't be unarmed! We're going to burn this place down! Next time..." he threatened with his eyes glaring dangerously at Wu-Pen.

Wu-Pen used a silk rag to remove the mucus calmly. "We'll see you soon."

"Yeah, you will!" Leroy shouted. "You'll see me very damn soon!"

"Yes, I will," he said as he watched the three men walking away.

Wu-Pen looked empathetically at the young man on the ground, still weeping and walked over to him. He knelt and put a hand on the young man's shoulder. He spoke in Chinese, "Yik Su, I'm sorry I wasn't here in time. Two years and you can go home." It was against Chinese law for a man to cut his queue, and the punishment was death if he returned to China without it. Yik Su would not be able to go back to China for any reason without his queue. If the Chinese were forced out of America, he would not have any place to go. If his family needed him to come home, Yik Su would not be able to go. If he reached the wealth he wanted, he still could not go back home to China. Wu-Pen added, "Vengeance will be repaid."

Bing Jue was angry and said, "Uncle, allow Uang and me to follow them and slit their throats in the darkness of the road."

Wu-Pen shook his head. "No. If they come back with fire, do as you will to protect our people. If not, we will do it my way on Sunday night. Remember Bing, a snake may strike fiercely and poison it's prey, but it will die too if it strikes a man with a gun. I have a better way. The fat one will die Sunday night in a way he never imagined, with much fear. He will beg and not be heard. Just as Yik Su begged and was not heard."

8

Martin woke up with a smile from a pleasant dream that he couldn't quite remember, but he knew it had to do with a blonde-haired lady; he was pretty sure of that anyway. His mother had gone off to her first day of work. The fire was burning in the cookstove, and he was warm and content lying on the hard floor where he slept. The apartment came furnished with two badly stained padded chairs and a table set in front of them. A small dining table with four chairs to eat on was near the kitchen, and a bed big enough for two was in the small bedroom. There were no other furnishing other than that. He laid where he was for a few minutes knowing his little sister Barbra was writing in her book of poetry in the bedroom like she did every morning. He eventually got up as the fire burned out and tossed in one of the last pieces of wood that were inside. He opened the back door and looked at the small back porch and saw there were only two pieces of wood left. He sighed heavily. He had hoped there was enough wood to last until the next day, at least.

He set out to see where he could buy a cord of seasoned wood, and he was pointed out of town to the Bowman's who made a living selling firewood to most folks who didn't cut their own. He walked quite a ways out of town past the sawmill and other mills and neared the homestead of the Bowman family. It wasn't hard to spot. They owned an impressive white two-story house and had three barns along the forest that had several logs piled up here and there and piles of cut blocks and multiple cords of split wood waiting to be sold. They also had three heavily built wagons to deliver the wood. He saw three young men stacking what appeared to be two cords in one of the solidly built wagons with higher sidewalls.

"Howdy," Martin said, walking up to the wagon. "I wasn't expecting such a long walk out here. I'm new to the area. I'm the new deputy sheriff, Martin Ballenger."

One of the young men about his age removed a worn glove from his hand. "I'm Jeff Bowman. Those are my brother's Sage and Rob. My Pa's around somewhere. The new deputy, huh? Well, what brings you out here?" Jeff Bowman and his brothers were muscular, and broad-shouldered men from a life of hard work yet had a friendly countenance and a naturally easy-going smile.

"I'm looking to buy some wood, and I heard this is the place to get it."

"You heard about right, yeah. It's what we do. The price depends on what kind of wood you want. We have fir, cedar, oak, apple, and pine. And if you want some pitchy kindling, we have a supply of that too."

"Oak would probably last the longest. How much for a cord?"

"For a cord of oak, you're looking at ten dollars and another dollar to deliver and rick it for you."

"What does rick it mean?"

Jeff frowned slightly. "It means stacking the wood up, so you know you're getting a true cord."

"Eleven dollars for that?" Martin asked, shocked by the price.

"If you want it delivered, yes. We don't give it away," Jeff said with a smile.

"Do you do deliveries on credit?" Martin asked curiously.

Jeff Bowman shook his head. "Not anymore, no."

"Listen, I'm new in town and a deputy sheriff, so I'm good for paying you when I get paid. But right now, I haven't got any money, and we haven't got any wood." He paused when he saw a big man walk up behind Jeff dressed in bib overalls. He was a gruff looking man. Martin continued, "My mother, little sister, and I really need it. My mother just started working at the butcher shop today, and as I said, I'm the new deputy sheriff, so we could pay for it when we get paid."

The big man spat on the ground. "Who are you?" he asked.

"Hi Pa," Jeff said. "This is the man you have to ask," he said to Martin.

"I'm Martin Ballenger," he introduced himself, reaching his hand out to shake.

"Isaac," is all the man said as he shook Martin's hand.

Martin continued, "Nice to meet you, Sir. I'm the new deputy sheriff in Branson. I was just explaining to your sons that my mother, little sister, and I just moved here and need some wood to cook with. If we could get a cord of oak on credit, that would be fantastic. We'll gladly pay you when we get paid."

"Are you working for the Sheriff or the Marshal?" Isaac Bowman asked.

"The sheriff, Tim Wright, Sir."

"Nope. If you worked for the Marshal, I'd do it, because we have a long-standing relationship with the Bannisters, they pay me on time, every time. The sheriff doesn't pay his bills, so now I want money in my hand before I do any business with him. Try the hardware store; they have bags of coal and wood for sale too. They'll give you credit, maybe."

Martin walked back to town irritated and a bit nervous that he wouldn't be able to get credit at the hardware store either. He went inside, and after some brief discussion, he was able to open up a credit account with the hardware store. Still, they couldn't deliver any wood until Monday, and it would be softwood, meaning it would burn faster and not as hot as Oak, for about the same price as the Bowman's wanted. It made sense, though, the hardware store bought the softwood from the Bowman's and then upped the cost to make a profit. Martin put a forty-pound bag of coal on his credit and took that home and threw some in the cookstove. It wasn't wood, but it would keep them warm and heat the cooktop for less than half the price.

Martin got bored at home, so he wandered out-side and went for a walk to show himself around town and introduce himself as well. He wore his badge proudly and his uncle's worn gun belt that held his .32 caliber Remington Pocket Revolver. He knew it was a small-caliber weapon for his profession, and he would upgrade soon enough when he could afford to, but it was the only gun he owned. It was a gift Martin's uncle gave him when his father divorced Sylvia ten years before. They had not heard from his father since he left and had no idea where he was now. Martin had been helping take care of the family ever since then. They had moved around a lot, but Martin now felt comfort-able and had high hopes that Branson was where they would call home for good. He was a deputy now, and maybe in a few years, he would become the Branson Sheriff.

He stepped into the small butcher shop and saw his mother laughing with a big heavy man who seemed to be enjoying her company. "Hi, Mother," he said as he stepped closer to the counter.

"Martin!" she exclaimed with surprise. "I want to introduce you to Henry. This is my son, Martin. He is the new deputy in town. I am so proud of him," she said with a proud smile.

Henry held a big hand over the counter to shake. "Nice to meet you, Martin. I'm sure our town's safer knowing you're out there. Do you like our community?"

"I do. I like it a lot."

"Good. Here," Henry reached into his pocket and pulled out a ten-dollar bill. "Your mother was telling me you needed wood. It's going to cost about five or six dollars or so, for a half cord of wood. The rest you can use for groceries, and that'll get you all by until payday. I was going to give it to her, but since you're here and maybe can get that taken care of and she can work a full day. Does that sound okay to you?"

Martin held the ten-dollar bill in front of him with widened eyes. He had maybe held a ten-dollar bill a few times in his life. "Sure. Thank you."

Sylvia smiled warmly at Henry. "I am so thankful. I can't thank you enough. You're a lifesaver, Henry."

He smiled kindly at her. "My pleasure."

She questioned Martin, "Have you gone to look for wood yet?"

He shook his head. "No, I was on my way when I stopped by here."

"I think Henry's right, a half cord would be sufficient for now to get us by, and I'll run to the store with what's leftover after work."

Martin shook his head. "If you make me a list of what you want, I can go get it. It's only noon, so I have time to get it all done."

"Oh, wonderful. Let me make a list real quick." Henry helped her find a pencil and a piece of paper to write on. Henry gave Martin one of his meatballs while he waited. Like usual, Henry enjoyed the response when someone new liked his spicy meatballs.

Martin took the list his mother made and went to the local market and inquired about adding to the credit bill they already owed from previous shopping trips. He explained his mother was working for Henry Redlin, and Martin proudly showed his badge to ensure that they were working hard to pay their bills to make a life for themselves. The store owner listened and agreed to allow them to add the items on Sylvia's list to the tab. Martin carried a heavy wooden crate of sugar, flour, and other necessities for cooking meals back to the house. He and Barbra put the goods away, threw some more coal on the fire, and he sat down on one of the chairs. Martin had charged a pretty hair brooch that he had stuffed into his pocket for Edith. It had cost a dollar and fifty cents, but it was worth it for a gift when he saw her tonight. He smiled because he had a ten-dollar bill to spend at the dance hall.

9

It was another sunny, cold Winter's day with a mere inch or two of snow on the ground. Matt wanted to take Christine for a buggy ride, but he wouldn't say to where. All he had told her was to dress warm and to trust him. Most of the time, when they went for a buggy ride, they either went South into the mountains or west through the heart of Jessup Valley. Today they were going North on a road she had never been on before. They had driven about five miles through the valley and nearing a high rolling hill covered with sparse trees and thick grass. Matt slowed the buggy to a stop and asked Christine with a daring grin, "Do you trust me?"

"Of course. Why would you ask?" She suddenly began feeling skeptical of it while looking at his sly grin. She was wrapped in a blanket and wore a knit stocking cap and fur ear muffs over her loose long hair that fell over her shoulders to her mid-back.

He smiled. "Because I'm going to ask you to close

your eyes and cover your head with the blanket."

"Why?" she asked, feeling uncomfortable all of a sudden.

He chuckled. "Because the road is going to get very rough and bouncy, maybe even a bit scary. But I would like for you to cover your face with the blanket and don't peek no matter what, okay?"

"Now, you're starting to scare me," she said with a hesitant smile.

"Trust me. I said we were going on an adventure, right? Well, we are. Trust me; we'll be fine. But you do need to hold onto my arm tight and be prepared for some rough riding."

"Where are we going?" she asked pointedly.

He pointed at the side of a very steep and tall grassy hill that rose above the road. The top of the hill seemed to be much higher than she wanted to ride in a one-horse buggy in the snow.

"No! It's dangerous. That's really high, Matt. And there are no trees to stop us if we slide."

Matt laughed. "Remember, there was something about trusting me? Honest, it will be fine. Just hold my arm tight and hang on. I won't let you fall out of the buggy, nor will I put you in danger. So, if you would do me a favor and cover your head with the blanket."

She took a deep breath. "Okay...but if we end up dead, I'm going to be really mad at you in heaven."

He laughed. "Okay, but if we don't die, you'll appreciate what I'm doing."

Christine laughed as she held on for dear life as Matt drove the buggy up the road to the northside of the hill and pulled off the road and over the rugged ground and up the more gentle slope of the steep grassy hill. The buggy rocked from side to side as it plowed over the shallow snow toward the top of the hill. It was a long climb, and despite the bouncy ride, she found herself trusting Matt and his ability to drive the buggy up the steep hill in slippery conditions. She held onto his arm with hers. When they got to the top of the hill, Matt turned the horse to face the south and stopped the buggy and set the brake. "Keep your head covered, until I say so."

He got out of the buggy and went to Christine's side and took hold of her hand to help her out of the buggy. "Don't open your eyes yet." He removed the blanket off her head and placed it over her shoulders to keep her warm. For a moment, he just watched her with her eyes closed. She was the most stunning woman he had ever known as the sun reflected off her skin, and a slight cold breeze gently caressed her hair. The urge to kiss her pressed upon him like an invisible hand pushing his face towards her. He resisted. It wouldn't be right to presume she would accept it. "Keep your eyes closed," he said as he maneuvered her to the edge of the hill and stood beside her, making sure she wouldn't slip in the snow and fall. He took a deep breath and exhaled. "Christine, open your eyes."

She blinked a few times to get used to the sunlight as it reflected off the snow on the ground. She looked up, and her eyes widened in amazement as her jaw opened a bit. Before her was the panoramic view of the snow-covered Blue Mountains stretching from east to west as far as her eyes could see and the beautiful valley laid out before it like the skirt of a wedding dress behind a beautiful bride. Matt grabbed her shoulders from behind and gently turned her around to look behind her. Her eyes widened to see the rugged and sharp peaks of the snow-covered Wallowa Mountain range that also stretched out from as far east to west as she could see. "Oh, my goodness! Matt, it's so...beautiful!" she gasped while slowly turning herself in a circle to take in the stunning beauty before her. To the east were miles and miles of rolling high grass prairie hills that were as large as the mountains they seemed. To the south were the broad-based Blues looking like thick white-capped swells upon the ocean with a spike in the middle of it, like a thumb sticking up higher than the rest. To the west was the opening to the rest of the world where the Oregon Trail passed through the mountains. The view was physically stunning from their elevation. "I have never imagined it could be so beautiful," she said in awe.

Matt leaned against the buggy and smiled as he watched her with her childlike innocence while she stared out in every direction captivated by the snow-covered beauty. Matt didn't say a word; he just wanted to watch her and the wonder of it in her eyes.

She turned to face him. "I would love to live right here! Oh, my goodness! Wouldn't you? Just imagine building a house up here. I'd want windows everywhere and a full wrap around porch with a porch swing on every side. Matt, it's so beautiful! Thank you."

He smiled. "I thought you might like the view. Do you see that big pillar over there like a thumb sticking up?" He pointed at Pillar Rock in the Blue Mountains. "This Summer, if you will allow me to, I will take you to our family cabin on Lake Jessup right at the bottom that pillar. It's quite beautiful there."

"I bet. Yes, I'd like that. You've obviously been up here before."

He nodded. "Yeah. It's a nice quiet place to come and sit down and just think." He reached behind the seat and pulled a tarp out of the small carriage and spread it out on the snow.

"What's that?" she asked, bewildered.

"A surprise. I had Regina and Mellissa help me with a picnic basket. I'm not sure what's in it yet, but I'll promise it's good," he said with a smile. "I thought we'd have a picnic up here." He pulled a basket out from behind the seat and set it on the floor of the buggy. He then reached behind the seat and grabbed a heavy blanket to lay on top of the tarp. "I couldn't let the view go without sharing a picnic with you."

She smiled appreciatively. "Matt, Isn't it kind of cold for a picnic?"

He laughed as he grabbed the basket. "It really is. But like I said, this is an adventure, not a sunny and warm picnic. Have a seat, and I'll make sure you are bundled up nice and warm."

Once they were seated comfortably next to each other and eating a salad, pieces of roasted chicken, and bread pudding, along with a bottle of brewed tea served in white china cups that belonged to

Mellissa. Christine, bundled in the blanket around her shoulders and the blanket she sat on wrapped around her legs, looked at Matt fondly and said, "Thank you. I absolutely love this."

He smiled warmly. "You're welcome."

They had talked a lot about many things, including how well Thanksgiving night had gone at the dance hall when Christine sang for most of the night. She was thrilled to have the opportunity and pleased beyond words with how well she was applauded. It had been a fun night indeed. Matt had already told her how good he felt about having reconciled with his father and his son. He felt free from two of the most substantial burdens that weighed upon him. The soot from those smoldering fires was finally extinguished. Now he had a joy in his eyes that remained even when talking about his father.

Christine realized she had most of the blanket they were sitting on wrapped around her legs. She unwrapped her legs and slid over on the blanket. "Slide over here," she said. When Matt moved over beside her, she leaned over him and pulled the other side of the blanket up over his legs and tucked it down between them so that the two edges of the blanket were all that was between them. With their shoulders touching, she said, "There. Now you can stay comfy and warm too."

Matt watched her with a grin. "Thank you. I don't think I've been tucked in since I was a kid."

Christine laughed lightly. "I am loving sitting up here with you and don't want to leave yet. Hey, I told you Edith and Paul ended their relationship yesterday, but I forgot to mention that I met your friend Martin. He is quite taken with Edith, I think. He seems like a gentleman. Edith isn't set on him, but maybe we could take them to dinner one of these nights? It might take her mind off, Paul."

Matt frowned. "He's not my friend. I don't even know him."

She placed her hand on his forearm. "He's not? He sure acts like you are. So why did you recommend him for the deputy position if you don't know him?"

"I didn't. Martin asked if I was hiring, and I told him to try Tim, but I wasn't half serious about it. I was quite surprised to see him with a badge. He doesn't have any experience."

"Oh. He told Edith and Helen you recommended him for the job. He even said he knew that I was your lady, but I told him we were just friends," she added quickly with an uncomfortable higher-pitched voice.

Matt nodded with a bit of sadness in his eyes. Christine had become the closest friend he had known since he was a teenager and in love with Elizabeth Ash, as she was known back then. Christine had become a friend that Matt found easy to talk to, and over the months, she had become a regular part of his life. Matt found himself wanting to be with her more often and missing her when he didn't get to see her for a day or two. Love wasn't a word Matt had used commonly in his lifetime, and he'd only said it to two other women in his life, Elizabeth was one, and Felisha Conway was the other. However, did he love Felisha? Their courtship was built upon letters mailed over time and distance. It was acted upon too prematurely to know what the other person was really like. Felisha knew who Matt was and what he did for a living, but when the time came to witness it, she was scared away. Matt knew her as a loving mother and a wonderful lady whose company he enjoyed. However, he would never know how jealous she was if it were not for his friendship with Christine. Was there any hell more miserable on earth than trying to live with a jealous wife who controlled a man's every move and suspected betrayal at every opportunity? Matt's life had been lived freely for too many years to be thrown into a dungeon of despair by an insecure woman who could not control her anger, tongue or reasoning when she was upset by an innocent conversation with a female friend. Matt certainly wasn't jealous of her when she spoke with her friends. He knew where he stood, and he was confident in her loyalty to him. If she would not give him the same amount of trust and respect, then quite frankly, he was more than willing to let her go.

Christine, on the other hand, never showed an ounce of jealousy. She knew who she was and was confident in herself. She would encourage Matt to talk with Felisha and always seemed to want the best for Matt without diverting his attention to another person's faults or to herself. Christine was a friend first and had been a friend in every way since he met her. His best interest was what she continually sought to make a priority. She was amazing, and Matt had fallen in love with her. He longed for her to become his lady and sometimes, he thought she wanted to be more than friends too, , but every time the subject got close to coming up, he was quickly reminded that they were just friends.

He responded dryly to her statement, "Yeah, we are just friends." Matt gazed out over the valley and mountains taking in the full beauty of God's Winter creation. Was there anything more beautiful than the mountains in the wintertime? Yes, there was one thing. Christine.

He failed to notice her downcast eyes and slight downturned lips that came over her expression. She spoke with a lack of emotion. "Thank you for bringing me up here. Matt. I've really enjoyed the view and spending time with you, but maybe we should start heading back."

Matt took a deep breath and hesitated as he furrowed his brow confused. "What? You just said you didn't want to leave yet. Are you getting cold?"

She nodded sadly. "Yeah." She was getting cold, but not near enough to want to leave such a peaceful and beautiful place with the man she was falling in love with. She didn't know how many hints she had to give him that she wanted to more than his friend. He wasn't so dense that he couldn't figure it out by now. It only left one other explanation, and that was he wanted to be friends and leave it like that.

"Oh. Okay, well, let's get you back home and warmed up." Matt stood up and held out a hand to help her up. She took his hand, and he pulled her up with his right hand and caught her with his left hand on her shoulder. For a moment, their eyes held contact while he adjusted the blanket around her shoulders to keep her warm. He longed to kiss her but refused.

"Thank you," she said, staring into his eyes until he turned away. She grabbed the basket while Matt folded the blanket they sat on and the tarp before they walked over to the buggy, where he stowed them and the basket behind the seat. There was an awkward silence that suddenly came between them and an uncomfortable tension that filled the air around the once peaceful and beautiful view. She put her foot on the rail to climb up, when she heard him say softly, "Christine."

"Yes?" she asked, turning to face him. Her brow furrowed when she saw his troubled expression. She put her foot on the ground to face him with her sincere concern. "What is it, Matt?"

"Come here for a minute, if you would." He took her by the hand and led her to the summit of the hill where they picnicked. He stopped and stared out at the view, seemingly troubled.

"Matt, are you okay?"

He smiled slightly and turned to look at her. His heart pounded, and he was more afraid than he ever remembered being. It was a different kind of fear than he was used to. It wasn't a fear of a bullet ripping through his flesh, but of the potential wound that could pierce his soul, right near the center point of the heart of a man. He could not go any further without letting her know he loved her, whether she felt the same or not. He took a deep breath and exhaled. He spoke nervously, "The first time I ever came up here, I was awestruck of just how beautiful the view is, especially in the wintertime. I never thought anything could be more beautiful than God's creation of combining mountains and snow. The combination is stunning. And then one day, I saw you, and I realize now that since I've gotten to know you that there is no one more beautiful to me than you. You are beautiful to me in every way. I love you, Christine, and I want you to be my lady if you would. I know I'm not much, but like the snow on the mountains, I think we'd make a beautiful combination."

She smiled slowly with a slight touch of water in her eyes. "I'd be honored to be your lady."

"You would?"

She grinned widely. She whispered, "Of course, I would."

"Would it be okay if I kissed you?" he asked with a slight hint of anxiety.

She laughed lightly. "I couldn't think of a better place for our first kiss."

He awkwardly moved forward and kissed her gently while his hands went to her cheeks. He pulled free from her lips and looked at her tenderly. "I've been tempted to do that for a while now," he admitted.

"So have I. I've been waiting and wanting to tell you that I'm in love with you too, Matt. I think we'll make a beautiful combination. The right combination."

10

Edith Williams, like the other ladies in the dance hall, was excited to hear that Matt and Christine were finally courting. She was confident that they would end up being married and live a happy life together. It didn't take long for the excitement Edith felt for Christine to become a personal reminder that she had yet to find love as real as Christine and Matt's. Edith had fallen for Paul Johnson quickly, and before she knew it, they were courting. It didn't take long for the relationship to become sexual, and she remembered Christine warning her not to give herself away before a wedding ring, but sex was the only way Edith knew to keep a man interested in her. When Edith was fifteen, she had fallen in love with an older man and ran away from her home to marry a man named Johnny "Denmark" Gottwells. He was a gambler that didn't have her best interest in mind. Running away with him was a mistake that had led her down a path of prostitution and abusive relationships.

How a man could promise to love her and vow to protect her like he had, and then turn around and beat her, use her, and then turn her into a prostitute for his financial gain was a good way to lose trust in men. After a few more so-called loves like that, she became cynical of relationships and men all together. Was it that she attracted the wrong kind of men or her folly in judgment that always ended up being the same story in another man? She had hoped Paul was a kind and gentle man who would fall in love with her and ask her to marry him as a gentleman should. At first, she thought he was sweet and charming, but every man starts out being kind, even the worst of them. In truth, Paul was a good man, and Edith felt for him in a way she had not felt for anyone before . Love was a word she didn't say easily, but she loved him. The walls she had created over the years were tough for her to let down, but Paul was insistent that he loved her. He treated her well, even after they had been sexual for some time. Just when she was growing confidant that she had finally found the real thing, Paul acted distant for a few days and then ended their courtship unexpectedly. He didn't give much of an explanation, certainly not a satisfactory one. All she knew for sure was he wanted to be single and didn't think he'd ever want to get married. His friend Sam hadn't been much help with information when it came to relaying anything substantial that Paul talked to him about either. All Sam said was, in his opinion, Paul had made a big mistake by letting her go. It did little to soothe her broken heart.

Christine was an exceptional lady with a far different history than Edith's own. They were as far apart on the scale of life values as any two women could be. However, Edith admired Christine for everything she represented in life. Her faith in God and the way she lived the things taught in the Bible she'd read daily, spoke louder than Christine's voice ever did. Christine didn't have to preach the Gospel, she lived it, and it was seen in her eyes as she cared empathetically for Edith and the other girls when they were scared, heartbroken, or damaged in any way. Christine would pray for them and let them all know Jesus wouldn't refuse any of them if they would give themselves over to Him, dust off their Bibles and read it and obey its words. All the girls had a belief in God, but few applied it the way Christine did. She was a Christian in word and deed. The way it was supposed to be, and the Lord was blessing her and Matt with each other. To Edith, it was a dream for them coming true.

It wasn't so long ago that Edith lived with the excitement of a future hope of love, and Christine was the one devastated. Even Christine, with all her values, had nearly fallen for a handsome and successful, but terrible man. In the depths of Christine's heartache and feeling like a fool, she met Matt. It was a friendship that grew day by day, and now their relationship was based upon their friendship and communication without ever kissing until today. Their foundation was built on a solid ground that would last. Edith wanted what they had found, that kind of security and trust. She wanted the inner peace and wisdom that Christine had as well. She wanted a man like Christine's too. Maybe that was why she took another look at Martin Ballenger. He was a nice man who looked at her with the same gaze that Matt watched at Christine with. There was no doubt about it; Martin was struck with adoration for Edith. He was handsome, not too successful yet, but he was a deputy with the Sheriff's Office and seemed to have more moral ground than the Sheriff himself. Martin was a man worth a chance to get to know anyway. He took her mind off Paul for a bit when she was with him if nothing else.

He had danced with her three times again tonight and kept himself busy at the bar buying drinks for himself and her. During the twenty-minute break that gave the ladies and the band a rest, Martin had asked to speak to her alone. He lead her to a private table away from Sam and Helen so they could talk. He sat across the small table from her with a drink and smiled at her kindly. "I feel like I must've known you in a past life, Edith, because I just can't believe how comfortable I am around you already."

She raised her eyebrows questionably. "Past life?"

He grinned. "I know it sounds silly, but it feels like it. What, have you never heard of that? I don't think I believe in it, but if I did, I'd swear we were married in a past life because I feel like I know you already. We just seem to fit; do you know what I mean?" He emphasized by locking his hands together.

Edith smirked questionably and placed her elbow on the table to lean her chin on her hand. "You know me, huh? Well, tell me a little bit about myself then.

I'm looking forward to hearing this," she said with an expectant smile growing as she took a sip of her small glass of pink lemonade disguised as champagne.

"Well, you're beautiful, obviously, but you don't think so. You would love to be married and treated right, but you haven't met the right man yet. Until now, that is. But you aren't so sure about that yet either. You will be. You have a sensitive heart, and it's broken right now, so you're really not looking for me or anyone else at the moment. What you are looking for is peace and a way to take the pain away. Now, if I'm not mistaken, you had a tough past and were abused by men and a bit of prostitution too. Don't worry; I'll love you anyway," he said with a wink. "Long story short, we're both still fairly young and have time to wait. I don't want to hurry you, but I hope one day you'll see me as more than just a suiter. Because I'll show what real love is and I'll make you happy whether we're rich or poor. And I mean that."

Edith's head had raised, and her hand fell to the table. She stared at him, taken back by his words. True, much of it was basic knowledge, but she was surprised by his boldness and confidence in being the one for her. She gasped questionably. "You don't even know me, Martin. You just met me last night."

He held up a finger to pause her. "I know. And like I said, it might sound silly, but I feel like I've known you forever, believe it or not. Look, I'm perfectly safe, I'm not trying to rush you into anything. But I think I'd be a fool to let you pass by me without letting you know I'm very interested in pursuing you. Edith, you're the most beautiful woman I've ever seen, and I'm caught like a steer on a rope or a fish in a net. You caught me." He spread out his arms innocently and finished with a smile.

Edith smiled appreciatively. "I didn't set a trap."

He laughed lightly. "I know. That's what makes this so amazing to me. I don't believe in past lives, but I think it's moments like these that make people think so. Interestingly enough, I talked to a spiritualist in Salem one time that said I would find love from the past. I have no idea what that means, but maybe it's finding someone new and feeling like old friends. All I know is I feel wonderful and comfortable when I'm with you. I'm in no hurry. I'd rather have a friendship and love like my friend Matt's and Christine's than to jump right into something. So please, take your time with me," he laughed lightly. She had told him the night before of her admiration for what Matt and Christine had. She had already told him about them courting.

She furrowed her brow and leaned towards him slightly. "That's what I want. I was very excited about them courting. Yeah, I agree, what they have is what I want."

He shrugged. "You know there's no reason why we can't have the same thing. I mean, why not? Well, unless you're not willing to get to know me, then that's a pretty good reason why we wouldn't," he laughed lightly. "But, if I'm worthy of getting to know at least, then why not? It could work out that way. I'm a pretty good guy, and I won't hurt you. I'm a good friend, and maybe that's all we need to know right now. I know you don't know me, so how about we agree to be friends. Can we start by being friends?" he asked and reached over the table to shake her hand.

She smiled slowly and reached out to shake his hand. "We can." He refused to let go of her hand and held it softly in his own on the table.

He explained, "I'm a romantic, what can I say? When the most beautiful lady in the world grabs my hand, I don't want to let it go. Do you mind if I hold your hand for a bit?"

"No, I suppose not," she snickered flattered by his words and attention.

"Good. So is there anything you want to ask me about?" he asked.

"I don't know," she laughed. "Just tell me about yourself, I guess."

"Okay. I'm twenty-seven and have been taking care of my mother and little sister for ten years now. I have worked on farms and a dairy mostly before coming here. I tried working for the silver mine when I first got here, but no way! I'm an above-ground kind of man. And now I'm a deputy sheriff. I hope someday to be the sheriff in two to four years. I think I can connect better with people than Tim does in an election."

"Probably. The Sheriff's not well-liked around here. So, tell me, why are you not married? You seem too nice and fun to be a bachelor," she asked quietly.

Martin took a deep breath and sighed. "I asked a girl once. She luckily said no, or I wouldn't be here with you." He frowned and continued, "She ended up choking on a radish not long after I asked her. It was very devastating."

"I am sorry. That must have been heartbreaking."

He could feel her fingers tighten around his hand, warmly. "It was unfortunate."

"Did you love her?"

"Well, I asked her to marry me." He smiled. "I worked for her father on his farm. She didn't want to marry a poor farm boy. What she didn't know is if she had said yes, we would have inherited that farm and been quite wealthy with me running it. Unfortunately, her parents came home from church and found her dead on the kitchen floor. There was a radish stuck in her throat. It was horrible. I couldn't work there after that; It was too painful. But I'm not a desperate farm boy anymore. I believe in love and lifelong marriage. I believe in taking care of and protecting my family, and someday, soon, hopefully, I'll be able to start my own family with a wife that I'll cherish and love very much. And then we're going to own this town. You and me, just watch and see," he laughed lightly while squeezing her hand gently.

She grinned widely. "What makes you think I'd want to marry you anyway?"

He raised his eyebrows knowingly. "You're still holding my hand. Let me ask you, were you attracted to me when you first saw me? You must have been because you invited me to stay after the building closed to get to know me. Am I right?"

She smiled slightly embarrassed. "Yes."

He tilted his head. "There you have it. Your old

suiter was the wrong man for you. But deep down, you already knew that, right?"

She frowned sadly. "I suppose I did."

He shrugged knowingly. "Of course. I think we're meant to be together, but that's just me. It takes two in a relationship as beautiful as Matt's and Christine's. But even they had to start somewhere, and I think we're right on their tail. Just you wait and see."

She nodded slightly. "You're weird, but I like you." She handed him a red ticket already signed by Bella to stay after hours again. "I was hoping you would come back tonight. Thanks for talking to me, but the bands starting in a minute and I have to get to work."

He smiled. "I'd love to stay after. Thank you. But as for now, I need to use the privy and then get another drink. Would you like one?"

"After we close down," she said kindly. "I'll be dancing until closing time, but then I'd love a drink."

Martin had already spent the ten dollars he had gotten from his mother, but he wasn't done drinking, and he needed money to buy drinks while visiting with Edith after the dance hall closed. He was there to impress her, after all. Martin wandered casually to the bar and scanned the top of it for any money laying out unattended. There were a few dollar coins and other coins in front of one man and down the bar a few dollar bills in a stack, but there was a group of friends standing near it talking loudly. One trick to stealing money under someone's nose was not making it visible and then directing the attention elsewhere. As the band prepared to start the next dance, the crowd of men were for the most part focused on finding a lady to dance with or continuing with their conversations. The lighting was brighter than he liked, and the area around the bar was crowded with men from all walks of life as it was a common place for the men to stand. On a table, he saw a five-dollar bill setting near the edge with two men sitting at the table, but their eyes were on a couple of the ladies across the room talking with each other. Martin casually glanced around to make sure no one was watching him and then walked by the table and expertly snatched the money up with a natural swing of his arm as he walked by. Martin then quickly tapped a man standing nearby on the shoulder who was talking to another man. He immediately began introducing himself to the two gentlemen as the new deputy sheriff.

A moment later, they heard, "Hey, where'd that money go?" one of the men at the table asked, looking around on the floor.

"It was right there. I just put it there," the other replied.

"Are you sure?"

"Of course, I'm sure. Did someone steal our money?" the first man asked.

Martin turned around to speak to them. "Gentlemen, I'm Martin Ballenger, the new deputy sheriff in town. Did you say someone stoled your money?"

"Yeah! It was sitting right there! It's all we had. Someone took our money."

Martin shook his head. "Thieves. If there's anything I hate, it's a thief! Well, let's see if anyone saw anything." He hollered before the band started up, "Excuse me. Excuse me! Listen up, folks, there's a thief around here, and he just stoled some money off this table. Did anyone see anything at all? I'm deputy Martin Ballenger, and I'm new in town, but I'll arrest whoever did it. How much did they take, fella's?"

"A five-dollar bill! It's all we had," one of the men said in disbelief. Both men appeared to be lumbermen.

"Someone stoled five dollars. If you've seen anything, let me know." He introduced himself to the men and shook their hands and apologized for not being able to help them after all when no one came forward.

Martin went out the front door and walked behind the dance hall, where a building served as one of the district privies along Rose Street. Inside, it was separated into two sections, one side had a wooden bench with multiple oval-shaped holes that dropped down into a cesspool, and on the other side, there was a four-inch metal channel in the floor with two holes that drained into the cesspool under the building. The smell was horrid, but it worked for relieving one's self. Martin urinated and then making small talk with a well-intoxicated man leaning against the wall while he peed. Martin pretending to be more intoxicated than he was, stumbled into the man and slipped his hand into the man's loose-fitting pocket and pulled out his thin wallet, and left the privy checking the wallet for money before he disappointedly tossed it to the side. He went back to the dance hall and ordered a drink. Martin paid with a five-dollar bill. The change he received, he put in his empty coin purse for drinks later.

He sat back down at the table by himself and watched Edith dancing with another man. Martin watched the man smiling at Edith and doing his best to win her attention. It was then that Martin noticed Edith was laughing at the man as they danced with the same smile she had when she danced with him. A sour expression began to take over his face with a surge of growing indignation. She should smile differently when she danced with other men because he was different than everyone else. He was special.

Sam Troyer pulled out the chair Edith had sat in and sat down across from Martin. "You better get used to it, Martin. Edith is a dancer, and she dances for a living."

Martin lowered his brow. "Why do you say that? I know what she does for a living," he answered snidely. He couldn't say he liked Sam that much since learning he was Paul's friend. Martin was a bit irritated that he sat down uninvited.

Sam grinned. "You look jealous, that's why. Listen, she just got her heartbroken by my friend. I suggest you don't get too attached, because they might be getting back together again before too long. I know Paul, and he's just trying to figure out his feelings. I suspect he'll take a few days to figure out how much he loves her and then come crawling back like a lost pup. They love each other; Paul just is a little slow in making sure of that."

Martin watched Sam with a cold gaze. "I think she's old enough and smart enough to make her own choice."

Sam shrugged his shoulders. "I never said she couldn't. What I am saying is don't get too attached. She's in love with Paul. There's a bunch of other ladies you could get to know. Edith is taken," he finished on a serious note.

Martin smirked without concern. "What business is it of yours anyway, Sam? Maybe she'll pick me over your friend. I'd appreciate you and your woman staying out of it and not interfering on your friend's behalf. Edith and I were made for each other."

Sam scoffed with an added laugh. "Right. We'll see about that." He stood up and leaned over, placing his hands on the table to speak lowly, "Listen, you're a deputy, and I'm not looking for any trouble, but I saw you take that money. I know you're a thief. I won't say a thing if you leave Edith alone, but if you cause any trouble for my friend and her, everyone will know you're a thief."

Martin's eyes narrowed as his face reddened a little. "I don't know what you're talking about."

Sam nodded. "Sure, you do. Stay away from her."

Martin's eyes hardened as he glared dangerously at Sam. "It's your word against mine. You better back off yourself, or I'll make up a reason to arrest you."

Sam laughed under his breath. "I'm afraid your boss already tried threatening me once. There's only one source of law around here, and that's Matt

Bannister, who happens to be a friend of mine. Your badge means nothing to me because I know what a piece of crap your boss is. After seeing you steal that money, I know you're about the same. Leave Edith alone, or I'll tell Bella, and you won't be allowed back in here."

"It's your word against mine," Martin said, trying to control the anger that was building inside of him. He showed him the red ticket Edith gave him. "I'm staying after to visit with Edith whether you like it or not. Tell anyone you want whatever you want, but soon she'll be with me. Tell your friend she's his loss and my gain."

Sam grinned and shook his head. "It's your heart that's going to get broke. But I look forward to seeing it."

"It's mine if it does, but I don't think so. I don't like you, Sam. You can leave now."

"Yeah, I don't like you either. I look forward to seeing you crying over your broken heart, though," he said and left Martin sitting alone.

Martin sighed irritated that he had been caught stealing after all, by Sam of all people. It could've been worse; he could have gotten caught in the act or pointed out as the thief by Sam then and there. It could have been much worse.

11

Martin gazed into Edith's eyes with a sincere expression. "I don't know why Sam would say that about me. I never did anything to him. Gosh, you know it's weird because I asked everyone in the dance hall if they saw who took the money. If I had taken it, someone could've said so then. Sam could have said something then. I would've been caught red-handed and lost my job and everything. Seriously, Edith, you have to ask yourself if I would have risked my job and my reputation, along with being able to come in here and talk to you. Would I risk all of that for a lousy five dollars? I couldn't steal a bucket of dung from a rancher without asking him if it was okay first. I'm honest like that! I didn't take any money. I don't know why Sam would say that. I just don't know other than he doesn't like me because I'm talking to you."

"Should we go ask him?" Edith asked. They were standing near the entry door leaning against the wall. Sam had told Edith he witnessed Martin steal the money off the table. Theft was not tolerated, and thieves were not welcomed back inside the dance hall permanently. As Edith's guest, it was only right for her to confront him about the stolen money before Bella did.

Martin shook his head. "No. Do you know why? Because I think I know what's going on. Sam doesn't want you talking to me because you're his best friend's lady, or he thinks so still. That's what this is all about. He and your friend Helen don't want you to find someone new. They hope you'll go back to Paul. I've seen this kind of stuff before, and they're going try to sweet-talk him into coming back for you." He sighed heavily. "I hope you'll remember me when they finally get him to listen. I don't think he honors you the way I do. I'm sorry, Edith, I never wanted to come between you and your friends, but they're messing with you and lying about me to keep you away from me. I think you're too smart for that, but just in case, do me a favor and don't let them steal you away from me that easily, please. I honestly believe we could have everything it takes to make a good life together, just like Matt and Christine. Or at least, I would like to explore that opportunity now that we're friends. I guess I need to ask, are you still interested in exploring that option with me as well?"

She appeared to be in deep thought as she thought about his words. "Martin...It's just so soon. I don't know. I'm confused and need some time."

He smiled a sad little smile. "Unlike them," he

darted his eyes into the ballroom to a table near the bar where Sam and Helen were sitting watching them. "I won't ever rush you to make a decision about me or…Paul. You'd think if Paul cared about you, he'd be here instead of me. You know, Sam suggested I try to court other women here like Angela, that's who he suggested. You see, Sam isn't concerned about me being a thief, or he never would've suggested I court anyone here. What he's worried about is me wanting to get to know you. Your friends, over there, have their own motives, and that's to get their little group back together. They don't care about your feelings or what you want. They're going to sabotage every relationship you have until they have they want. Look, at them, they're just staring over here, wondering what we're saying, and it's killing them not to know. If that's the kind of friends you want to have, that's fine. I don't let my friends dictate my life, though." He took a deep breath. "Listen, Edith, I'm a good thing, and I am interested in you. You're the most beautiful lady I've ever known, and twice as beautiful as Christine, by the way. I'm going to go so you can think things over, but just remember, those two friends of yours may try to control you, but you have to pull away from them someday and make your own decisions. I'm not a thief, that's just another trick to get me out of the picture. And if I confront Sam about it, I'd want to punch him in the face, and I don't want to be kicked out of here." he said with a sad smile. "I have a loving heart big enough to carry us both through life. I'm serious about getting to know you. The real you. I'll bet your old flame never said that, did he?"

She shook her head sadly.

"Of course not, or he would be here instead of me. Anyway, I hoped to give you this at a better time, but I wanted you to have it. When I saw it, I thought it was beautiful, just like you. And I want you to have it whether you believe me or not about the theft accusation or even if you go back to your old flame. There's not a lady in the world who could wear it better than you." He pulled a white square box with a red bow tied around it out of his coat pocket and handed it to her.

"What's this?" she asked, surprised.

"Open it," he suggested with a pleasing smile.

She untied the bow and lifted the top of the box. Inside was an attractive metal hair brooch decorated with green leaves and a red rose at its center. She grinned widely. "Thank you, Martin. I love it."

"You'll wear it?" he asked.

"Of course."

"Good. I'm glad you like it. I can't wait to see you wear it. Well, I suppose I better leave so you can visit with your friends."

"Martin…" she said quickly. "You don't have to leave. We can sit at our table and talk. You still owe me a drink," she said with a smile.

He smiled slowly. "Well, let me ask you, are you interested in getting to know me better?"

She grimaced playfully. "Yeah, I guess I am."

Martin came home late and was feeling quite excited about his future. His evening had started a little rough when Sam confronted him, but it had ended well after two hours of conversation with Edith. Sam and Helen had left the ballroom when Martin and Edith sat down away from them, and most of the other ladies had their private conversations with other men. He had only seen Matt Bannister for a second when he came by to tell Christine goodnight, and then she went upstairs for the night. The night was even better than the night before. Edith was an amazing lady, and he was sure he had finally found the one lady that would make his life complete.

He fumbled with the door key and stepped into the main room of their apartment. He was surprised to see a lantern hanging from the ceiling still lit, and his mother Sylvia sitting in a chair glaring at him with a cross expression.

He smiled with the influence of alcohol and the exuberance he felt from another great night spent in Edith's company. "Mother, I had such a wonderful night! I have found my soul mate. Finally, Mother, I know I have found her. She's so beautiful and sweet. You're going to love her." He sat down in the cushioned chair, separated by a small table from her.

She asked curtly, "Where did you get the money to drink? I told you to buy a half cord of wood and a few items. Not a bag of coal! How much money is left, Martin?" Her eyes burned into him.

"Mother, didn't you hear me? I found my soul mate."

"I don't care about your damn soul mate! I care about feeding my family until payday. How much money did you spend?"

Martin laughed slightly and waved a hand as he said, "All of it."

"What do you mean all of it?" she asked heatedly.

"I spent all of it. I don't have any money left. But we have coal and some food. We'll be fine."

"Why didn't you buy a half cord of wood like I told you to?"

He sighed heavily. "It was too expensive. I got coal because it's cheaper, and I got the food on your list."

"Yeah, I saw the food. You got what I wrote down for you to get, but why did you get a hair brooch for a dollar fifty? What kind of brooch costs a dollar fifty, and where is it?" she asked heatedly.

Martin giggled. "I got it for Edith, and she loved it. I think she'll look fantastic with it."

Sylvia stared at her son, angrily. "I don't give one cent about this Edith or your soul mate! I'm wondering what we're going to do for dinners this week until I get paid next Friday. You get paid at the end of the month. My pay is going to be low because a few dollars will be coming out to pay for that ten dollars over the next few weeks. I only make five dollars a week, Martin! We don't have money for you to go drinking! We have rent coming up, and that's coming out your pay first thing. Now how did you get this crap and go drinking too?"

Martin was getting annoyed. "Don't worry about it. I charged it all at the store."

Sylvia grimaced and ran her hand through her hair. She spoke heatedly while keeping her voice low, trying not to wake the neighbors. "Are you stupid, Martin? How much did you charge?" She sat at the edge of her chair turned towards him.

He shrugged. "Close to ten dollars or so, but I got a lot of stuff. We're fine."

Her eyes glared into him harshly. "You charged ten dollars, and we need ten dollars for rent in two weeks? That's twenty dollars right there we have to pay. I gave you ten dollars to buy wood and food, and now I am ten dollars more in debt than I was this morning! Coal smoke gives me a headache, Martin! You know that. We came here to make a new start, and we're already drowning because of you!"

He sighed with irritation. "Mother, I can get money anytime. Don't worry about it."

"Martin, we'll talk tomorrow, because I am very disgusted with you right now!"

"Mother, it will all be fine. I'll take care of everything. Do you want to hear about Edith?"

"No, I don't! I want to go to bed and get some sleep. Your sister and I are going to church tomorrow with Henry. Would you like to go?"

"Church?" he asked with disdain. "No. Who's Henry?"

"My boss, Henry Redlin. He asked me to join him at church. I think it will be good for us to go. I haven't been to church in ages. It wouldn't hurt you to go either."

"I have my own church."

"Really? What might that be?" she asked skeptically.

Martin narrowed his eyes with irritation. "Why are you going with him, anyway?"

"Because Henry's a very nice man and he invited

Barbra and me. He invited you as well if you want to go with us?"

Martin shook his head with a growing resentful sneer. "Borah was nice too, remember him? I could show you the burns on my back if you don't. Howard was nice, too, remember him? He nearly beat you to death. And Jessie, that prince who went after Barbra? Yeah, he was nice too, wasn't he?" he seethed with his eyes burning into his mother. "How about you just leave the men alone, okay? You can't pick them without them hurting you or one of us. I won't let this one near Barbra, and I don't care how nice you say he is. If he takes an interest in you, he's bad!"

Sylvia's teeth clenched together tight as she stared at her son with tears building up in her eyes. "How dare you?" she asked quietly. "I've done nothing to hurt you two."

Martin slowly shrugged and held up his hands in emphasis. "What did they call, Steve, oh yeah, how about leaving us with Hawk?" He glared at her angrily. "Keep your friend Henry away from Barbra and me. Nice means nothing, every man you meet is nice, Mother! Even if they're the most wretched human beings alive."

Sylvia began to sob. "I've told you and told you I am sorry for that. How many times do I have to plead for your forgiveness before you stop shoving that in my face? I've told you I am sorry for leaving you both with that bastard! I would never put you in harm's way." She buried her face in her hands while she cried.

Martin watched her emotionlessly with a cold glare in his eyes. "Forgiveness doesn't remove scars, Mother. Borah burned me with his cigar again and again. Howard just hit a lot. Jessie nearly raped your daughter if it wasn't for me coming home. Where were you? You left her with him even after she told you he was trying to touch her! And Hawk? No, Mother dear, forgiveness does not heal the scars."

"What do I have to do before you stop blaming me?" she asked desperately with a raised voice.

Martin shook his head slowly. "There's nothing you can do. It is your fault. Just keep that fat boss of yours away from here and away from my sister."

"Are you ever going to forgive me for bringing those awful men into our home?" she asked weakly through her anguished tears.

He scoffed slightly with a wicked grin. "It was never our home! We were always going from one man's home to the next. You warmed their bed, and Barbra and I were just dogs to kick around and use. You say you didn't hurt us, but you put us there. And you kept putting us there over and over again!"

"What choice did I have?" she cried out loudly. "Your father wasn't there to help support us, was he?"

"Nope, he wasn't," he answered simply. "But if you were loyal to him, maybe he would've been."

"I was loyal to him!" she yelled. "I never mistreated that man, but if I went out to pee, he was wondering who met me there! He accused me of committing adultery, but how could I when I could hardly leave the house without him accusing me of something? No! He left on his own accord. He was the one whoring around every chance he had! Not me. I was abandoned with two children and no money."

Martin shook his head calmly. "I wonder what's worse leaving your family, or putting your children in the hands of one cruel man, one after the other for years? My father made his choice, but he didn't take me to Borah's house or Hawk's. Those were the choices you made. Not mine or Barbra's."

"Don't you think I know that!" she yelled as she stood up and went to her bedroom doorway bawling. She turned around. "Are you going to blame me for everything bad that's ever happened to you, Martin?"

He held his arms outward defensively and then pointed at his wrist. "Yeah, maybe you better go to church because it wasn't the sins of my father that put this scar of a cigar burn on my wrist, now was it?"

Sylvia slammed the door behind her as she went into her room, crying bitterly.

Martin raised his voice loud enough for her to hear, "Don't ask me to go to church again!" Martin said as he went into the kitchen to find some jerky he bought at the store.

12

Matt and Christine had gone to church and sat with Albert and Mellissa Bannister's family during the service. There was going to be a potluck after church, and although the church building was large enough to hold the congregation, it didn't have the kitchen space or a space large enough to hold the tables needed for a potluck. Reverend Eli Painter rented the bottom floor of the Branson Community Hall for the potluck so the food could be warmed up, and there'd be plenty of room to eat and socialize after the church service.

Matt and Christine filled their plates with good food and sat with Albert and his family and a few others at one of the tables and enjoyed a nice lunch. When they had finished eating, Matt took their dishes back to the kitchen, where a few of the older ladies in the church were washing the dishes and putting them away. Like most potlucks, after eating, there was time to socialize, and everyone intermixed and spoke of everything from politics to new babies and quilt making. Matt didn't mind talking to people, but he had an idea and waited patiently for Christine to finish a conversation with Mellissa and a few other ladies from the church. When she was ready to break away from them, Matt took her by the hand and began to leave the potluck, but before he could get very far, Henry Redlin called out to him and led a lady and a teenage girl over to Matt and Christine.

"Matt, I'm glad I caught you before you left. I wanted to introduce you to my friend and new employee, Sylvia, and her daughter, Barbra. This is the famous U.S. Marshal Matt Bannister and his dear friend, Christine Knapp. Wait…are you two courting now?" he asked, looking at their hands held together.

Matt smiled. "We are."

"Fantastic! Congratulations," Henry said sincerely and shook Matt's hand.

Matt glanced at Sylvia and reached his hand out to shake her hand. "We met once. How do you like our town so far?" he asked, maintaining eye contact.

Sylvia smiled slightly embarrassed by how she had flirted with the Marshal when she first met him. "I love it. My son's the deputy, and Henry was good enough to give me a job as well. I think we're going to like it here a lot," she said, shaking Matt's hand. She turned her attention towards Christine. "My word, you are beautiful."

Christine smiled. "Thank you. You are very pretty yourself, and your daughter is stunning. How old are you, Barbra?"

Barbra lowered her eyes self-consciously. "I'm fifteen." Barbra was five foot six and had thin features. She had a long and narrow face but had the prettiest big blue eyes and brown shoulder-length hair. She was a beautiful young lady, though, by her mannerisms, she had no idea how attractive she was.

Christine continued, "You are a beautiful young lady, to say the least. You shouldn't hide your face; you have no reason to. You're stunning."

"Thank you," she said with her face turning red.

Christine said to Sylvia, "She gets her beauty from her mother, no doubt."

Henry nodded. "There's no doubt about that. Her boy's a handsome young man too, but he didn't want to join us today."

Matt explained to Christine, "Her son is Martin Ballenger, the new sheriff's deputy."

"Oh! I've met him. He's been talking with my friend Edith at the dance hall."

"Wait," Sylvia said thoughtfully. "Are you a dancer there?" she sounded surprised.

"I am."

"Oh. I wasn't expecting that. Martin told me about this Edith, but I thought she was a…" she paused and shrugged her shoulders apologetically.

"No," Christine said with a slight chuckle. "She's a very good friend of mine and all we do is dance. That is all we do," she emphasized.

"Oh, good. I always hoped Martin would meet a nice lady to settle down with."

Christine smiled. "Maybe someday if he proves to be the man she is waiting for. However, she just ended a serious courtship with a gentleman and isn't ready to move on yet. So, let Martin know to give her some time to adjust and get over Paul."

Matt spoke to Henry, "Thank you for bringing the meatballs. They were delicious as always."

Henry smiled. "You're welcome."

Barbra looked at Matt curiously. "Can I ask you a question?"

"You bet."

"Why do you wear your gun to church?"

"Barbra!" Sylvia admonished her.

Matt chuckled. "It's fine. To answer your question, it's because there's a lot of people who don't like me. And the people who don't like me, you probably wouldn't want to dislike you. So, I don't let my guard down, not even in the church. There are certain places where people do not expect to be attacked, and being at church is one of them. Those who want to harm me know that as well. The best thing I can do is be prepared, even if it's unlikely."

"Should my brother wear his gun to church and everywhere too?"

Matt grimaced. "I've seen too many young deputies become arrogant with a gun on their hip. There's a sense of power and arrogance that's fairly common when a young man puts on a badge for the first time. Unfortunately, the combination of arrogance and a gun has gotten a lot of them killed within the first year of the job. That's why I keep my deputies low on experience on a very short leash. No, I don't think he should. It could lead to trouble he may not be ready to handle."

"He's wearing it everywhere now," Barbra said.

"Wearing it is one thing, it's the thinking you're too important with it that is the biggest problem. My advice for your brother is to stay humble."

Henry said, "It was good talking to you, Matt. I just wanted to introduce you to Sylvia and Barbra. The more people they get to know around here, the more at home they will feel. I think I'll go introduce them to Albert and Mellissa now."

Matt shook his hand again. "Nice to meet you, ladies, again. Henry, I'll be seeing you soon."

After they parted ways, Matt took Christine's hand gently and led her out of the main room towards the exit door and untied the rope that closed off the stairway leading upstairs.

"What are you up to?" she asked questionably.

"You'll see." He led her upstairs to the main dance floor. It was a wide-open wooden dance floor with a stage at one end for the band to play at community dances. He lead Christine to the center of the dance floor and turned towards her putting his hand around her waist. "Can I have this dance?"

She smiled affectionately with her eyes shining brightly into his. "Surely, Mister Bannister."

They danced closely together in the silence of the room with her head resting against his shoulder. "I think I could dance with you forever," he said lightly.

She stared into his eyes and stopped dancing. "I would like that," she whispered.

He moved forward and kissed her.

Albert Bannister saw Matt kissing Christine

and cupped his hands over his mouth and yelled forcefully, "Whoa! You're not married! Get away from her." He then laughed as he walked onto the dance floor with his wife, Mellissa. "I think we'll join you," he said with a humored smile.

Matt laughed lightly. "There's a law forbidding Blacksmith's from dancing. At least there should be. Step on my toes one time, buddy, and you're going downstairs head first."

Albert laughed, "I'm just trying to keep you out of trouble! Up here, all alone kissing a beautiful lady...Yeah, this is what big brothers are for."

Mellissa grinned happily. "Never mind him, go back to what you were doing." She smiled at Albert fondly. "Leave them alone. You're such a brute." They began dancing in the silence as well.

"It came from upstairs," a voice was heard saying from the bottom of the stairs. "Someone's upstairs."

Matt sighed lightly. "I think our moment of solitude is over." He peered over at Albert and shook his head. "You had to yell, didn't you?"

Albert laughed. "Sorry."

Christine spoke softly as they danced. "It doesn't matter. I'm happy in your arms just the same."

The sound of footsteps climbing the stairs sounded like a heard of cattle as a group of people came up to the dance floor. Some began dancing with their wives, and others just loitered around to continue their conversations while watching them dance.

Henry Redlin came upstairs with Sylvia and Barbra. He laughed when he saw the people dancing without music. "I love my church family. Sylvia, any chance you'd like to dance?"

Her eyes opened wide with surprise. "Sure," she answered.

On the dance floor, Henry danced respectfully with Sylvia. "Thank you," he said. "I'm not the most handsome fella in town or any town for that matter..."

"Don't say that," Sylvia began.

"No, it's true. I know I'm not handsome at all. It doesn't take much more than looking in the mirror for me to know that. So, thank you for coming to church with me, and for this dance. I appreciate it."

Sylvia smiled warmly and lowered her face. She asked with the sound of a burdened heart, "What's the worst thing you've ever done to someone, Henry?"

He frowned. "I don't know. Maybe a joke I pulled on a friend of mine, and I didn't think about how embarrassed he'd be. I apologized for it, and I felt bad. You? What's the worst thing you've done?"

Sylvia took a deep breath. "That's not so bad, Henry."

"Well, he didn't appreciate it. I should've considered his feelings more."

She paused the dance to look up at him sincerely. "Henry, are you really that nice?"

He seemed surprised by her question. "It wasn't a nice joke."

Sylvia chuckled. "You're a very rare kind of man, Henry."

He grimaced and shook his head slightly. "I don't think so. I'm pretty plain. So, what's the worst thing you've done to someone?"

She shook her head sadly. "It doesn't matter. I

was just asking because most of the men I've known hurt my children and me."

He shook his head, compassionately. "Well, no one should have ever harmed your children or you. I'm sorry to hear that. But if you're expecting me to be a monster, I'm not. I might look like one, but I'm not one."

"You don't look like a monster." She pulled herself closer to him as they danced. "That's the worst thing I've ever done, Henry. I left my kids with monsters." She had tears in her eyes.

Henry frowned as he stopped dancing and looked at her with genuine caring.

She continued, "I never thought anyone would ever hurt my children, but they did. And it's my fault for putting them in the homes of men I thought I knew. I didn't," she said with tears welling up in her eyes. "Martin reminds me that it's my fault all the time."

"Did you allow it, or did you get them out of there?"

"I got them out as soon as I found out. I loved my children and wouldn't stand for anyone hurting them. But every man I met and fell for turned out to be a monster, it seemed. Until I said no more men and struggled to raise them alone."

"You can't blame yourself for someone else's actions. But I can understand your regret for putting them in a place like that too. Once the damage is done, you can't take it back. It's unfortunate because children should never be harmed in any way, to begin with. Hopefully, those men will face the consequences for what they have done, and if not here on earth, they certainly will when they face the Lord at their judgment. The Lord says vengeance is his, and sometimes that's where it happens. In the most terrifying court imaginable with a judge, you can't lie to, because he already knows. What I'm saying is they're not going to get away with it. No one will. So in the meantime, you and your children need to heal. You need to forgive those monsters for what they've done. But more importantly, you need to forgive yourself even more so."

"I don't know if I know how," she said softly. "How does one forgive such wickedness? And how can I forgive myself when I can see the scars on my son's arms? He still blames me, Henry."

He took a deep breath. He spoke softly, "Out in the oceans; there are giant icebergs, big pieces of ice bigger than this building. Most of the iceberg is underwater, and it's still pretty big. I've never seen one, but I've read about them and seen pictures. Unforgiven hurts, or people are like one of those icebergs. The depth of how bad we're hurt is buried deep within, deeper than what shows on the outside. How do you forgive something so massive that there seems no way to forgive someone for it? The answer is like an iceberg. It melts a little at a time, and the more that melts away at the surface, the more it rises out of the depths. You forgive them every day, and every time they come to mind. The damage they caused is so infuriating that it's hard to get rid of it all at once, so you do it one day at a time. And gradually that massive iceberg can no longer sink a ship but can keep your glass of sun tea cold. And then the next day, when that last little bit of ice is gone, you realize you have forgiven them, and you are free of that burden." Henry paused. "That's how you do it, Sylvia. But you have to be willing to forgive; otherwise, that massive iceberg of hate, bitterness, or guilt is going to sink your ship. And that brings a lot of casualties along with it. I don't want to see you fall, so make the decision to forgive yourself and the men who harmed you and your children."

She listened closely. "Thank you, Henry."

"I hope it helps. As far as Martin goes, he has to make his own choice. But you can't keep hanging on to the guilt like you are. You have to forgive yourself."

Reverend Eli Painter walked upstairs and looked around with concern. "Folks," he hollered, "we didn't rent the upper floor. So please, come downstairs. Whoever untied the rope had no right to do that. I would hate to be charged for the cost of the whole community hall when we only reserved the bottom floor. So please, all of you, come downstairs before we're charged a full fee."

Albert Bannister kept dancing with his wife as he said, "Sorry, Reverend, but I'm dancing with my wife. I think we can all say, forget it. We're dancing."

Matt added with a growing smile, "It's my fault, Reverend Painter. Albert will take care of the fee if they charge you for it," he teased. "No, I'll take care of it." He grinned with a slight laugh.

Henry stopped dancing and raised his hand to get everyone's attention. "No, I'll pay the entire fee myself, Reverend, because the time spent with this lady has been worth every second. And I want to keep dancing with my new friend for as long as she's willing to dance with me."

Sylvia smiled gently. "It will be my honor to dance for as long as you like. Thank you, Henry."

Reverend Eli Painter shook his head slightly. "Well, I won't argue with a blacksmith, butcher and a U.S Marshal. That's a losing bet there. So, there's only one thing to do, and that's going down and get my wife. I think we'll dance too." He said with a wink and a smile.

"Billy, boy," a lady told her teenage son, "Run home and get your fiddle and hurry back. We're having a church dance!"

13

Leroy Haywood didn't need his friends to be mean or cruel. He had walked into town before church was out and spent a few hours drinking before he left the saloon with a good dose of alcohol in his system. He wanted to stroll through Chinatown in the daylight while all of the rats were out of their holes before he walked back to the Slater's Mile. He entered Chinatown and chuckled as he pushed the first skinny Chinese man down to the ground he had come across. The man happened to be carrying a duck that got away when he fell.

"Where are your women?" he asked. "You un-natural heathens prefer ducks?" he laughed as the man scrambled after the duck he had been carrying. Leroy walked one block after the other, knocking over tables of food, goods to be sold, and slapping the Chinese men across the head as he walked along. His foul mouth and curses were not understood by the Chinese he swore at, but the tone was clearly not friendly. The Chinese who saw him coming either closed their shop and got out his way or humbly nodded and walked away as quickly as they could. Leroy was entertained by the panic he was causing, and he felt powerful as he watched the Chinese scatter like cockroaches a block ahead of him. It was fun to cause chaos, and he loved every minute of it. What he couldn't quite understand was why he seldom saw Chinese women. Leroy's wife had left him recently, but he couldn't say he cared. She cooked, and that was all she was good for, really. He had no attraction to her and went to the brothel when the urge arose. He liked living alone and felt a surge of energy like he was alive again when he thought about going home. It was still daylight and early for him to go back on a Sunday afternoon, but he didn't mind at all after a weekend of carousing and drinking. He didn't have to put up with his woman, and that was something to look forward to anyway.

He walked block after block causing as much damage and harm as he could. A small dog came at him barking continuously. "Oh, what a cute little pup," Leroy said, calling it over with its wagging tail. He stepped forward and kicked the small dog as hard as he could in the ribs. The dog flew and rolled to a stop and limped painfully out of sight behind the building.

The dog's owner, a middle-aged man in black clothing and his long hair in a queue, ranted in Chinese angrily with concern for his dog.

Leroy stood where he was and watched the man

challenging him as he chuckled. "What are you going to do about it?" he asked with a pleased smile. "Go make stew, huh? Let me speak china man-ish, deadpuppyyummy," he laughed as he made the hand gesture of using a fork to eat with. He smiled as the man went inside. "You're welcome for the meal!" he laughed and started walking farther down the block.

He came to the block where he had been confronted by Wu-Pen and his two guards the evening before. He recognized the building and red door that Wu-Pen and his men had come out of. Leroy laughed to himself and walked over to the door, unbuttoned his pants, and began peeing on it. The Chinese on the street who saw him turned away in a hurry and moved past quickly. Leroy lifted the stream of urine upwards, sideways, and even in circles to cover as much of the door as he could. He laughed like a mad man as he did so. "Hey in there, open up and have a bath!" he laughed. "I'll piss on you all."

He finished and began buttoning his pants when the door opened. Wu-pen stood in the doorway with his guards right behind him. Wu-Pen was smiling.

"Piss on you and all you heathen Chinese rats! Go back to China, you slits!" Leroy yelled, pointing at Wu-Pen.

Wu-Pen nodded politely. "If it saves trouble with you, we will do so. Right away, Sir."

Leroy chuckled. "Yeah, you better! If you don't leave, I'll do to you what I did to that other English-speaking China rat. I'll whip your hide right off your back with my whip right here in front of all your fellow cockroaches. Get out of my town or my friends and I will burn you all out!"

Wu-Pen showed no trace of emotion as he bowed humbly. "Yes, your honorable, sir. If you can come back tomorrow, this whole place will be empty, I promise you."

Leroy smiled with the power that swelled through him. "You better! Next time I'll bring men with guns, and we'll shoot you all down like rats in a barrel."

"Yes, sir. As I suggested, if you can come back tomorrow. Have a good day." Wu-Pen said, closing the door. He turned to face his guards with hardened eyes, and his breathing became heavy with the fury he was feeling. He spoke in Chinese, "Tonight that man will learn what it means to suffer. He will not go unpunished. Tonight, our vengeance begins. Have the door and stairs scrubbed clean of that man's foul scent, and the ground covered with fresh dirt! The temple needs to be cleansed, and then rest for we will have a late night."

Bing Jue asked, "Shall I follow him to his home?"

"No need. I already know all I need to know." When the miners damaged the Marshal's Office, Wu-Pen volunteered his craftsman to repair the office as a favor for Matt arresting the men responsible for killing two of Wu-Pen's friends and the scourging of Ah See. He offered to pay for the damages and made sure the work was completed correctly. What he did not inform the Marshal of was one of the men was a skilled locksmith and, while repairing the door locks, pressed each key on

Matt's keyring into small blocks of clay to recreate the keys in the privacy of his own home. Wu-Pen had a copy of every key Matt Bannister owned, including the key to his house. Wu-Pen had the keys to Matt's entire life. If Matt needed to be disposed of, Wu-Pen had a key to do that as easily as he would Leroy tonight. He had already gone into Matt's office undetected and went through his files to get the names, addresses, and read the arrest report on Leroy and his friends. Now was the time to settle the debt of justice that the court of American Law failed to do. It would start with Leroy experiencing hell and not being able to do anything about it, while everyone else in the world slept peacefully. "Tonight, that fat man will live a nightmare."

14

Bella's Dance Hall stayed closed on Sundays, and the ladies were free to do whatever they wanted to do within reason. They were all encouraged to go to church, but only a few did. Most slept in and then rested after a week of dancing and doing chores around the dance hall. Some had potential courters who would come and visit with them, while others had Bella's blessing to leave the dance hall in the company of a gentleman to spend the day together if the gentleman had gained Bella's confidence. Relationships that had bloomed like with Sam and Helen's and Edith and Paul's had her blessing to leave the confines of the building. However, new gentlemen, like Martin Ballenger, despite being a lawman, had not yet earned Bella's trust and were refused permission to leave the building. Edith was irritated, but Martin was willing to remain in the main ballroom to visit with his potential lady.

Martin and Edith sat at a small table for two and

showed no interest in sharing a conversation with Helen and Sam. There was a thick tension between the two men, and it wasn't hidden under the slight acknowledgments of politeness for the sake of the two ladies who were best friends. Even so, the breakup of Paul and Edith had caused Edith to start withdrawing from Helen and focused on her friendship with Rose Blanchard and the one man who made her feel desirable at the moment, Martin Ballenger.

Sam and Helen decided to leave the dance hall to remove themselves from any possible confrontation and walked a block when they saw Matt and Christine walking back towards the dance hall on the boardwalk. They walked hand in hand and shined like many couples do when the excitement of a new love is present.

"You two look so happy together," Helen said with a joy-filled smile.

"I think we are," Christine replied with her beautiful smile. "We just came from our church potluck that turned into a spontaneous dance. It was so fun, wasn't it?" she asked with an excited grin.

Matt nodded. "It was."

"So, what are you two out doing today?" Christine asked.

Helen grimaced slightly and waved back towards the dance hall, annoyed. "Oh, we're going out for lunch and then play a few games of pool at the billiards. We would go back to the dance hall, but Edith is there with Martin, and they're acting strange. This whole thing with Paul and Edith has caused a lot of friction between her and I. She's been talking to Martin a lot lately, and he's feeding the fire between us, I think. He doesn't like Sam, and now Edith does not like Sam either for calling Martin a thief. And you probably noticed, but she's more of Rose's friend than mine now. She hardly speaks to me now that Paul broke it off with her and Martin's come into the picture. Nah, we just don't want to be there when Martin's there."

Matt asked Sam, "Why are you calling him a thief?"

"Because he is. I watched him take five dollars off a table the other night, and when the men noticed it had been taken, Martin turned around and got everyone's attention to say he was a deputy and would arrest whoever took the money, which it was him! He played it off like a great thief, though."

"Did you call him out on it?"

"Later, I did. I told Martin I saw him take it and suggested he not get too caught up in Edith. He tried to threaten me, but I told him you were a friend of mine. I will tell you, though; he isn't quite right in the head, I don't think. He gets a real dark look on his face when he gets mad. I wasn't scared, but his expression took me back a bit. I don't know what it is, but I didn't like him the moment I first saw him. You've met him right, Matt?"

Helen answered, "Of course he did. He recommended him to the Sheriff for a job."

Matt shook his head slowly. "I never recommended him for the job. He asked me for a deputy's position, and since I just took Jed from the Sheriff, I suggested he ask Tim for a deputy's job, in jest, I might add. I didn't think Tim would hire him." He laughed lightly.

Helen spoke frankly, "He's telling people you recommended him to the sheriff for the job."

"No, I didn't. He's a thief, huh?"

Sam nodded. "He'll deny it and blame me for trying to put a wedge between Edith and him, but if you know me, you know I'm telling the truth. I don't think he's right, Matt. And Edith won't listen to Helen or me. Have you noticed that, Christine?"

Christine wrinkled her nose questionably. "I know she seems to like him a lot so far, and I have noticed her spending more time with Rose for the past few days."

Matt spoke, "Maybe we should go talk to Martin and see what we think of him," he suggested to Christine.

"What do you think of him, seriously?" Sam asked.

Matt tilted his head with a half shrug. "I don't know him, and I haven't talked to him more than a hello. So, I couldn't say one way or the other. But I'll make it a point to visit with him a bit when we get there."

Matt and Christine walked into the dance hall and saw Martin sitting at a small table at the farthest point away from the main tables. He was talking with Edith; Rose had joined them. Matt walked Christine towards their table, and the three of them quieted as they approached. The expression on Rose's face revealed they had been gossiping either about Christine or Matt either one.

"Hello," Rose spoke awkwardly.

Matt smirked with a touch of humor. Gossip was nothing more than hens cackling in the hen house about another hen who had more character than the cackling hens. Gossip was the same wherever it went. "Hello. I sure hope we're not interrupting."

"No, not at all," Martin answered as he turned his chair towards Matt. He wasn't allowed to wear his gun belt in the dance hall but noticed Matt was wearing his. "You might want to take your gun belt off, Matt. Bella doesn't allow guns in the dance hall."

The comment, though innocent, irritated Matt. "I'm the one man that is above that rule, thank you. We met your mother and sister at church today. I think they had a good time. I invite you to come next week."

Martin shook his head, uninterested. "Thank you, but no. I'm surprised that my mother went. She's never been a churchgoer. It surprises me that you are too. I wouldn't think you'd go there with your reputation, you know."

Matt shrugged lightly. "My reputation comes from just doing my job. But knowing Jesus and accepting his salvation is far more important than anything else. Of course, I go to church."

Martin laughed and glanced at Edith. "That's being said by a man who whipped a grown man to tears and made him bellow like a starving cow with a willow switch!" He looked back at Matt with a smile, "That's not part of your job, that's the abuse of power. I would've arrested him maybe for beating that girl, but not whip him like that," he finished with an arrogant smile.

Matt narrowed his eyes with irritation. "If I re-member correctly, you stood right there watching him beat that little girl for not pronouncing a word correctly, and you did nothing. Don't tell me what you would've done in the presence of these ladies when I know you'd do nothing! You don't need a badge to stop someone from beating a child. And if you were wise, you wouldn't think you know more about doing my job than I do." He watched Martin's face intently and caught the quick flash of fury that passed by like a fleeting glimpse of his darkness hidden inside. It was a glimpse of the same kind of rage Matt had seen before many times.

Martin laughed uncomfortably in front of the ladies and replied lightly, "Ah, you got me there, Marshal. I was just joshing with you a bit. I apolo-gize if I irritated you."

Matt shook his head. "I'm probably not the best man to irritate. I do have that reputation you men-tioned for a reason. And it's not for being nice if you get on my bad side."

Christine spoke quickly to Martin, "Your sister is so pretty. And your mother looked so happy when she was dancing with Henry. You have a wonderful family."

His eyes revealed a deep hostility for a second, it was harder for him to control, but covered it quickly with a fake smile. "Why was she dancing at church?"

"We had a potluck after church, and it turned into a dance. It was wonderful. Your mother and Henry danced the whole time, I think. She was so happy."

A scowl of resentment crossed his lips. "How

wonderful. Isn't dancing forbidden in church? Isn't it a sin for you, Christians?"

Christine chuckled. "Well, I guess if it were, I wouldn't have a job."

Matt watched Martin's facial expression and seen the twitches of anger around his lips and hardening of his eyes. His fists were tightening and his shifting in his chair. It only took a second, but it was clear Christine's answer irritated him more than he was already.

Matt turned to Edith. "How are you doing, Edith?"

"I'm okay."

"Good. I'm sorry to hear about the breakup between you and Paul. He's a good man, and I thought you two would you know, get married."

She frowned and shrugged her shoulders. "He doesn't want to."

Martin added quickly, "It's his loss and her gain. I think Edith is beautiful and phenomenal in nearly every way. How do you like the brooch I got her?"

She smiled at him and bent her head over to show the pretty metal hair comb with leaves and a red rose painted on it. Despite the new brooch, there was a sadness in her eyes.

Matt ignored commenting on the brooch. "I think Edith's a pretty special lady myself, and I think she needs to take some time before hurrying into another relationship," Matt said while looking in her eyes. "Right?" he asked.

She smiled and nodded as her eyes grew moist.

"Oh yeah," Martin agreed. "Time is the key to everything. I hear you and your lady took your time. I know Edith wants a relationship like yours. She's told me about that, and so do I."

"It takes time. Speaking of which, I have to go." He addressed Christine. "Walk me outside?"

"Of course," They stopped at the bottom of the stairs in the entry of the dance hall. She turned and faced him with her hands in his. "I'll see you tomorrow?"

"Of course. How about we have lunch at the Monarch Restaurant at noon?" he asked.

She shook her head with a crinkle of her nose. "Can we try some Chinese food? Dave brought some home the other day, and it was delicious. It's only a couple of blocks from here?"

"We'll try it. Okay, I must go check in on my deputy and make sure all is well before I go home. I'll see you tomorrow, Beautiful." He kissed her in a long embrace. "I'll see you at lunch. Goodnight."

15

Leroy Haywood slept peacefully in his bed when he was awoken abruptly by a hand forcefully covering his face with a moist cloth. He tried to sit up and fight whoever it was attacking him, but a blunt, hard blow to his ribs sent a paralyzing shock through him, and he took a deep breath. His world went as black as night.

Leroy opened his eyes, disoriented for a moment while he focused on a candle burning in front of his face. He was sitting upright on a kitchen table chair and couldn't move due to his body being tied firmly to the chair. Wide strips of fabric about four inches wide tied his wrist and elbows to the back of the chair securely. His chest was tied tightly to the back of the chair, holding him upright. His hips were tied down as were his lower thighs and just below his knees and ankles. Strangely, both of his big toes were tethered tightly upwards to his ankles by strings. He pulled and strained to break free of the cloth bonds, but he couldn't budge from his position. He couldn't stand forward or tip the chair sideways. He became aware of two figures standing one on each side of him holding his chair in place. The only part of his body that he could move was his head. He tried to yell furiously, but there was a thick rag shoved into his mouth and a strip of the silk tied around his mouth to hold the gag in place. He couldn't move, and he couldn't yell. He was in his home still, but the house was pitch black except for the candle shoved in front of his face. He couldn't see past the candle to see who had tied him up.

The candle pulled back and slowly revealed the kind and smiling face of the same older Chinese man who Leroy had spat on the other night and whose door he had urinated on that day. With a kind smile, the Chinese man lowered himself to his knees on a small pillow he had brought and set on the floor in front of Leroy.

"Now you see me," he spoke softly in English. "Good, good." He pulled a small metal box out of his long black coat pocket that was about four inches long and two inches wide, and about an inch and half thick. The cover was decorated with a dragon. The top cover of the box slid out to open the box. In the dim light of the candle, Leroy could make out the features of the two men standing on each side of the chair. They were the two guards who had made a mockery of him and his friends the other night in Chinatown. Neither man appeared to be friendly.

Leroy tried to speak, but he couldn't. He was angry, but growing more afraid in his helpless situation. He tried to scream and demand to be released but realized it was only entertaining the man kneeled in front of him.

"You might wonder who I am; My name's Wu-Pen. You might wonder what I'm going to do to you? I'm not going to kill you, no," he said, shaking his head. He took a deep breath and added, "But nature's a cruel lady, and one of the cruelest ladies in nature is this little beauty." He reached for a pair of bamboo tweezers and slid the cover of the metal box partway open. He reached inside with the tweezers and gently pulled out a small Black Widow spider by the fat shiny black belly. He looked up at Leroy and smiled. "The Black Widow is a very dangerous lady, but most gentle if left alone. She is very much like us Chinese. She is very much like me. But if you push her, she will bite. Sometimes she has mercy and delivers no venom, but if you keep pushing her, she will poison you. Either way, with or without poison, the bite will still hurt." He moved the tweezers down to the front of Leroy's tethered big toe just under his nail and pressed the spider against the skin. The spider bit him.

Leroy screamed through his gag and tried to break free to no avail. The fear in his eyes and panic of his muffled voice made Wu-Pen laugh lightly. "I don't think she delivered her justice." He rubbed the spider against the front of his toe again. The spider bit down and held on for a second. "There," he said, pointing his finger at Leroy. "You shouldn't have made her angry. You shouldn't have killed my friends out at the granite quarry." He moved the spider to Leroy's other big toe and held spider above the candle to get it angry and then set it against his toe. The spider sank its fangs into his toe while Leroy tried to break free again. Wu-Pen spoke in Chinese, and one of the two men with him took a short knife blade and cut a small hole in Leroy's long johns just above his knee. Wu-Pen put the spider into the hole and dropped the spider down inside of Leroy's long johns.

Leroy screamed through his gag, trying to plead for his life. Tears were coming down his cheeks while his eyes begged for mercy.

"Shhh. You'll scare her with all that intimidating yelling. Sorry, I don't speak that language. Do you remember calling me a rat?" He opened the box to the next segregated compartment and reached in for a larger Black Widow spider. "Oh, yes, you do." He spoke in Chinese again, and the same man with the blade began to unbutton the bottom half of Leroy's long johns over his belly. "You shouldn't have hurt my friend; Ah See. Ah See's brother found this black beauty for you."

Leroy tried to break free with all the fury he had, but the binds held him pinned to the chair tight.

Wu-Pen set the spider against Leroy's fat and hairy stomach. The spider drove its fangs into his skin and refused to let go when Wu-Pen gently pulled it back. He laughed, amazed. "This lovely lady doesn't like you. She must know of your deeds."

Leroy began to weep in helpless fear.

Wu-Pen shook his head as he pulled the angry spider back from Leroy's belly. "Don't cry, baby. For such a big and mean man, it's quite entertaining to see you so afraid of a little spider. Let's see if she'll kiss your fears away?" He put her mouth against his belly again. She buried her fangs into his skin again and injected another shot of her venom. "Oh, yes! Do you remember calling me a slit? Of course, you do," He laughed and then spoke in Chinese to his guard named Bing Jue. Bing Jue immediately slit a hole in the crotch of Leroy's long johns.

Leroy began shaking his head and begging through his gag. Tears slid out of his eyes.

Wu-Pen smiled. He held the Black Widow close to the candle in front of Leroy's face for him to look at it. "I love these dark ladies. They are so beautiful in every way and so gentle if you are caring enough to be respectful with them. Do you see her red hourglass? Do you?" he asked sharply.

He nodded as he sobbed in fear.

"She is nothing except danger for the fool who harasses them. Or the fool who gets dressed without checking for them." He dropped the spider down through the hole into his crotch.

Leroy began to squirm with a deep yell. His eyes opened wide as a panic shot through him, and he started crying out in terror.

Wu-Pen laughed. "She bit again. Good." He reached back for the metal box and opened it to the third chamber. He pulled out a large Black Widow with a massive round belly. It was much larger than the other two. He frowned. "I had my people look for the biggest Black Widow they could find. This fat lady was in an old shack out on a farm. I've had her for a few days now, and she has not eaten. She's been saving all her poison for you. You spit on me, remember?" He spoke in Chinese, and Wu-Pen's other guard Uang Yang untied the cloth from his mouth and pulled out the wadded-up fabric in his mouth. Leroy tried to scream, but his cheeks were squeezed tightly to force his jaw open. Quickly Bing Jue grabbed his tongue with a pair of small pliers and pulled it forward, exposing his tongue.

Leroy, in a panic, did everything he could to get away or plead for their mercy.

Wu-Pen smiled wickedly. "You should not have done what you did. As I said, I am very much like a Black Widow. I will leave you alone and step gently until you threaten me or hurt my people. And then I will bite you, and my bite leads to much pain before certain death." He used his tweezers to force the giant spider onto his tongue. The spider resisted at first but then drove its fangs into Leroy's tongue. The first bite was quick. Wu-Pen aggravated the spider over the candle and set it on his tongue again. It bit down into his tongue and injected a hefty dose of venom. He let the large Black Widow loose in his mouth, and the two men let go of his tongue and cheeks and quickly closed Leroy's mouth. One held it tight while the other tied the strip of silk from the bottom of Leroy's chin to the top of his head tightly. Every time Leroy moved his tongue, the spider bit again.

Wu-Pen leaned back on his heels to watch comfortably. "The burning sensation will turn to cramping, then much pain. It will be excruciating, and it will be hard to breathe. But I am merciful; with your mouth closed, you will drown in your own stinking vomit before the pain becomes unbearable. And I will watch," he said with a friendly smile. He added, "Don't fear being alone. You're two friends will soon follow you."

16

The death of Leroy Haywood was curious if nothing less than suspicious. Dr. Bruce Ambrose had discovered eleven spider bites from the tip of his big toes to his leg, crotch, belly, and multiple bites on his tongue and inside of his gums. He found three Black Widows, two alive inside of his long johns, and one large dead one inside of his mouth. The one in his mouth had been crushed by pressing it into his teeth with his tongue. Leroy's long johns, grotesque and foul as they were, had two fresh cuts in them about where the bites were found. The oddity of it indicated foul play of some kind, but there were no marks on his body aside from the bites. There was no bruising of his wrists from his hands being tied together or bruising anywhere else that one would expect from a murder of this suspected type. There was a small cut on his inner cheek where it may have been done by pressing his cheeks against his broken tooth, and that was the only indication of foul play. Oddly, there was vomit inside of his mouth, but very little on his lips or the bedding. It was too suspicious, and an autopsy would have to be performed. With his findings, he got a hold of Matt and went over the facts with him as he knew them while the body was being moved to the funeral parlor for an autopsy that he would do shortly.

Matt sent word to Christine that he had to cancel lunch with her and then took Truet Davis with him out to Leroy's small company cabin to investigate a potential crime scene. Leroy was a big and strong man, and no one would be able to subdue him to submit to eating a Black Widow without a fight. Could it have been a coincidence of natural occurrence? Black Widows normally didn't run in packs, nor cut their access holes into a man's long johns, so no, it was intentionally done. However, there were no clues. Leroy was found in bed with his eyes wide open in terror, and his mouth clenched shut tight by his co-workers when he was late waking up for work. Matt searched around the room, and although there were spiders, none were Black Widows. Nothing seemed out of the ordinary mess of his usual living conditions, except for a few drops of white wax on the floor in the middle of the main room. A few drops of wax from a candle was the only clue he had. There were no burnt candles in Leroy's home. He lit his place by a lantern that was out completely. Matt pulled the nearest chair out and seen a drop of wax on the edge of the seat and small splatters of wax on the side of the leg. It gave a good indication that Leroy was tied to the chair, and someone used a candle for light. Unfortunately, not one person out at the Slater's Mile heard or seen anything suspicious at all. There was nothing else to be found, not a muddy footprint, not a speck of blood or anything else that would help discover what had happened during the night.

Matt and Truet went back to town to the Fasana Furniture & Undertaker's Parlor to look at the body and find out what Dr. Ambrose and Matt's Uncle, Solomon Fasana, who was the only undertaker in the county had discovered during the autopsy. They walked down into the basement and entered the preparation room for the mortuary business.

Dr. Ambrose spoke to Solomon Fasana, "I'm excited to see Mitchell. I haven't seen him since our college days."

"If he's doing so well in Chicago, why is he coming here, surely, there's better money-back east?" Solomon asked. He was in his mid-fifties and was a businessman with salt and pepper hair and a well-trimmed gray beard on his square face. Unlike his older brothers Luther and Joel, Solomon wasn't as thick and broad, but taller, thinner and more of an upper-class gentleman. It wasn't that he was too arrogant to visit with his family; it was more of the fact that he had married a wealthy lady from Boston and brought her to Branson. She didn't appreciate the humor or lowly blue-collar status of Solomon's family.

Dr. Ambrose chuckled. "Mitchell's already made a fortune. He wanted to experience the wilderness and unsettled lands while he could. He's thinking about buying a house in Portland and starting a practice over there. He wants to hunt and fish when he wants to and experience the west coast."

Matt frowned. "Who's that, Bruce?" he asked the doctor.

"Oh, my best friend from college is coming here next week to visit for a few days. He's a very renowned surgeon now in Chicago named Mitchell Ryland. He's giving up the city to try some rural living while it's still wild. He saw a picture of a sturgeon caught in the Columbia that was twenty feet long and the salmon, and that's about all it took. He wants in on the adventure before it's all settled."

"Nice. You should send him elk hunting with my brother Adam, you heard about his elk hunting experience, yeah? You can't get more adventurous than that."

"I think that would be too much for him. Would you like to know what I discovered about our fat stinky boy, here?"

Matt nodded, "I would."

Dr. Ambrose was able to see the body in better light and discovered that there were no ligature marks like one would typically see from a rope, but there was some slight bruising on his forearms by something broader than a belt. His lower legs revealed the same very slight discoloration of having tried to force himself free of something flat, non-abrasive, and about four inches wide. None of the three men had ever seen anything like it before.

One thought kept going through Matt's mind. He turned to Truet, who stood back from the table where Matt and the other two men peered at the slight bruising. "Leroy was too big and strong of a man to subdue without a fight. Unless someone put a gun to his head, but even then, I don't think he'd let anyone tie him up. I think he'd fight. There's only one person I can think of who could make Leroy do whatever wanted with one hand. Wu-Pen's guard Bing Jue. And it makes sense, doesn't it? Leroy killed two Chinese men and scourged Ah See, and nothing was being done. The court just wiped it away like it was nothing at all."

"Yeah," Truet agreed. "They'd have a reason. I don't know anything about Chinese culture, but not many white folks use anything else except rope to tie someone up. And most wouldn't touch a Black Widow. Who even thinks of that?"

Dr. Ambrose spoke, "The amount of venom he had injected into him would have killed him for sure, but the same faint markings are on the bottom of his chin. His mouth was tied shut. One of the symptoms of a Black Widow bite is severe abdominal pain and vomiting. The vomiting is what killed him. He drowned in his own vomit. It didn't have anywhere to go with his mouth tied shut, so it went into his lungs. And you think the Chinese did it?"

Matt nodded. "I can almost guarantee it. The problem is they left nothing behind for me to prove it. Truet and I will talk to Wu-Pen and question him, but I can already tell you he's not going to admit to anything. They were too clean and efficient; I mean, there's not even one muddy footprint. There's nothing except wax drops from a candle. And even if he had white candles all over, three-quarters of the people living around here have white candles too." Matt exhaled deeply. "The neighbor's dog barked, I guess that's something."

Dr. Ambrose yawned. "Well, I suppose I can classify his death as a homicide since that's what we're finding."

Matt shook his head. "Don't do that, because if you do and rumor gets out that Chinese are suspected of it, we'll have fifty to a hundred innocent dead Chinese on our hands, if not more. Chinatown will be burned down and half of our city burning with it. Technically, the spiders killed him, right?"

"Well, yeah, but they didn't happen by accident. It wasn't natural by any means."

Solomon Fasana added, "You can't lie on the death certificate, Matt. It isn't right."

"I'm not asking anyone to lie. I'm asking you to be blatantly precise. The spider's venom caused his death, yes or no?"

"The spiders wouldn't have bitten him if they weren't placed on him," Dr. Ambrose explained.

"That's not what I asked. Technically speaking, was it the spiders or the men that killed him? What caused his death the Black Widow venom or a man? Let me make this very simple, who bit him a poisonous spider or a man?" Matt asked sharply with his glaring at the doctor.

"The spiders, obviously."

"Then, there you go. Leroy died of multiple bites from Black Widows."

"There's more to it than that, and you know it,"

Dr. Ambrose said heatedly.

"Of course, I do," Matt fired back. "And it's my job to figure that part out. If you want to put pending investigation, fine do that. But do not let the town know it was a murder because then there's going to be a hell of a push back that we won't be able to control, and many innocent men will be killed. I want to avoid that. This is where we can. We can control what's said here. And I can't arrest someone without evidence even if they are Chinese, because I can't prove it was them. And I won't hang someone if I don't know for a fact that they are guilty. And we all know if I arrested a Chinese man for this, he would hang whether he was innocent or not."

Dr. Ambrose nodded. "Alright. I'll cite his death as asphyxiation due to multiple Black Widow bites. Investigation pending. That way, if you do find something to arrest with later, we can come back to it. Sound fair enough?"

"Sounds perfect. Right now, I think Truet and I are going to see Wu-Pen and see what he says. Thank you, gentlemen."

Chinatown was one block over from Rose Street on Flower Lane. It continued to grow steadily with buildings lined up on both sides of the street, including laundries, restaurants, stores, and various other businesses. Quite a few of the buildings on Flower Lane had no sign or indication of what kind of business was offered behind its doors. Other more obvious ones had tarp-covered awnings over the tables full of vegetables and other goods for sale. The melting snow on the street created a muddy mess as it did everywhere in town, but the Chinese were in the process of making boardwalks along the road, and in some places, stone walkways with perfectly laid stones cemented in place. Rumor had it that there were Chinese bordellos where Chinese women were housed, even though they were rarely seen. More commonly known were opium dens and gambling halls, but there was no way of identifying them to the outsider who didn't know where to look or couldn't speak or read Chinese. Finding a wanted man of Chinese origin would have been a difficult task if they wanted to hide him in the strange and different design and customs of a foreign culture.

Matt and Truet rode their horses down Flower Lane and nodded to the Chinese in a friendly manner. The people smiled and nodded to their greeting with kindness. When Matt tried to inquire about where to find Wu-Pen, he had run into a brick wall when it came to finding any help locating him. It seemed no one knew what he was saying and shook their heads and waved their hands with an innocent smile. Matt remembered that Wu-Pen had given him a card with red Chinese writing on it that he had told Matt to show anyone if he ever wanted to see him. They rode back to the Marshal's Office and got the card and went back to Flower Lane. Matt showed the card to a Chinese man on the street, and he immediately signaled for Matt to follow him and led them up Flower Lane to a two-story wooden building with a red door. The building was plain and straightforward, with no windows on the front at all. The only noticeable symbol was the tarp-covered awning and a bright red door. The man motioned for Matt and Truet to dismount their horses and follow him inside. Not having any place to hitch their horses, the Chinese man hollered to two men on the street in Chinese, and they dropped what they were doing and came over to hold the reins of the horses while Matt and Truet went inside. The kind Chinese fellow made hand gestures to communicate that the horses would be safe.

Inside, there was an everyday looking entry where the man grabbed a rag and immediately began washing the boots on their feet with a bucket of water and a dry towel. It was most uncomfortable for Matt to have a man clean his dirty boots, but the fellow was insistent. Matt understood when the fellow led them through a door and entered a beautiful large room that had a clean and waxed beautiful oak floor. The large room appeared to be a temple and was decorated in vibrant colors of silk banners with dragons and lions encircling the tall ceiling of the room. At the far end of the temple was the altar, and a large brass gong in an ornamented painted red frame, a decorative covered golden bowl of incense smoked lightly revealing a strong aroma of a sweet fragrance. There were multiple figurines of various kinds and sizes were set about, such as a pair of large golden lions, creatures that looked like dogs to Matt, but had dragon-like faces as they snarled their teeth.

The friendly Chinese fellow who had led them to the temple removed his shoes and walked in his cotton socks. He was stopped by an old Chinese man in an orange robe with the front half of his head shaved and wore a queue. The fellow who led them knelt and bowed in front of the man in orange, he spoke in Chinese and remained on his knees while the man in orange left the room and soon came back and spoke in Chinese. The fellow who had brought them there stood up and motioned for Matt and Truet to follow the man in the orange robe before the friendly Chinese man quickly departed with a smile. The old priest led them up a narrow staircase hidden behind a paneled wall and into a hallway with many doorways along the long hall. There was a door at the end of the hall as well. A Chinese woman in a beautiful ornamented gown of multiple colors stepped out of one room into the hallway, seeing them, she smiled and quickly stepped into another room and closed the door behind her. She was stunning for the brief second they saw her. The priest knocked on the door at the end of the hallway. Upon hearing a voice inside, he opened it and motioned for Matt and Truet to go inside.

They entered a large office, and the first thing Matt noticed was the two guards, Bing Jue and Uang Yang, were observing them carefully.

"Marshal Bannister, come in," Wu-Pen spoke in a welcoming manner while standing from behind his large desk. "It is so good to see you coming here to see me. Sit, please." He motioned to the two chairs in front of his beautifully ornamented desk. It had elegant carvings of flowers on the sides, and the top edge had an intricate carving of flowering buds. The chairs hand carved flowers that matched the desk.

"Thank you," Matt said, looking around the office with admiration for the decorations and the skill it took to craft the many sculptures of tigers, snakes, and flowers that were on shelves around his office. He was careful to notice where the guards stood in the room.

Wu-Pen continued with a friendly smile. "Can I get you anything? Tea, water, something to eat?"

"No, no, thank you. Can I ask why the man downstairs insisted on washing our boots? That was kind of odd."

Wu-Pen chuckled good-naturedly. "How should I say this? It's cleaner than cleaning American's feet."

Matt laughed lightly. "I suppose so." He paused to look at Wu-Pen carefully. "I came by to let you know that Leroy Haywood, the man who killed your friends and whipped Ah See, was found dead this morning."

Wu-Pen frowned. "I wish I could be sympathetic, but under the circumstances, I cannot." He continued with interest, "How did he die if I may ask?"

"Spider bites. Eleven Black Widow bites. It was bizarre to find."

"Eleven? Where would he find so many at once? It seems like a terrible place?" He translated in Chinese to his guards. Both raised their eyebrows questionably, but neither spoke a word.

"No, there were only three spiders, but they repeatedly bit in specific places. It seems someone tied Leroy down and directed where the spider's bit." He leaned forward to be understood correctly. It also gave him a moment to casually un-thong his revolver's hammer as unnoticeably as he could. "Wu-Pen, Leroy was a big man, and I believe someone murdered him late last night. No one would have been able to tie him up and force a Black Widow into his mouth if he wasn't quickly subdued without a trace of a struggle. The only person I can think of that could do that is him." He nodded at Bing Jue, Wu-Pen's guard.

Wu-Pen raised his eyebrows, surprised by the suggestion. "Yes, Bing could, and he did as you have seen in your jail not long ago. But he did not. Bing is always near me, and he does what I tell him to do. I assure you he is not responsible for this, and nor am I." He shrugged with a smile. "Though I am glad to hear he is dead, we did not kill him. You should know that what Bing and Uang can do with their hands and feet is a lifetime of studying the art of fighting, but others walk our streets from China who can do the same. It could be any one of those men out there who could have controlled that big fat man as easily as Bing or Uang could have. Unfortunately, our friends found in the quarry pit and Ah See were not trained in the same way. Or," Wu-Pen suggested slowly, "the person you're looking for may not have been Chinese at all."

Matt nodded. "True, I have no evidence proving one way or the other. I am at a loss on this one. He was too big and tough not to put up a fight, but there was no evidence of a fight. He was tied to a chair, but there's barely any marks of what held him there despite any fight he may have put up. If someone wanted to kill him, they would've; he was tortured by someone who wanted to see him tortured. A lot of people didn't like Leroy, but most folks would be satisfied just shooting or stabbing him; this was much more than that. This murder was ruthless and sadistic and most uncommon for an American to do. That doesn't mean it wasn't, but Americans are very straight forward when it comes to killing someone. They don't take their time to enjoy a slow death, usually. Americans just do it and get away as fast as they can, so they're not caught. But someone subdued and tied him to a chair, cut two holes in his long johns and put Black Widows down his drawers and one in his mouth and then tied his mouth shut. And once he had drowned in his vomit, they put him back in bed nice and comfy like. They even pushed the chair back under the table. That's not how American's do things around here. At least not in my experience as a lawman. Wu-Pen, there was not even a muddy footprint. And that's definitely not American. As I said, I suspect it was someone who could control Leroy, and there's only one person I've seen who could do that."

Wu-Pen smiled while shaking his head. "Yes, but Marshal, as I said, what Bing did many of the Chinese can do with any training at all. I assure you; it was not I, and I hope you do not suspect Bing or Uang. They were here all night with me. You may be right, it may have been a Chinese man, but I have not heard of it until now. If I hear of anything that might help you identify the man responsible, then I will let you know. You seem to care about the Chinese people, and we will help you when we can. We are friends, yes?"

Matt nodded. "Yes, we are. And I would hate to think you were involved in this."

He grinned happily. "Fortunately, I am not. I would not risk all I have to be arrested by you."

"Can I ask you something?" Matt asked.

"Yes."

"Who are you? I mean, what do you do here to have such an elegant office and guards everywhere you go?"

Wu-Pen smiled. "I'm the high priest of the temple. I am also, how would I say, the president of the Chinese Benevolence Association as well. In short, I help my people."

Matt nodded. "Very good."

When Matt and Truet left, Wu-Pen opened his drawer and pulled out a key ring with the four keys to Matt's world.

Bing Jue spoke in Chinese, "Do you want him dead?"

Wu-Pen shook his head. "No. He will be a useful friend to us. He's just doing his job and is very good at it. We do need to be careful, but if ever needed, we have the keys to ending his life." He held up the keys and smiled. "We'll wait a month before killing the man who lives alone, Roger Lavigne. Patience, my friends. Vengeance doesn't always have to be soon."

17

Henry Redlin was feeling nervous. He peered in the mirror and combed his black hair over with the help of some hair oil. He had trimmed his beard and still saw nothing appealing about himself. He was overweight, had a round face with beady eyes and thick eyebrows that kind of matched his black beard. His worst feature, by far, was his sizeable nose that didn't leave much room for anything else to be desired. He was fifty-three years old and had never been married or courted too many women. In the world of romance, he was inexperienced and, for the most part, had never considered himself to be much of an offer to a lady of value. He had all but given up on ever falling in love, but then Sylvia Ballenger walked into his shop. She was an attractive lady who was going through some hard times and willing to work to support her family. One of the qualities that he appreciated in her was her sense of humor, and the way she could make him smile. It had been a week since he had taken her to the church potluck and danced with her. He had pitched in to pay the fee for the church to use the dance floor, and it was worth every penny. Since that day, he had been working ten-hour days, and Sylvia worked right beside him even though her workday was through at closing time. She stayed late and helped him clean-up for the last hour every day, and she often worked through lunch or had lunch with him. They got along well and laughed throughout most of the day. He found himself falling for her a little more day after day. He found it hard to fall asleep from the excitement he felt just to see her the next day. His youth had been resurrected, as he felt rejuvenated and alive. It reminded him of when he was a teenager and had his first love, who eventually crushed his spirits and married another man far more handsome than himself. He had no idea if he was reading too much into it, or if Sylvia was genuinely interested in him, but Henry hoped so because he was falling for her.

The only thing that bothered him was that Sylvia wasn't a born-again Christian, she believed in God, but had no relationship with Jesus the Christ. It was a cautionary tale because he would not start a business with a partner who didn't share his core beliefs, and it's not wise to be unevenly yoked. A business partner who didn't share the same set of values could lead to differences that could tear the business apart from the inside out. It was even more essential to be equally yoked in a marriage. He had never spoken of marriage with her, but he invited her to church the week before, where they danced at the potluck and had a great time. He asked her back to church today. There was no potluck or anything special going on other than a time of worship and a sermon. To his great joy, she accepted his invitation, and after a sermon focusing on Jesus' birth and the angel appearing to some shepherds out in a field and telling them to "Rejoice, for a Savior has been born to you, He is the Christ, the Lord." And then the sky was filled was angels singing, "Glory to God in the highest, and on earth peace to men on whom his favor rests."

Reverend Painter spoke, "All throughout the Bible when an Angel appears to someone, its first words are fear not, because Angels are so mighty and awesome that they can terrify us. If those millions of Angels bow to one Lord and obey Him, and yet they scare us, then how awesome is our God? I think this passage lets us know a little about that. The sky fills with angels, thousands of them, and they are singing in one voice, better than any choir we will ever hear on earth, 'Glory to God in the highest, and on earth peace to men on whom his favor rests.' Can you imagine that? Three Kings are going to see a baby. There is about to be a bloody massacre of every male child two years old and younger throughout the land to kill this one baby. And God sends his Angels to tell a few lowly shepherds on a hill that a baby was born, and those shepherds got to see the heavenly choir like no one else ever has. Keep in mind that shepherds in those days were some of the lowliest people in the society. So why did God send the heavenly hosts to see shepherds of all people? The answer is simple, from Kings to shepherds, God sent his Son, Jesus our Lord, the Christ, to save all whom his favor rests. On whom does his favor rest? The Angels just announced the birth of a savior, Jesus. His favor rests on those who humbly come before the Lord and lay down their lives to pick up the cross, repent from their sins and follow Jesus Christ as their Lord and Savior. From the highest of society to the lowest of society, it doesn't matter where you are; Jesus wants to forgive your sins and accept you into God's family. You've never done anything so wrong that Jesus can't forgive you or will shun you. You can be forgiven right now, and now is a good time to get to know Jesus. If he's worthy enough for the Angels to worship him, then maybe we had better too, huh? Jesus was worthy to be the lamb sacrificed for our sins and making us perfect when the time comes for us to enter heaven. He's the only way into heaven. That is the reason why he was born and the reason why the Angels filled the sky and sang the song they did. They were rejoicing at the miracle of salvation that's available for all of us. There was no other reason. Our salvation is so important to God that the angels were celebrating and worshipping in great joy. Do not let the importance of the birth of Jesus slip by you like some simple Christmas story. It is crucial, and it is the most valuable gift you could ever receive. God wants you with Him; He wants to help you in times of trouble and in times of plenty. He yearns for you to come to him and fill that empty space in your soul. The question becomes, are you going to accept that gift of salvation and have peace with God, or are you going to spit in his face and reject all that God has done for you? What did He do for you? Jesus is the son of God, and he went to the cross willingly to die one of the worst and most painful deaths imaginable for your sins. His blood being shed on that cross and his death and resurrection are the New Covenant. Jesus is alive and well today folks, and as the Old Testament prophesied, none of his bones were broken while on the cross. Blood is made in the marrow of the bones, and that means his blood is eternal. The Bible says the simplicity of it will be a stumbling block for many. That means they can't believe salvation could be so simple to have. We can't earn it or work hard enough for it, as many will try to do. Folks, it's a gift worked out by God to enjoy an eternity with us. He loves us that much. The choice is yours. Think about it, though, because it does have eternal consequences. But like it says in the book of Joshua, 'As for me and my house, we will serve the Lord.' If you want to as well, now is the time to accept Jesus as your Savior."

To Henry's joy, Sylvia and her daughter Barbra both stood up and accepted Jesus as their Savior. It was the beginning of a new life in Jesus Christ. He was excited for them, and Henry was proud to be a part of it. He took them both to lunch to celebrate and took them home. It took some courage on his part, but he asked Sylvia if he could take her out for dinner at the Monarch Restaurant later that evening. She accepted without a moment's hesitation.

For the first time, Henry was smitten like he was a teenager again. His feelings couldn't be denied; he was falling for his employee, the one thing he had never imagined he would do. He dressed in his best suit and borrowed a buggy from the livery stable and drove it over to pick Sylvia and drove her to dinner.

Inside, they sat at a side table in the high society restaurant and ate their meals, which was the best meal Sylvia said she had ever had. They made some small talk and shared a dessert of chocolate cake with a scoop of ice cream.

Henry watched at her with a smile. Sylvia had her hair brushed and falling loosely like always with her bangs held up out her face with a hair comb. She wore the same dress she had worn to church for the past two weeks. By the Monarch Restaurant regular customer standards, she was in worn-out casual wear, but Henry knew it was her best dress. "You look very pretty tonight," he said gently.

She widened her eyes and wrinkled her nose doubtfully. "Have you seen some of the ladies in this place? I look like an old maid compared to these women in here," she said with a laugh. "But thank you. And thank you for bringing me here, in a buggy no less! I've never been so spoiled."

He grinned pleased. "I haven't noticed the other ladies."

She scoffed lightly. "Oh, hogwash!" she laughed softly.

"I haven't." He took a deep breath and forced himself to continue, "I need to ask you a question..."

"Uh-oh, am I being fired? You don't have to pay me for all the time I'm staying after work to help you."

He shook his head with a nervous smile. "No, you're not being fired, but you might want to quit after I tell you something."

She frowned with concern. "What?"

"I'm glad you're working for me."

She laughed. "Oh! I quit. If I'm making you happy or glad, I quit. I never wanted to make my boss happy."

"I wasn't done," he chuckled. "I'm not the most handsome fella in Branson..."

"I quit!" she exclaimed in playful jest.

He spoke nervously, "I can't help how I'm feeling, and I'm becoming...ah...smitten with you. I enjoy working with you, and I don't want that to end. I don't want to cross any lines or intrude on any boundaries you may have, but I think it's only fair to let you know that I am thinking about you all of the time and just don't want to scare you away, I guess. You could do better than me, and I suppose I shouldn't have said anything, but..."

"But what?" she asked seriously.

"I can't get you off my mind. I think about you all of the time. I go to bed..."

"Ohh...Henry, keep it clean," she teased with a smile.

He laughed loudly. "Nothing like that! No, I can't sleep because I'm excited to see you in the morning. I don't know," he shrugged shyly, "But do you think I'm out of line?"

She nodded her head slowly. "It depends."

"Depends on what?" he asked with a hint of concern.

"What you're going to do about it?"

He was awkwardly thrown off coarse. "Well, nothing. I'm not firing you or anything. I don't want you to quit on me. I'm just trying to say I like you is all."

She shrugged. "I like you too."

He sighed, "No, it's more than that. I like you a lot, and I was wondering if... we could. Well, I was wondering if it would be okay if I...courted you?"

She couldn't help giggling softly. "I was hoping you were going to ask that. The answer is yes. I would like that a lot. Henry, I don't find you unattractive at all. I would love to be courted by you."

He smiled. "Great!" He reached into his pants pocket and pulled out a gold ring with a small diamond on it. "I know it's terribly soon, but would you accept this ring? It's just my commitment to be courting you and only you with intentions of marrying you. Are you okay with that?"

She held her left hand out for him to place the ring on her finger as her eyes glossed over with moisture. "I'd be honored."

He slid the ring onto her finger. "Thank you for coming into my life, Sylvia."

Her lips pressed against each other tightly as she wiped her eyes. "Thank you. Barbra's going to be so excited. She really likes you."

"I've never had children, and I'm getting too old to have any little ones, so if you don't mind, I'll just adopt yours, and we'll do our best to make sure she has everything she needs to live a good life now. I know you told me about all those animals you were mixed up with before and all of that cruddy stuff. I promise to be the opposite of those men and treat you and your kids right."

She covered her mouth to stop from sobbing, but a tear slipped slowly down her cheek. "You're going to make me cry."

He smiled compassionately. "From here on out, life's going to become a good thing, okay?"

She nodded quietly as her lips tightened. It was the best day of her life so far.

18

Edith Williams had not been feeling well for a while; she was occasionally nauseous when she stood up, a bit sick to her stomach throughout the day, her chest felt tight, and had occasional headaches. Christine had asked her if she missed her menstrual cycle, but she had not. It was the first time she feared being pregnant, but she had a monthly period. It came a few days late and was a lighter flow than usual and didn't last long, but it was a menstrual flow just the same. However, her menstrual cycles had never been precisely on schedule or consistent with the flow. Over the past week, her symptoms had increased, and she was vomiting and nauseous more often now. By the signs, Bella was concerned about Edith being pregnant, but since Edith said she had a monthly, Bella was more worried about the chances of her spreading a virus or whatever it was to the other ladies. Fearing she had the beginnings of Tuberculosis or Typhoid Fever or any other contagious disease that swept through communities like the Black Plague, Bella walked Edith to the office of Doctor Ambrose to have her examined. Edith laid on the medical table while the doctor examined her. Bella stood beside Edith holding her hand with an anxious expression on her face. It wasn't rare for one of the girls to catch a cold or maybe the flu by dancing so close to men who were sick but felt well enough to dance anyway. Bella feared the worst and hoped she wouldn't have to close for a week or two to isolate her ladies from the general population if it was a severe disease. An anxious expression-filled Edith's face while she waited for the doctor's diagnosis. Dr. Ambrose had asked a lot of questions and hadn't said too much since he began examining her. Her anxiety grew the more he studied her and didn't say anything.

Bella must've been growing anxious as well, as she asked, "Well, Doctor, does she have Leprosy or...?"

Dr. Ambrose was listening to Edith's stomach carefully with his stethoscope. He pulled the two ends out of his ears and looked at Bella. "Not quite Leprosy." He glanced at Edith, "Well, young lady, I can't hear the murmur of a second heartbeat in there, but I'd say, you are about twelve weeks pregnant. I do hope you know who the father is."

"What?" Edith asked in horror.

Bella spoke heatedly, "Of course she knows who the father is! My girls are not whores, Doctor. She was courting the father until just recently." She glared angrily at Edith and then sighed heavily. "Edith, I always told you girls to keep your honor and wait for marriage. Now you know why. You're going to be a mother, and so we need to start preparing you for that."

Edith was in shock. "I can't be pregnant. I don't want to be pregnant!" She covered her face with her hands and began to weep bitterly.

"Stop crying," Bella spoke sharply, "It isn't going to do you any good. You knew the consequences of laying down with a man long before today."

"I can't be pregnant," Edith whimpered. "I had a monthly."

Dr. Ambrose asked with interest, "When did you have one?"

She shrugged like a little girl in trouble. "Three weeks ago."

"Was it normal like always, or was it a lighter flow? A lighter color, and only a day or so long?"

"It was lighter, but I still bled. I still had my monthly! I never missed my monthly."

He nodded as he listened to her. "That wasn't your menstruation cycle, but that doesn't mean you didn't have some blood loss here and there, which you might have mistaken as your monthly cycle. You had mentioned earlier you've always been a little inconsistent with the heaviness of the flow and day of the month. It's not that uncommon to have some bleeding during the first months of pregnancy, which explains why this is such a shock to you. Anyway, a child is growing in you, and in about six to seven months, your baby will be coming into the world."

"Can you take it out of me?" she asked Dr. Ambrose with a look of desperation in her eyes.

He narrowed his eyes with repulsion. "No. I'm here to save lives if I can, Miss Williams, not kill a baby. What you're asking for is an abortion, and I will not do that. You may not want that baby right now, but I assure you, you'll love it more than anything else in this world. Trust me on that, okay? I won't be held accountable for killing a baby, and I hope you won't go elsewhere to do that either. I suggest you get used to the idea of being a mother because around mid-June or so; you're going to be one." He smiled softly and put his hand on her shoulder. "You'll be fine. All those fears you feel right now will disappear just as soon as you hold your baby for the first time. Honestly, you'll love your baby."

"No, I'll be living on the street," she said and began crying again.

Bella sighed. "Let's go back to the dance hall, where you can get some rest. We have time to figure out what we're going to do. I sure hope you saved most of your money over the past few years. Have you?" She was irritated by Edith's irresponsibility.

"Most of it. Bella, I don't want to quit dancing. I don't want to have a baby." She began sobbing and wound up in Bella's arms. Bella held her for a moment and spoke softly, "Sweetheart, you'll be okay. I've never thrown anyone out onto the streets, and I won't do that to you."

Christine had just bathed in the bathtub and walked towards her room in the dance hall covered by her robe when she saw Rose Blanchard come out of Edith's room with a joyful smirk on her lips. "Edith's old nag from red creek was beaver dammed," she said as she passed by Christine.

"What?" Christine asked, not comprehending. She went to Edith's room and seen her being consoled by Helen and one of the other girls named Angela. "What's wrong?"

Edith was sobbing, Helen glanced up at Christine. "She's pregnant."

"Ohh," Christine sighed and then glanced down the hall towards Rose's room with disgust. She stepped inside to kneel and hug Edith. "It's going to be okay, Edith. You know you have friends here, and we'll be there for you the whole time. It truly will be okay." She reached forward and grabbed Edith's hands to pull them from her face. She smiled caringly. "Your baby is going to be beautiful, you know." Christine's eyes filled with tears, and she began to weep as Edith moved forward to hug her.

"I'm so scared!" Edith sobbed.

"I know."

They broke the hug, and Christine wiped her eyes. "Have you told Paul yet?"

Edith shook her head.

Helen spoke, "We'll be going over there pretty soon. I'm going to walk her over there."

"What if he wants nothing to do with me or the baby?" Edith asked through her reddened eyes.

Christine frowned empathetically. "Then, you raise that baby on your own."

Edith looked at her with a sorrowful expression.

"I don't want it, Christine. I want it out of me." She covered her face and began weeping again.

Christine grabbed her wrists and pulled them down and held them down to look into Edith's eyes. "Listen to me. I had a baby girl," she swallowed emotionally. "I told you about my baby girl named Carmen. She was beautiful, Edith. I loved her more than anything, and I watched her take her last breaths in my arms. There was nothing I could do for her. It was the most horrendous experience I've ever been through, and I would give anything to have her back. My baby girl is buried out on the Kansas prairie somewhere in an unmarked grave," she spoke emotionally of losing her baby girl to Influenza on the wagon train coming west with her husband four years before. She shook her head. "Don't you ever tell me that you don't want that baby inside of you again. You have no idea what love is until you hold your child. He or she may be an inconvenience at the moment, but that's not the baby's fault." Christine placed Edith's hands on her belly. "You're going to become a mother. Be proud of that and be the best mother you can be. Now, go clean yourself up and go tell Paul, he's going to be a father. And you both better love this baby, because I know all of us will. Now, go tell Paul."

Rose's voice could be heard down the hall, telling another girl that Edith was pregnant. Helen spoke incensed, "Do you hear that? Rose is telling everyone that she's pregnant like it's funny or something. Just a few days ago, she was Edith's best friend, and now she's spreading rumors around like a disease."

Christine shook her head slightly. "It doesn't matter. Some people are like that, but Helen and I are not," she said to Edith. "Rose is Rose, and her integrity and the ground she walks on is weak. Never mind her, you go get beautiful and go talk to Paul."

Edith frowned. "What if Rose tells Martin?"

Christine grimaced. "So what? Are you in love with Martin?"

Edith shook her head. "No. I think I should be the one that tells him, though."

"I can ask Bella to talk to Rose about that. The only person she listens to is Bella. In the meantime, don't worry about that."

"Rose is going to tell him because she wants Martin," Edith said sadly.

Helen smirked. "Oh good, maybe he'll marry her and get her out of here for at least one day before I get married so that I can enjoy just one day of quiet, at least."

Christine laughed lightly despite herself. It brought a small smile to Edith's lips.

19

Edith and Helen walked across Main Street and heard Martin Ballenger calling to them. He was about a half-block away and jogged towards them after getting their attention.

"Don't mention anything to him, please," Edith asked quietly.

Helen tightened her lips slightly agitated. She did not like Martin at all. "It's not like he's not going to find out eventually," she remarked snidely.

"I know, but not today."

Martin came to a stop with a slightly reddened face from the cold air. "What are you two girls doing out and about in this cold? I think we're getting some more snow tonight by the feel of it and the clouds over yonder. It was a bit warmer yesterday, I think."

"Yes, it's cold," Helen sounded uninterested in talking.

Edith smiled uncomfortably. "What are you up to today? Making any arrests?"

"No. Mostly, I'm just delivering mail for the

sheriff right now." His eyes focused on Edith. "You look beautiful today, even though you look a bit troubled. Is something wrong?"

Edith shook her head quickly. "No, nothing's wrong."

"Are you sure?" he asked, looking at her intently.

She gave her best intentional smile. "I'm sure."

"Okay. I just wanted to make sure my lady is doing well. So, where are you two ladies going?"

Helen answered intentionally, "Sam's house. And he probably wouldn't want you coming along with us."

Martin frowned and peered at Edith questionably. "You're not going there, too, are you?"

Edith nodded. "Yes. Helen wanted me to go over there with her."

Martin took a deep breath as a flash of anger crossed his expression. He bit his bottom lip before asking, "Not to talk to your old beau, Paul, though, right? You know he'll try to get back together with you, right?"

Edith took a nervous breath. "Well, if he's there, I'll say hi."

Martin motioned towards Helen, annoyed. "You know she's trying to trick you into going over there so he can play the poor pity me story. Do you think if Christine's former beau tried that, she and Matt would be what they are today? Didn't you tell me that Christine and Matt were made for each other? You said they had a beautiful love story together, right?"

"Hmm, mm," she agreed.

His eyebrows came together as he emphasized, "Then don't let Paul and his friends steal you away from me, not after all we've shared together. You're the only woman in the world for me, Edith. We were made for each other. Just like Matt and Christine were," he said sincerely as he put his hands on her shoulders affectionately.

Edith motioned a hand wave towards him uneasily. "No, of course, he won't steal me from you. That's not even a question."

He smiled slightly with relief as his shoulders relaxed. "Good. Can you promise me Paul is past history and you feel nothing but remorse for ever agreeing to court him? Can you promise me that?"

Edith answered uncomfortably. "Of course, I can."

His smile faded just a bit, and his eyes grew a touch harder as he said, "Then let me hear it, so I don't have to worry about you going over there."

Helen raised her eyebrows questionably. "Seriously?"

Martin glanced at Helen coldly and then back at Edith with a warm expression. "I never asked for much except for you to just be honest with me. If I have nothing to worry about, then you should be able to tell me that just fine. Right?"

She grinned with a slight awkward chuckle. "Right. Okay, fine." She straightened herself up and stared into his eyes, intentionally fighting a smile. "I feel nothing for Paul, and you have nothing to worry about by me going over there. You need to trust me," she added with a playful slap to his chest. She glanced at Helen quickly to see her squinted eyes, and her jaw opened with surprise and perhaps a touch of confusion.

Martin exhaled with the warmth of reassurance. His voice turned affectionate, "I keep thinking about how our first kiss was so magical. It was like coming home to a long-lost love after a long time apart. Our whole life could be like that, you know. Every time I kiss you, it feels like the first kiss. I know that snake, Paul and others have mistreated you and hurt you, but from this moment on, our lives are only going to get better." He tried to paraphrase what his mother had told him Henry had said to her.

Edith's eyebrows lifted with interest as his words touched her. She spoke anxiously, "The first kiss was amazing. Martin, it really was. But it's really cold out, so we need to get going." She was beginning to shiver.

"Wait a minute. I was thinking, maybe you, me, and Rose and Tim could all go out to dinner before work one of these nights? I'd love to get you out of the dance hall and around town," he asked.

Edith nodded. "That sounds great."

"Awesome, I'll let Tim know," he said with excitement. "Alright, I'll let you two go. Remember, though; you're my one and only one. So don't let that fool sweet talk you back to him, or I'll have to kill him." He chuckled. "Just kidding." He leaned forward and pressed his lips to hers. They engaged in a long kiss with their arms around each other and came apart slowly after a few moments.

Helen watched slack-jawed and wide-eyed.

"You're mine, beautiful. I'll see you tonight," Martin said before walking down the street without saying anything more to Helen.

"You didn't tell me you kissed him!" Helen charged irritated.

"Helen, you're not my mother, and you're not Bella, so what's it matter to you?" she asked defensively.

"Because we're friends and you're carrying another man's child," she spoke softly.

"I didn't know that until today, now did I?" she asked defensively.

"You know it now! Why were you kissing him just now? You do know you're only enticing him to continue this foolish belief he has that you're the only woman in the world for him! Edith, there's something wrong with him, and you need to break whatever you have going on with him off. What if you tell Paul about the baby and he wants to marry you, what are you going to do about Martin then, huh?"

Edith gasped. "Paul ended our courtship because he never wants to be married. Martin is a good man, so why would I want to ruin a relationship with him before I know what Paul's going to say? I'm having a baby whether I like it or not, and I haven't saved up enough money to live on my own forever. I'm keeping my options while I have them. If Paul disregards me, then Martin will have to be the one who marries me. You've wanted to get pregnant so that Sam would marry you! You've even planned it that way, and it didn't work. Now I am pregnant, and I never wanted to be! I have to find someone to marry, or I'll be forced back into whoring. And I don't want to do that!" Her voice shook with fear as the truth came to the surface.

Helen stopped walking and looked at her friend, compassionately. "You're not going to be on the streets. As Christine said, you have too many friends who love you. I am your best friend, and you'll live with Sam and me if need be. I'll help you raise that baby, but Edith, get away from Martin. If there was ever a creep on the streets, it's him. I think you're too close to see how weird he is, but you heard what he said about Paul. The man's insane. He wasn't kidding; I don't think."

Edith wiped the slight moisture from her eyes and pulled herself together. "He was just kidding, Helen. Martin's harmless. We'll see what Paul says, but in truth, I do like Martin. He's kind of romantic in a way. You heard what he said about the future."

"My bedpan has more romance in it than Martin. Sam doesn't like him, and he likes everyone. Martin's a thief, a liar, and who knows what else. But he's no good." They turned onto Lexington Lane and walked to cottage number Seventeen. Helen knocked on the door with anticipation of seeing her man. Edith was as timid and scared as a nervous mouse facing a farrow cat ready to pounce.

Paul Johnson opened the door wearing his dirty work clothes. His bib overalls were covered with flakes of sawdust with oil and grease stains in the blue denim material. He wore a long-sleeve brown sweater under the overalls. He was surprised. "Oh! Hi...Come in. Sam is changing his clothes and washing up in his room."

Helen snickered. "Perfect," she said and stepped past Paul and knocked on Sam's door before entering in uninvited and closed the door behind her.

Paul closed the front door and spoke at Edith uneasily, "How are you?"

She nodded quickly. "Good. You?"

"Good. I'm just working, and that's about it."

She frowned as he turned away from her to step into the small kitchen area. "I haven't seen you at the dance hall."

He shook his head. "I guess I don't feel like dancing." He sat down at a small table and began untying his work boots. "I've been going to Ugly John's Saloon and playing cards a bit."

"Oh." she stood awkwardly in the middle of the room. "I wanted to talk to you."

He tossed one boot against the wall and began untying the other. "Talk."

"Well…I'm…"

He interrupted quickly, "I heard you were already courting someone else. Congratulations," he said bitterly, looking up at her.

"No, I'm not. I'm not courting anyone," she said with a surprised grimace.

"That's not what I heard. I heard he's there late every night and has been since we ended our courtship. It didn't take you long to find someone new, did it?"

"I didn't end our courtship. You did," she said pointedly.

He shrugged uncaringly.

She gasped, "Paul, I need to tell you something, and I'm afraid you're not going to like it." Tears filled her eyes. Her hands fidgeted nervously.

He leaned back against the chair and sighed. "What? You're getting married?"

She shook her head. "No. I'm going to have your baby."

"What?" he spat out, surprised.

"I'm six weeks pregnant, according to the doctor. I found out today."

Paul sat still as the news was absorbed.

"Aren't you going to say anything?" her voice quivered as the fear and desperation became evident.

"What do you want me to say?" he asked, raising his hands hopelessly. "Is it mine?"

Her eyes narrowed. "Of course, it's yours! I haven't been with anyone else," she finished angrily.

He shook his head quietly. "So, I'm going to be a father," he spoke softly to himself.

"And I'm going to be a mother."

He glanced up at her quickly. "We're going to have a baby?"

She nodded. "Yes. Whether you like it or not, we are. I know you don't want to get married. But I thought you should know."

He stood up. "Edith, I didn't tell you the truth. It isn't because I didn't want to get married. I do want to get married, but I wasn't sure you were the one I wanted to marry, so it made no sense to keep courting." He paused and then added, "My folks didn't think I should marry a girl from Rose Street. They expected more than that from me."

"I'm not a whore on Rose Street, Paul," she spoke, heatedly. "But you got what you wanted, so maybe I am. I don't know." She began to weep softly with a painful expression.

"No, you're not." He put his arms around her shoulders to embrace her. "I never lied to you other than that. I love you, Edith, I was just a bit confused and dismayed by my folks saying that and wondered if it was true. This time I have spent away from you has been hard. I would've come to you and asked if we could fix it, but I heard you were already courting someone else. I figured if you're courting someone else already, then my parents were right. So, I'm going to ask you right now, are you courting someone else? Because that's what I'm hearing."

She wiped her eyes as she stared into his. "No, I am not courting anyone else. Who told you that anyway, Sam?"

"No. Sam said you weren't to his knowledge, but said the new deputy was spending a lot of time with you. The men at work are the ones who told me that. So, you're not courting him?"

She shook her head. "I've already told you I wasn't. Martin's a nice man and has become a friend, but there's nothing between us. Nothing even close."

Paul swallowed and took a deep breath. "Edith, I've missed you, and I don't care what my parents think, I'm in love with you and want to raise our baby with you. I don't have a ring or anything of the sort, but if you marry me, we could start a family."

Edith began sobbing and lowered her head into Paul's chest as she hugged him.

"Is that a yes?" he asked with a laugh.

She nodded. "Yes," she wept. "Oh, yes, I'll marry you."

"And your friend, the deputy, you'll stop letting him stay after hours?"

She laughed. "Yes, I'll let Martin know tonight. I love you so much, Paul! I've missed you so much."

"I've missed you more, Edith." He kissed her in a passionate embrace.

20

Martin was in high spirits when he entered the dance hall. He had gotten a draw off his wages from his new employer and friend, Tim Wright. He bought himself a new pair of black pants and new blue and white pinstriped shirt with his badge pinned to it. Martin looked nice in his new clothes and felt as good as he appeared. He hung his gun belt and coat upon a brass hook on the wall inside of the entry of the dance hall. Martin greeted the security guard Phil Mears and went inside the ballroom to buy a drink and a dance ticket. He saw Edith dancing and watched her with a sense of pride, knowing that beautiful yellow-haired lady dressed in a pink and lavender dress that so many other men in the building wished they could have belonged to him. She was his lady and would be for the rest of their lives.

Across the room, Sam Troyer was sitting at a large table with four chairs against the wall with a taller man about the same age with neck length black hair and a beard. Sam pointed at Martin while speaking to the dark-haired man, who stared at him with a smirk. It irritated Martin, and he wanted to know what Sam was saying to the stranger, but in the scheme of things, it meant nothing. Martin was the happiest man in the room and had every reason to be. Love was hard to find, but finding the love of a lifetime with the one person made for him was the greatest miracle in life. He may have thought he was in love with a few other ladies over the years, but he had been wrong all along. Edith was the right woman for him; he had no doubt. And she was feeling the same way about him. Kissing her took his breath away, and he never wanted it to end. If he could hold and kiss her all night long, it would be something he would never get tired of doing.

He leaned against the bar and watched Edith finish the dance. She was smiling as the man guided her arm in arm towards the bar to buy her a drink. The gentleman bought her drink, and they talked as she drank the small glass of champagne. Martin maneuvered closer and handed her a dance ticket. "Let's dance, beautiful."

She smiled awkwardly. She took Martin's ticket and took him by the arm as they walked out to the dancefloor to wait for the next dance.

"I would love to give you the biggest kiss, but I know you're working," he said with a smile.

She smirked slightly to acknowledge his words. She appeared to be uncomfortable and distant.

"Is something wrong? You seem very quiet," he asked. He noticed she was keeping further away from him than usual.

"I'm just tired. How are you?" Her voice had a dryness to it.

"Good. How could I not be?" he laughed. "I have the most beautiful girl in the world and a job that's going to make me the Sheriff someday. I'm excited about our future," he said as they began dancing. "Are you sure you're okay? Did I say something wrong?" he asked when she had given no response to his excitement.

"Yeah, I'm fine. I'm just not feeling well."

"Do you want to stop dancing? We don't have to finish the dance," he asked gently.

"No, I'll be fine. How about we just dance," she said shortly. She was trying to avoid any conversation at all.

It was becoming apparent that she didn't want to talk to him for some unknown reason, and it ate at his thoughts. He hadn't done or said anything wrong that he was aware of, and the only thing it could be was her seeing Paul again. His jaw clenched as he thought about it. "Edith, have I angered you? I notice you're not talking to me. Is there something wrong?"

She shook her head sadly. "Honestly, you haven't done anything wrong."

"Did that piece of crap Paul say something to upset you?" he asked, trying to control his hostility at the thought of her going to Paul's house.

She stopped dancing in the middle of the dance and reached into her pocket to hand him a red ticket to stay after hours again. "Martin, I can't talk about it right now, but I need to talk to you after we close tonight. I'll talk to you then, okay?" she asked with moisture clouding her eyes.

Martin frowned with concern. "Edith, talk to me, what's going on?"

She shook her head emotionally. "I can't. Not right now. I'm sorry," she said and left the dance floor in a hurry towards a doorway leading up a few stairs to the stage that was covered by a large red curtain.

He grimaced and walked back to the bar and ordered another drink. His stomach tightened into a knot, and his breathing grew labored as he tried to figure out what may have happened with Paul. He glanced over and noticed Sam and the taller man with dark hair watching him. Sam seemed to be enjoying himself at Martin's expense. He had enough of the staring and walked over to Sam's table. "What's going on with Edith?" he asked sharply. "Why do you keep looking at me?"

Sam motioned to his friend sitting beside him. "Have you met my friend Paul? Paul, this is Martin. The sheriff's new deputy."

Paul nodded without so much as a word as he eyed Martin carefully with a slight smirk to his lips.

Martin's breathing deepened as he realized Paul was Edith's former beau. He was beginning to make sense of why she wasn't talking to him now that he knew who was with Sam. Martin's eyes grew darker. "You're the one that broke Edith's heart a couple of weeks ago?" he asked, already knowing.

Paul nodded regrettably. "I am. But we're back together now."

Martin bent forward slightly as the wind had been sucked out of him by the stunning announcement. His face flushed as a wave of disbelief stunned him. He shook his head as he spoke heatedly, "No, I'm afraid you're wrong. We're courting, her and I. Unless you think kissing her today and every day was meaningless. So, you can tell her goodbye and walk away now. I won't allow you to interfere with us. If you know what's good for you, you'll leave right now and never talk to her again. I'm serious about that." He paused, expecting a response, but none came. Sam watched him with a humored grin, and Paul stirred his drink while shaking is head with a smirk on his lips. Martin continued, "Look, she gave me a red ticket. I've gotten one every night for two weeks now. Starting the night, you broke her heart. Don't try to tell me you're back together with her. As I said, Edith is mine, and I won't let you interfere. I'm warning you, leave here and stay gone!" His eyes glared at Paul intensely.

Sam waited for Paul's response expectantly.

Paul smiled slowly and looked up at Martin. "You didn't kiss her."

Martin pointed towards the stage. "You can ask her! I'm telling you, don't get in my way, or I'll hurt you!" he sneered with a low voice.

Paul was slightly taken back by the venom of the unexpected threat by a man Edith said she wasn't courting. "Well," Paul said calmly, "I'll tell you what, if she did kiss you, then you can have her, and I'll back so far off that you'll never see me again. But it isn't because I'm afraid you're going to hurt me,

I'm afraid you don't scare me much at all, deputy or not. I know your boss, and he's not worth a dime's worth of cow dung either. So, you can take your little shiny badge and shove it up your ass! Now we've said our peace, and you can walk away."

Martin snorted a disgusted laugh. "You ask her. Hell, I kissed her today when she was on the way to your house! It was a nice long kiss too."

Paul narrowed his eyes, growing irritated. "I'll ask her."

Martin smiled victoriously. "Yeah, you do that!" He stepped over to the bar and ordered another drink and gulped it down before ordering another. He was angry, and the pressure was building up in his chest with every beat of his heart like it was pumping more force into his chest with every heartbeat. He watched Edith come out of the side door that went up onto the stage and walked towards him at the bar.

She stopped in front of him and sighed with an apologetic expression. "I apologize, Martin. I shouldn't have left the dance floor. Do you want to finish the dance, there are still a few minutes if you do?" she asked. "Or if you want to, you can dance with someone else." She held out a dance ticket for him to take back.

His lips twitched with anger and bit his bottom lip. "Why would I want to dance with someone else?" he asked, keeping control of his voice.

"I don't know. Maybe because I walked out on you?" she asked with an uneasy shrug.

He nodded slowly, with his eyes boring into her.

"Maybe, or could it be because Paul is over there, and you don't want to be seen with me?" he asked pointedly.

She sighed heavily. "Can we talk after we close tonight?"

He grabbed her arm firmly and began walking her towards Paul and Sam's table.

"Let me go, Martin!" she pleaded. "You're hurting my arm!"

"Not until he knows the truth!" He stopped at their table. Squeezing her arm, he ordered, "Tell him! Tell him we've kissed, and you don't want him! Tell him he doesn't matter anymore!"

"No, Martin! Let go of my arm; you're hurting me!" She cried out while trying to pull her arm out of his grasp, but he held her tight.

Paul and Sam both stood up quickly. Paul spoke harshly, "Let her go, now!"

Martin perplexed, stared at Edith, and loosened his grip. "What do you mean, no?" he asked with a stunned slack jaw that hung open.

"No!" She declared while pulling her arm away from him. She stepped towards the protection of Paul at the end of the table. "I've never kissed you! What do you think I am a whore? Paul and I are courting, and I wish you would leave me alone! I was going to tell you that nicely later tonight, but after this, I don't care about your feelings! I never have, and I would never kiss you! That's disgusting. Now, I wish you would just leave me alone!"

"What?" he asked, stunned. "Edith...why are you doing this? He's just going to hurt you again. What about the future we planned for a life together?

You're going to ruin everything good and...loving that we had going for us. We were like Matt and Christine and all that they have. Remember, it's what you wanted!" he finished growing hostile.

Sam laughed as he and Paul sat back down against the wall. "Yeah, Edith, don't ruin Matt and Christine's relationship!" he quipped.

Edith laughed lightly as she sat down on Paul's lap. "You're not Matt, and I'm not Christine. I'm me, and my heart belongs to Paul. It always has. Sorry, Martin, but there was never anything between us. Nothing at all. As I said, I was going to explain it to you nicely when we closed, but after dragging me over here and hurting my arm. I don't care anymore. I won't be manhandled again by anyone."

"Edith?" he asked with great sincerity as he stared at her with his eyes glazing over. "What about us?"

She put an arm around Paul's shoulders. "Martin, Paul, and I are going to be married. I suppose you're going to have to move on without me. Rose is free, and she likes you. Maybe she's the real one for you," she said with a condescending smile and glanced at Paul and Sam as they laughed.

Martin's lips snarled, and his eyes grew darker and narrowed in his growing rage. He held out a hand for her to take in hers. "Come on!" he ordered.

She grimaced. "No! Just go away, Martin."

He grabbed her wrist and yanked her off Paul's lap to the floor. Paul stood up quickly as did Sam. Paul pushed Martin backward. "Get your hands off her!" He glared down at Martin for a moment and then bent over to help Edith up off the floor. "Are you okay?" he asked with concern.

"Yes, I'm fine," she said, shocked by Martin.

"Edith, let's go!" Martin demanded with a hard glare. His eyes clearly expressed his fury, and it startled her.

Paul had enough of him. He pointed his finger in Martin's face and shouted, "Go away before I bust your head open!"

Helen Monroe hurried over to Edith and asked, "What's going on over here? Edith, are you alright?" she asked with concern.

"I'm fine."

Martin pointed at Helen. "Ask her; she was there! Helen, didn't Edith kiss me today?" His eyes pleaded with her desperately.

Helen shook her head with disgust. "Hell no! Why would she be kissing on you?"

Martin was incensed. "You lying, whore!" He drew his hand back to slap her face with an overhand palm, but it was quickly blocked by Sam, who stepped in front of Helen and threw a hard-right fist that connected with Martin's jaw and sent Martin down to the floor.

Sam yelled, "Leave her alone, Martin! I told you not to get too attached to Edith. I told you Paul and her would get back together. Now get the hell out of here before I bust you up so bad you have to be carried out of here! And if you ever raise your hand to my woman again, you'll never think clearly again!"

Martin's face turned into a wild scowl as he got back to his feet. He growled from deep within and ran forward to tackle Sam. Martin wrapped his arms around Sam's waist and lifted him and slammed him down on the floor. Martin tried to stay on top to hit Sam, but Sam wrapped his arms around Martin's body and held him close as they rolled on the floor, trying to get the upper position. Paul and a few other men stepped in and pulled the two men apart and held them to keep them from fighting. Both men wanted to continue the fight and reached for each other as they cursed bitterly to be released.

The security guard, Phil Mears stepped in between them. "What's going on here?"

Martin spoke first, "He hit me!"

Paul argued, "Martin was going to hit Helen when Sam stopped him! He pushed Edith down, too."

Phil spoke to Edith and Helen. "Are you two all right?"

Helen answered first, "He's causing trouble, Phil. He's trying to break Edith and Paul up, and that's what this is all about. He was going to hit me, though, yes."

"I was not!" Martin yelled. "I'm a deputy sheriff, and I am arresting Sam for assaulting me." He pointed at Sam. "You're under arrest! Come with me now, or I'll come back with Tim and a few of the others, and we'll drag you out of here by your hair!"

Edith shouted, "You can't arrest him for something you started! Get out of here and leave us alone! No one wants you here."

"What about us?" he asked desperately, leaning his body forward. "Edith, why are you acting this way? I trusted you. I'm falling in love with you!"

Sam and Paul both chuckled.

Edith stared at him and shook her head slightly. She spoke coldly, "You mean nothing to me. Now please leave and don't come back."

He held up the red ticket. "Can we talk tonight, please?" he begged.

"No! I don't ever want to see you again."

Bella walked quickly to the skirmish and demanded to know what happened. She didn't care to listen to either Martin's side of the story of Sam's, she looked at her two girls and asked them. When they told her what had taken place, she turned and faced Martin. "Martin, I need you to leave my building at once and never come back. I will not have my ladies manhandled!"

"I didn't touch her!" he yelled.

"I don't give a damn. You need to leave, and you need to leave now! You're no longer welcome here, ever!"

"I'm a deputy sheriff! You can't stop me from…"

"This is a privately owned business, and unless you have official business with a matter of law, yes, I can, and I will. We have security, and if that's not enough, we have the Marshal. Now get the hell out of here. Now!" she shouted.

"Can I talk to Edith?"

"No, you may not talk with Edith. Phil throw him out!"

Phil grabbed his arm and began to take him towards the door. Martin started to cry out, "Edith, please…talk to me. Give me another chance! Edith, I love you, please."

174

Bella grabbed his coat and gun belt and took them outside of the dance hall where Phil had led him. "Here are your things. Good night, Martin and goodbye. Phil, if he tries to come back inside ever again, crack his head open."

"Yes, Ma'am," he answered. He addressed Martin, "Don't come back."

Martin was upset and, in his anger, began to cry as he spoke: "Please, give me another chance."

Bella answered, "No. Phil, close the door."

"Yes, Ma'am. So long, Martin," he said with a smirk and closed the dance hall door.

Martin stood on the street, staring at the door with a growing sneer. "Edith," he yelled, "How can you do this to me? I won't let you go! You belong to me!"

21

Martin burst through his apartment door and slammed it shut behind him. He screamed in anger and tried to catch his breath from his pounding heart and hard breathing.

Sylvia came out of her room, wrapped in a robe. "Martin, be quiet! We have neighbors. Now, what are you screaming about?"

He glared at her with his teeth clenched as his chest rose and fell with his breathing. "She lied! She said we never kissed, and now they're courting again! She lied! She said she was never interested in me, but she was! I know she was; we kissed! We were falling in love; I know we were! Now suddenly, she wants to change her mind? Well, I won't let her! She's going to marry me or no one at all!" He paused to catch his breath and stared at his mother with water-filled eyes that seemed to be about to spill over. He continued emotionally, "She has to marry me, Momma, she's the one for me."

Sylvia sighed and shook her head. "Martin, if she lied, then hon, she's not the one. Remember, Lois, you thought she was the one too, but she wasn't."

He fumed. "Of course, I remember Lois! Why do you have to bring her up? Edith is not some teenage infatuation. I love her, Mother!" He sat down in a chair and quietly began to weep. "How am I ever going to be happy if she won't talk to me? I'm so tired of losing. When am I ever going to win the heart of the only girl that I want? She got me kicked out of the dance hall for good, Momma. I can't go back in there anymore." He sniffled and wiped his tears away.

Sylvia sat down in the chair beside his. "Martin, you'll find love eventually. It takes time. But chances are you won't find it in the dance hall or a saloon, maybe you should come to church with us, and meet some young ladies who want a good man to marry."

"I'm not going to church."

Sylvia frowned. "You know Martin since I have been going to church and praying, I feel a lot happier than I ever have. When you accept Jesus as your savior, he comes into your heart, and I don't know, but I am different now. I am happy for maybe the first time ever, and I'm excited about life. You don't need a girl in your life to be happy. That kind of happiness only lasts until the first argument, or a bad mood comes along perhaps. It's not lasting. You need a relationship with Jesus, and then you'll be happy with yourself.."

Martin glared at her scornfully. "I don't believe that. You can go to church if you want to, but I have my own beliefs. And why are you bringing up church anyway?" he asked, becoming more aggravated. His voice rose, "I just told you Edith lied and is ruining everything, and you want to bring up church?" He stood up and turned to face his mother and cursed bitterly before adding, "Why don't you just leave me alone?"

Sylvia scolded him, "Why don't you lower your voice! We have neighbors, and I'm sure they don't appreciate being woken up on a work night."

"It's not that late, and if they're not awake, they should be!" he yelled towards the wall.

The neighbor banged on the wall a few times in anger and yelled, "Shut up!"

Martin stepped forward and kicked the wall and yelled, "You shut up! I'm a sheriff's deputy, and if you think you're tough, I'll blow your head off! Don't bang on the wall again!"

"Martin!" Sylvia yelled, standing from the chair to get his attention. "What is wrong with you? Huh? What?"

"Don't you listen? No, you don't. What was I thinking? You have Henry now, and he's all you care about! Henry, oh, Henry." He shook his head with disgust as he glared at her. "What's with the ring anyway? Did he pull it off his dead wife or something? He isn't going to marry you! He's just going to use you and try to sweet talk Barbra out of her knickers, just like he will you…"

"Enough, Martin!" Sylvia shouted. "Henry has done nothing but be nice to us."

He rolled his eyes. "Yeah, I know! Just like everyone else, huh? You're putting your daughter in danger by being around him. I won't let you put her at risk anymore. Take that damn ring off right now!" he ordered and held out his hand.

Sylvia scowled and shook her head lightly. "I'm not giving you my ring. And you must be drunk if you think you can tell me what to do. Maybe you need to go outside and cool down for a while."

"Mother, I need your ring," he said, still extending his hand outward.

"For what?" she asked, appalled that he'd even ask for it.

He exhaled and let his hand fall. "For Edith. I don't have a ring to ask her to marry me with. Can I have yours, please?"

"No, you can't have my ring! What are you talking about anyway, Martin? You just met her."

"And you just met Henry!" he screamed in her face. "What makes Henry any different than Edith, huh? We met them on the same day! Why can't I feel for Edith the way Henry feels for you, huh? There's no difference. You're just selfish and enjoy seeing me lose the love of my life while you wear that stupid ring and prance around here like some kind of special high and mighty person now that some man likes you for a week or two!" He paused to glare at his mother. "I'll break you up. I won't let you find happiness if I can't have it too. I'll kill him and blame it on Paul."

Sylvia slapped him across the face. "Don't you ever speak like that again! If your so unhappy with your life, then do something about it. But do not stand in my house and threaten my friend or me ever again, or you can leave and not come back! Do you hear me? You're almost thirty years old, and you want to take my ring to give to some girl? Are you out of your mind? I'm sorry that girl lied to you, but that's not my fault or the neighbor's fault. You need to get a hold of yourself and stop! Just stop, Martin!"

"Stop what?" he screamed.

"She doesn't want you! Okay? Find someone else and let her go."

His eyes grew wild as he glared at his mother. He spoke through his gritted teeth. "I can't let her go! I love her! She belongs to me."

Barbra came out of the bedroom she shared with her mother and shook her head at Martin. "Are you going to brand your name on her? You talk like she has no choice about who she wants to court. Obviously, it's not you."

Martin stepped forward and shoved her as hard as he could. Barbra flew across the room and landed on the floor next to the back door. He continued forward and shoved his finger into her face while he seethed, "Shut your damn mouth before I bust your teeth out!"

Sylvia grabbed his shoulder and spun him around and pointed at the door. She screamed furiously, "Get out! Get out of my house and don't come back until you can apologize to your sister and can act like a reasonable human being! And if you can't, then go away! But don't you ever lay your hands on her again, or you'll never be welcomed back."

"Fine! You know what? Both of you can go to hell!" he hollered and left the apartment and slammed the door behind him. His voice could be heard screaming at them from outside, "Mother, you're a whore! You both can go to hell! I hate you both!"

Sylvia stared at the door with her mouth open shocked by how she had seen her son behave and what she now heard.

Barbra sat up and got back to her feet. "He's doing it again, Ma. I don't understand why he can't act like a normal person. Do you think Henry would act like that if you rejected him?"

Sylvia shook her head with tears burning her eyes. "No. I'll talk to Martin tomorrow when he calms down. Are you okay?" she asked, looking at her daughter. Her tears rolled down her cheeks.

"I'm fine. Are you okay?" Barbra asked and then hugged her mother as she began to weep.

22

Martin walked back to Bella's Dance Hall and walked around the building, looking for a way in without going through the front entryway where Phil Mears stood guarding the door. There were only a few first-floor windows, and they all had bars over them to protect the ladies. The only way inside was to go through the main door. Martin stood in the cold, watching the door waiting for Phil to leave the entry. Twenty minutes later, Phil stepped away from the entrance to enter the ballroom and left the front door and entry open. Martin took a chance and darted forward and went up the steps through the opened door and quickly slid through the ball-room's entrance hiding his face with his hands as he did and ducked behind a couple of men standing by the bar talking. He peeked around the men and saw a glimpse of Sam and Paul talking at the table. He scanned the dance floor and saw Edith dancing with an older man in a suit. Edith danced with a joy on her face that she didn't have when she was dancing with Martin earlier. Martin couldn't believe she would be smiling and having a good time while knowing he had been kicked out of the dance hall permanently. It was wrong, and he needed to make it right. He saw Bella in her usual place near the other end of the bar laughing with a couple of men. Martin took a deep breath and walked towards her.

Bella saw him coming and lost her smile as a nasty scowl came over her face. She pointed at the door and spoke sharply, "Out! You are no longer welcome here. Turn around and leave, Martin, and don't come back!"

He raised his hands in a defensive position. "I'm sorry. Just give me one minute, please."

"No." She waved a hand towards Phil to get his attention. He had gone to a table of a few young men who were getting rowdy to quiet them down to a respectable volume.

"Bella, please, can I just talk to you for a minute?" He cursed angrily as Phil came near. "I'm sorry. Doesn't that mean anything to you? I want to come back here. Bella, please! Let me stay."

Phil frowned and grabbed Martin by his arm and pulled it behind his back and forced it upwards with his right hand and grabbed his hair with his left hand and forced him towards the door. "Let's go!"

"Bella, let me stay!" Martin yelled, bringing the attention of almost everyone in the dance hall. "I have to talk to Edith, damn it! Edith, I love you! Don't do this to me, Edith! You're my lady!" he yelled as Phil tossed him off the top of the stairs down a short distance to the hard snow-covered ground below.

Phil pointed at him. "Martin, if you come back, I will break your arm! Stay away from here."

"Phil...Come on. You know Edith and I are courting. Tell Paul, for me, will you? Come on, Phil, you know I'm better for her than he is. Please," Martin begged desperately with watering eyes.

Phil shook his head. "Go home, Martin." He closed the door.

Martin waited in the cold for another hour for closing time to come. It was Eleven on a Monday night, and almost every man needed to go home and get some sleep for Tuesday morning's workday. Martin watched the men leave and gasped when he saw Paul step out onto the porch with Edith. Her arms were around him, and Paul leaned down to kiss her. Martin's heart pounded with explosive bursts as his fury burned within him. He wanted to step out into the open and confront them both right there, but he knew they'd just go back inside, and he'd still be standing in the cold. He clenched his jaw and endured the sight of another man kissing his lady. Paul let her go as he and Sam began walking away. Edith and Helen remained on the porch for a moment as they watched them walk away. Edith grinned with excitement as she stepped back inside.

Martin followed Paul and Sam home. He remained hidden as much as he could, but neither Sam nor Paul ever looked back behind them. Once Martin followed them to their home, he knocked on their door.

Paul opened the door and was startled to see Martin glaring at him.

"Can we talk?" Martin asked quickly.

"No. No, we can't talk. What are you doing here?" Paul asked, stunned to see him.

"I want to talk to you."

Paul shook his head. "No." He closed the door as Sam asked who was there.

Martin knocked again.

The door was pulled open by Sam. "Go away before I finish what we started! That's your only warning." He slammed the door closed in Martin's face.

Martin bit his lip in anger and pulled his .32 Caliber Remington Pocket Revolver out of its holster. He knocked again and stepped closer to the door expecting it to be opened. When Sam yanked the door open, Martin had the revolver pointed at Sam's face. "Yell at me again, Sam! I dare you!" he said sharply as he stepped uninvited into their home, forcing Sam backward. He kicked the door closed behind him while he held the gun on Sam.

Paul stood in the kitchen area staring at Martin in disbelief.

Martin glared dangerously at Sam, who held his hands up and was too scared to speak. Martin spoke harshly, "Not so tough now, are you? You got your wish, didn't you? They're back together just like you, and that fat pig of yours wanted! This is your fault!" He pulled the revolver back quickly and slammed it across Sam's head. Sam fell to the floor, holding his head. Martin aimed the gun at Paul.

"Please...don't shoot," Paul begged. "I'll do anything, okay? Just don't shoot me."

Martin's lips twisted into a sneer. "I'm giving you both a choice. Leave Edith alone and never talk to her again, or die. What's it going to be?"

Paul shook his head with his hands up defensively over his face to deflect any shots that may come. "I'll never talk to her again. Not ever! Please, just don't shoot me." The fearful expression on his face left no doubt to his sincerity.

"I've kissed Edith! I even kissed her today. I'm not the one lying. We were courting until you showed up. She's supposed to be with me, not you!"

Paul shook his head. "You can have her!" He cried out fearfully.

"You said you'd never be seen again if I kissed her. Well, I did!"

"I believe you! Please, I already said I'd leave her alone. Trust me; I'm done with her for good. You can have her."

Martin peered down at Sam, who was sitting against the wall, holding a lump swelling up on the side of his head. Martin snarled and kicked Sam in the face with a right boot as hard as he could. "And you keep your nose out of my business! What Edith and I have is none of your business! If you ever intervene again, I will blow your head off!" he shouted. He took a breath and spoke more reasonably to Sam, "Now, I need you to talk to Bella and tell her it wasn't my fault. Tell her it was your and Paul's fault that Edith fell and that you lied about me trying to hit your lying pig of a woman. Sam, are you listening, or do I need to kick you again?"

"I'm listening!" Sam replied sharply.

"Good. I need back in the dance hall and the good graces of Bella. Who's going to help me with that?" he asked, slowly letting his eyes roll over the two men.

"I will," Paul said. "Look, I'm finished with Edith. If I had known you were courting her, I never would've been there tonight. You have my word on that. She swore she wasn't courting you. I asked her because that's what I heard, but she said she wasn't. She lied to me too. I have nothing against you," Paul said through a shaking voice.

Martin nodded. "You both have one day to make things right with Bella and Edith too. If Bella doesn't let me in there tomorrow night, I'll come back here and leave you both wishing you had tried harder. I know where you live, and I can make life hell for you both. See?" He pointed at his badge. "I could kill you both and go arrest some drunk vagrant for it and get away with it. Don't test me, fellas. You both have one day to make this mess you made right again." He pointed the gun at Paul. "I'm going to marry Edith, or no one is. Do you understand me?"

"Absolutely. No argument here, buddy. And listen, I have to work tomorrow, but after work, I'll be talking to Bella and Edith. And that's the last time I'll ever be there."

Martin exhaled and smiled slightly as he took a deep breath. "Okay. Yeah, I think we have an understanding." He waved the gun between the two of them. "And this talk stays between us, right?"

"I'm not saying anything!" Paul exclaimed.

"What about you, Sam? You're not saying much. Do we have a problem?"

Sam glared up at him with a slightly bloody nose while holding his head. "My head hurts!" he shouted. "But no, we don't have a problem. I won't say anything."

Martin nodded as he relaxed with a feeling of excitement, starting to build within him. "Then tomorrow I'll have my lady back. Okay, fellas, I hope I don't have to come back unless it's to go get a drink with you, two, sometimes."

Paul shrugged exaggeratedly. "Sure."

Martin put the revolver back in his holster and walked to the door. "Thanks, fellas," he said and walked out of the house.

Paul let his body slide down the kitchen cabinet and sat on the floor with a dumbfound expression on his face. "What the hell?"

Sam glanced over at his friend and shook his head without saying a word.

"Crazy...that was crazy."

Sam nodded. "The only person I'm talking to is Matt Bannister in the morning. Or should we go tell him now?"

Paul scoffed. "In the morning. With our luck, he'd be out there watching to make sure we don't."

Sam nodded. "We need to lock the door."

"In a minute. I'm shaking too much to stand," Paul said and exhaled, trying to relax. "I'm starting to think he kissed Edith after all."

Sam smiled despite himself. "He seems crazy about her anyway."

Paul widened his eyes and exhaled. "No doubt."

23

Matt Bannister stepped out of his office, carrying a new wanted poster that had come in the mail. "Gentleman, this is important," he said as he stepped into the main office where his deputies had their desks. "We have a new wanted poster that you all need to pay attention to because he might just be in our neighborhood. Boys, let me introduce you to Bo Crowe." He unrolled the poster, and there was a drawing of a hard-looking man with long black straight hair, a strong face with a beard, a slightly bent nose, and a cockeyed left eye that wandered to the left rather than straight. He was wanted for robbery, rape, and burglary. There was a five-hundred-dollar reward for him.

Nate Robertson gazed at the drawing of Bo and asked, "Do you think he'll see us coming?"

Jed smirked. "Just stay slightly to his left. Not too far left, though."

Nate laughed.

Matt spoke seriously, "Do not take this man lightly. He's one of the Crowe Brothers I mentioned last week. They're just over the mountain, and I don't know if Bo is hiding out here in Jessup County or not, but we do know he has a lot of family over in Natoma, the Sperry-Helms Gang. I'm going to tell you all right now, if you see this man, do not confront him alone. His eye may look a little funny, but he's a dangerous man. So, nobody try to face this man alone and definitely don't face him if he's with his brothers or the Sperry-Helms Gang."

"Boss," Nate said, borrowing Jed's name for Matt. "Are we ever going to go to Natoma and confront them?"

Matt answered thoughtfully. "At the moment, I don't have a reason to go over there. I am going to wire the Natoma Sheriff and ask him to contact me if he sees Bo. But until then, no. As to your word ever, I hope not. I hope the Sperry-Helms Gang decided it was safer for them to find legitimate jobs and go straight. Because quite frankly, unless our favorite worthless sheriff, Tim, comes clean on who took Pick out of his jail and hung him, my hands are tied legally. There's nothing else I can charge them with or accuse them of doing. But if the Natoma Sheriff sees Bo over there, then yes, we will go there to get him. And if we have to confront the Sperry-Helms Gang in the process, then they'll have to choose what they're going to do. We will bring Bo in one way or another. Does that answer your question?"

Nate nodded uneasily with the thought of facing the notorious gang.

Jed smiled as he watched Nate. "And you're fighting beside me because I can't wait to watch you wet your jeans in the middle of a gunfight."

Nate shook his head with a small smile. "Not me, Jed. Phillip would, but I'm good."

Truet Davis spoke softly in deep thought, "Just hope it never comes to that. Having bullets flying past you isn't much fun, fellas. Is it, Matt?"

Matt shook his head. "No, it's not. It can be downright scary. Nate, you're the only in this room who hasn't killed a man before, and I hope you never do. But if you're given no choice, do not hesitate to pull the trigger. You aim to kill, and you pull the trigger."

Nate smiled. "You've told me that before."

Matt nodded with a serious expression on his face. "Good. Remember it. Because wearing that badge increases your chances of it happening. If you can go your whole career without using your gun, fantastic, but I doubt it will happen if you're going to work for me. If you worked in the Sheriff's Office, maybe, but we don't run and hide from the bad guys here. The Sheriff does."

Jed spoke, confirming Matt's words, "Ain't that the truth. Tim Wright's good at looking good, but he ain't good at much other than looking it and taking credit for other people's work."

Nate smirked. "Is that why he liked standing next to you, so that he could look really good to the ladies? Comparatively, that is?" he laughed.

Jed smiled. "I don't have to look good to the ladies; I'm married. And my woman thinks I look alright. She never said I looked good, just alright," he joked. "Now Truet's the handsome one. He's got every lady in town looking at him; just most are too nervous to talk to him. He looks so handsome."

Truet smiled handsomely. "Yeah, but I found the lady that's won my heart. And I even got her brother's permission to court her after a while," he grinned. "And I'm riding over there to Willow Falls tomorrow. So I won't see you all for a few days after today."

Matt laughed lightly. "Why don't you tell them why?"

Truet didn't look too pleased. "Annie wants to build a fence line in the middle of winter. She has all the supplies but isn't strong enough to dig the post holes in the frozen ground. But she says I am."

Jed grinned. "So you're going to set fence posts?"

Truet nodded. "Romantic, isn't it?"

Jed asked, "It can't wait until Spring?"

"Apparently not. Everyone's too busy with the ranch and other projects. She needs me to build this fence as soon as possible. She's trying to get her horse business going, so I'll go help her out."

Nate spoke, "It sounds like she needs to hire some more help."

"This spring, she will be hiring some help."

The door opened, ringing the bell tied above it. Sam Troyer and Paul Johnson stepped into the office. "Matt, we have to talk to you about Martin," Sam blurted out quickly. "He threatened our lives last night. He forced himself into our house and held us at gunpoint and threatened to kill us!"

Matt frowned. "For what?" he asked while he sipped his cup of coffee.

Paul sputtered, "Because he wanted me to leave Edith alone!"

"Tell me what happened," Matt said and listened to all that they told him about the night before. When they finished talking, Matt said, "Well, let's go talk to Tim and see what he says."

"Matt," Paul said slowly, "If Martin sees us talking to Tim and not Bella, he might be crazy enough to come back over and shoot us. He followed us home just to see where we lived."

Matt shook his head. "My words not good enough. You both need to be there and tell Tim what happened yourselves. You can't let Martin scare you away from telling Tim what his man did. That's exactly what Martin wants you to do. Don't worry about him; I'll take care of that before I leave. Let me grab my coat, and we'll walk over there."

Sheriff Tim Wright sat behind his desk with his deputy Bob Ewing in a chair in front of him, talking over some things when the door opened. Tim glanced up curiously when he saw Matt and the other two men enter his office. "Gentlemen, what's going on?" he asked with a hint of concern. It seemed every time Matt came into his office; it was usually bad news concerning him.

Matt spoke as he stood along a wall allowing Sam and Paul to step in front of him, "Where's Martin this morning, Tim?"

"I sent him to run a few errands. Why?" Tim asked.

"I'll let these men explain."

Paul and Sam told Tim Wright what had happened the night before. Tim interrupted a few times to ask a question or two but listened until they had finished talking. Tim shook his head. "Well, I mean, that's not right what Martin did. That's not right at all. But Edith told you they weren't courting?"

Paul nodded. "Yeah."

Tim raised his hand a bit as he laughed. "I have to tell you, I am surprised, because I was there when he met her, and she wanted him to stay late. He's stayed late every night for two weeks or longer now. Since you two stopped courting anyway. He talks about her every day. It's almost annoying because she's all he talks about, and I can tell you they have kissed and a bit more than that because he was flying as high as an eagle over that one. I heard about it for days. So, I don't know what she's saying, but he's saying they're courting. I can see why he might be a bit angry, especially since she just dumped him like a used bedpan when you came back around."

Matt spoke from his place by the wall, "That still doesn't give him any right to threaten them or to do so with a weapon."

"Of course not," Tim agreed.

"Wait," Paul said with a quizzical expression. "You're telling me they were courting?"

"That's what he's been saying, and by what he's saying, I'd hope so. I know he's excited about courting her."

"And they did kiss?" Paul asked, sounding betrayed.

"Well, yeah," Tim answered simply. "Listen,

Martin talks about her a lot, and he doesn't mind sharing the details about her and what they do. If you know what I mean, …she's a wild one. I'll spare you the details since she's your lady and all. But you know what I mean. Anyway, Martin should be back before too long, and I'll sit him down and tell him that was absolutely unacceptable, and he had better never do anything like that again. I'm tempted to take his badge over this, but I think I'll talk to him and see what he has to say for himself. Drawing a weapon on you two is not going to be taken lightly. I assure you, you won't have any more problems with him, and if you do, let me know right away."

Paul nodded. "Alright."

Sam stared at Tim with a bit of hostility in his eyes. "Martin hit me with his revolver and then kicked me when I was down. He pointed his gun at me and threatened to kill us both, and all you can say is you'll talk to him? What about taking his badge away and throwing him jail?" He turned to Matt, "Does that sound reasonable to you?"

Matt tilted his head with a slight shrug. "I think the sheriff has the right to talk to his deputy before making any decisions. It's only reasonable, right?"

Sam sighed with disgust. "Yeah, we know the kind of decisions he makes. Well, we've said all we can say. Paul, let's go." He turned back to the Sheriff. "I will tell you this, if your deputy comes to our house again looking trouble, I'll shoot him myself."

"As long as it's self-defense, you have that right. Listen, I'm not condoning what Martin did. I'm quite surprised by it, and I'm shocked, really. He's such a fun-loving and easy-going young man. I want to hear his explanation of what happened and why he felt like he could do that to you. I may still fire him, but I want to hear him out before I do."

"Right," Sam said as he and Paul left the office.

Matt asked Tim, "If you don't mind, I'd like to stay here and confront Martin with you? The only reason I ask is because if we're going to have a mad dog loose on the streets, I want to know it."

Tim frowned. "Matt, I know you don't have any respect for me or how I do things, but Martin is my deputy, and I would prefer to confront my deputy in private. Bob is my lead deputy, and between us, I think we have this under control. No hard feelings, I hope, but I'd prefer you not to be here."

Matt nodded. "I understand. Take his badge, Tim. He's not able to control his emotions, and that's bad for everyone."

Bob Ewing nodded in agreement. "I agree. The kid's an idiot. Take his badge and let him go."

Tim frowned at his deputy. "You just don't like him."

"I never have," Bob said plainly.

Matt asked, "Why is that, Bob?"

Bob looked at Matt and exhaled. "Because he hasn't got a clue what he's doing. Martin's a lazy, whining, know-it-all punk with no respect. I've had to work with him for two weeks now, and he's driving me crazy. Mark Thiesen is a young man too, but Mark wants to do the job and learn. He's dependable. Martin's a loose wheel that carries no weight and won't shut up about that woman or about anything else he doesn't know about, includ-

ing the job. I can't stand him, and I encourage Tim
to take his badge before I kill him myself."

Tim spoke shortly, "I think that's enough, Bob."

Bob shrugged. "I'm just saying my peace."

Matt walked to the door. "I'll talk to you two
later. Let me know what happens, please."

Martin sat in front of Sheriff Tim Wright's desk with
Bob Ewing and Tim, interrogating him about what
happened the night before. Martin was furious that
Paul and Sam had gone to Matt Bannister instead
of Bella. He clenched his jaw while listening to Tim
lecture him about the expectations of a deputy and
how he had failed to hold to the proper expectations.
Bob glared at Martin like he was a piece of trash,
and Tim looked disappointed in him. For the most
part, Martin acted like he was listening and tried
to appear apologetic, but more than anything, his
mind was reeling with fury over them going to Matt
instead of making things right with Bella. He had
given them an easy choice, and all they had to do
was make things right with Bella. Now he was still
forbidden to enter the dance hall and in trouble with
his boss. It irritated him all the more.

Tim said pointedly. "Give me one reason why I
should keep you as a deputy."

The words raised Martin's eyebrows with interest. He was suddenly wary of losing his job. "I
already told you it didn't happen like they say it
did. I didn't enter their house with my gun drawn.
Yeah, I followed them home, and I knocked on the

door to ask Paul to leave Edith alone. It wasn't even a question, I told him to leave her alone, but I didn't pull my gun until they cornered me in their house and threatened to beat me up. Look at me; they're both bigger than I am. I'm a small man; I didn't go there to fight. Sam had already tried to whip me in the dance hall. Look, I was angry and thought I'd try to be reasonable, but they were unreasonable, and now they're trying to get me fired to ruin me. They already got me kicked out of the dance hall, and I didn't do anything wrong other than wanting to talk to Edith!" He paused to take a deep breath. "I'm sorry, but they're lying. Just like Edith lied to him."

Bob added, "That's not a reason to keep you hired on here."

"No, Bob, it wasn't," Martin said sharply, unable to keep his anger under control as he glared at Bob. "That was an explanation! And I don't owe you an explanation. I owe the Sheriff an explanation, not you."

Bob took a deep breath and shifted in his chair and glanced at Tim with annoyance.

Martin addressed the Sheriff, "I'll tell you why you should keep me as a deputy, and it's simply because I didn't do anything wrong. If your woman was lying to you and seeing another man, wouldn't you want to confront him? It's the same thing, and neither of you can tell me you'd be nice about it either. Bob, you'd beat the other man senseless, and I know you would! I didn't do anything either of you wouldn't have done. But I didn't do it the way those two said I did."

Tim spoke with a slight smirk, "So, why should I keep you?"

Martin raised his shoulders with a shrug. "Because I love what I do, and I'll be worth keeping."

Tim nodded. "I agree. Martin, I will give you another chance if you promise to leave those men alone. Don't even talk to them again. Agreed?"

"Fine."

"Good." He turned his attention to Deputy Ewing. "Bob, can you go order our lunch or something. I need to discuss this more in-depth with Martin."

When Bob left the office, Tim said, "I told Paul you and Edith had been courting since they broke up. He didn't seem so happy to hear that, and he knows Edith lied about kissing you too. And I may have hinted to a lot more." He smiled. "So, I doubt they'll be getting back together after all. You know I was kicked out of the dance hall too, so welcome to the rejects club, Martin." He paused for a short chuckle. "I was thinking about what you said yesterday, and yeah, Rose Blanchard is a very pretty lady. I'd like her. So, I need you to get back into Edith's good graces, so you'll be welcomed into the dance hall. Then we can do that double dinner date with her and Rose. I'd like to get to know Rose better, that's why I laid the groundwork for Paul and Edith to split up for good. Martin, my friend, Edith's all yours now."

Martin grinned. "She always was. But I'll see if I can talk to her and smooth everything over. Last night was our only bad night, and that was because of those two liars. I think I want to talk to her before they do. And I'll get that dinner set up with Rose too. I'll be back later."

Tim leaned back in his chair after Martin left. There were a lot of women in Branson, but most were either married or not so attractive. There was a handful that were single, attractive, and old enough for him to court, but the one he liked the most wasn't interested in him. And she was his best friend's sister. Debra Slater was a lovely blonde lady and had few suitors who were good enough for her father and brother to accept. Not even Tim was good enough for her family, not that she wanted him anyway. It was a blessing when Bella's Dance Hall opened because it brought several clean and attractive women to Branson, who would sooner or later be looking for a husband. Tim had no desire to marry, but he was more than willing to meet and pursue Rose Blanchard. She was a beautiful red-headed lady who had been overshadowed by Christine Knapp being everyone's favorite dancer. Now that Christine was courting Matt, Rose was becoming the newest favorite of many of the men in Branson. Tim had his own unspoken motives, and that was either to court Rose or if that didn't work out steal Edith away from Martin, which he didn't think would be that hard to do. Martin had nothing to offer her.

24

Martin stood at the front door of the dance hall peeking through the narrow edge of the dark curtain of the window looking for anyone that he knew that he could convince to unlock the door. He knew the front door would be locked and that Bella and her husband would probably be in their apartment or the office. The security guard Phil Mears would be sleeping as he stayed up later than anyone else and slept most of the day. There were certain ladies Martin knew wouldn't open the door for him, but he watched the stairs in his limited view hoping to catch sight of one or two of the more simple-minded ones coming down or going back up the stairs so that he could get their attention. He may have looked like a perverted fool standing at the door peeking through the curtains to others on the street, but he didn't care. He needed to talk to Edith, and that was all that he cared about. Paul was ending his relationship with her, so now Martin and Edith were free to continue their relationship.

He knocked on the window quickly when he saw Rose Blanchard coming down the stairs in her robe. She peered curiously at the window and walked over to the door. She lifted the curtain and made a half-humored expression.

"What are you doing here?" she asked quietly through the window.

He grinned happily. "Can you unlock the door? I need to speak with Edith."

Rose glanced nervously behind her and then answered, "I can't. I'd get in a lot of trouble."

"No, you won't, because if you let me in and tell me where Edith's room is, I'll be in and out before anyone knows."

She pressed her lips together tightly and shook her head quickly. "Hmm, I can't."

Martin lost his smile and raised his voice slightly, "Rose, open the door. I'm a deputy sheriff, and unless you want to go to jail for hindering the duties of a law officer, I'd open the door right now. You can't keep a lawman out of a business, Rose. It's against the law. Now, please, unlock the door and let me in. I won't tell anyone who let me in, okay. Just unlock it and disappear."

"Ohh," she groaned and reached over and flipped the lock open and opened the door. Martin stepped inside quickly and closed the door behind him. "Where's Edith?" he asked lightly.

"In her room. She's not feeling well…"

"Where's her room?"

"Upstairs. The third one on the right."

"Thank you," He ran up the stairs and entered

a long hallway with rooms on both sides of the corridor over the ballroom floor below. He was startled to be facing Christine Knapp as she walked towards the stairs.

She screamed in fright and then cried out loudly, "What are you doing up here?" she was horrified to see him upstairs. "You're not supposed to be here! You need to leave!" she ordered loudly.

Martin didn't have time to think as other doors opened, and ladies peeked out to see what was happening. Shouts and little screams alerted the other ladies. Christine stood in Martin's way to the third door on the right. She was pointing towards the stairs and ordering him to leave. He hadn't come this far to be forced back down the stairs, so he clenched his fist and drove it into Christine's stomach, which doubled her over, and then pushed her as hard as he could backward. She fell to the floor hard and was unable to breathe. Helen Monroe cursed him from down the hall and came running at him. He sneered as she got closer, and he hit her in the face with a solid right fist when she got close enough. She fell to the floor near Christine, holding her face and began wailing loudly. The other girls started screaming and hiding in their doorways.

Edith peeked out her door and seen Martin with a crazed expression reaching out for her. She slammed her door shut as quickly as she could. "Get out of here, Martin!" she yelled fearfully.

"Edith open the door!" he yelled and forced it open by ramming his body into it, the force of it knocked her backward. She backed up to the far wall. He stepped inside her room and looked at her with an innocent but troubled expression. "What is wrong with you? Do you think I'm going to hurt you or something? I just wanted to talk to you and tell you it's okay; we can be together! Paul doesn't want you anymore, and now everything's okay."

"No, no, it's not!" Edith demanded as she pressed herself against the back wall protectively. She was frightened for her safety. "Martin, please get out of here!"

"No!" he exclaimed with a quick grimace. "Look," he pulled the red invitation to stay late out of his pocket. "I have an invitation to talk with you, but I wasn't able to use it because of those friends of yours. They got me kicked out, and I didn't do anything. How else am I supposed to see you, huh?" he asked. "Now, you're going to talk to me, Edith."

The calls for Bella, Dave, and Phil were echoing up the stairs, and Martin knew his time was getting short. He kicked a pair of boots on the floor over to her. "Put those on, and let's go talk. Hurry up."

Fearful tears clouded her eyes as she shook her head. Her voice quivered as she spoke softly, "I'm not going anywhere with you. You have to get out of my room." Her body was beginning to shake visibly.

His eyes and voice softened a touch. "I need you, Edith. We're soul mates, remember? And soul mates are never complete without the other half. We have to go, get your boots on," he explained.

A determined scowl formed on her face. "Get out of my room! And leave me alone!" she screamed. "I don't want anything to do with you, Martin. Get it through your head; we'll never be together! I don't ever want to see you again. Now leave!"

Martin's eyes grew strangely dark as a wicked sneer appeared on his face that sent a cold chill down her spine. A strange growl came from deep within his throat, and he grabbed her and shook her in his hands. "Get your damn boots on, and let's go before I throw you out the window!"

"Get your hands off her!" Bella ordered loudly as she stepped into the room. Her husband, Dave, was right behind her.

Martin swiftly jerked Edith forward while maneuvered behind her to put her between Dave and himself. He held Edith close to him with his left arm wrapped around her neck, Edith fought him, but she froze petrified in fear when he drew his revolver and pointed it at her head with his right hand.

"Shut up!" he hissed in her ear. Her body trembled with her desperate and helpless muffled sobs.

"Oh, my lord!" Bella gasped, horrified. "Martin, please, don't hurt her. Please."

Dave raised a hand to try to calm Martin down. He was nervous. "Son, put the gun down."

"He's got a gun!" one of the girls screamed out in the hallway. The sound of panic and crying came from the girls in the hall.

Christine's voice was heard in the corridor, saying, "Angela, go get Matt as fast as you can. Tell him to hurry! Go now!"

Martin glared at Dave. "Back away! I'm taking her out of here for a while. And that's all. Don't make me kill her! Back away now!" Edith began to sob heavily and wail out with gut-wrenching cries of terror.

Dave shook his head. "Son, you can't do this," he said softly, hoping to calm Martin down.

Martin shouted, "Who's going to stop me, you? Matt? I have a gun and a badge. I can do what I want. Now back away, she belongs to me, not you. Go!" he demanded and began to walk her forward but almost tripped over her slow, unwilling steps. "Down the hall! All of you. No, that way!" he ordered Dave, Bella, and the other girls to walk to the opposite end of the hall to clear a path to the stairs. He pulled Edith out of the room and began walking backwards towards the stairs dragging her with him.

Edith was sobbing and begging for someone to help her and pleading with Martin to let her go. Martin told her to shut up and kept pulling her back towards the stairs while keeping his eyes on Dave down the hallway.

Christine stood at the top of the stairs with her back pressed against the wall, wondering how she might be able to help her friend, but there was nothing she could do. Helen Monroe's face was bloody from being hit by Martin. She longed to help her friend but was being held back by Bella. Helen dropped to her knees, crying out futility wanting to help her friend. The chaos down the hall kept Martin's attention on Dave as he stepped forward, trying to convince Martin to let Edith go. Martin stepped backward towards the staircase. Christine glared at Martin with a furious expression as he backed up and stood in front of her. She said, "You better let Edith go and run because Matt's coming.

He won't let you get away with this."

Martin snarled and quickly slammed the back of his hand that held the gun into Christine's face as hard as he could. She cried out and covered her face with both hands, and started sobbing as blood started flowing between her fingers. She bent over and stepped towards the opposite wall to put a hand out against the wall to brace herself as she watched as the blood dripped heavily onto her other hand. Bella yelled out a string of obscenities and came quickly to Christine's side.

Martin pointed the gun back at Edith's head. He shouted above all of the curses and ladies yelling at him. "If Matt kills me, it will be over Edith's dead body! And if that's how it has to be for us to be together, then so be it!" He spoke brutally in Edith's ear, "Loving you for eternity doesn't sound so bad to me anyway!"

Edith's eyes opened wide in terror as her wailing became more profound and more desperate as he held his left arm around her throat tightly. He began stepping backward down the stairs as quickly as he could without falling. Dave stood at the top of the stairs looking like he wanted to kill Martin if he could. Martin stepped off the last step with his eyes on Dave and froze when he felt a gun barrel pressed against the back of his head. He heard the hammer being pulled back until it clicked.

Phil Mears spoke in his deep voice, "Put the gun down, or I'll close this place down for a day while we clean up your brains. I'm not joking, Martin. Put it down now!"

"Phil…" he said with a hate-filled scowl. He was angry that he had focused so much on Dave that he forgot about Phil. "If I'm going to go, so is she. We're connected her and I. We're soul mates. We could spend eternity together if we both go now. Go ahead and pull the trigger."

"Think so?" Phil asked, looking around Martin's head to see his pistol. He could see Martin's finger was on the trigger. "There's no reason for anyone to get hurt, Martin. How about we all just calm down for a minute, okay? I'm going to put my gun away. Don't hurt Edith. This is just a big misunderstanding, right?"

Martin chuckled wickedly with his back to Phil. "Now you look weak, Phil. I would've pulled the trigger."

Phil still stood behind Martin and knew if he let Martin turn around and put Edith between them, he would lose any opportunity of saving her. He spoke softly, "Martin, I'm going to throw my gun over by the stairs, so don't be startled by that and pull the trigger, okay? Just to be safe, when you remove your finger from the trigger, just for a second, I'll throw it. None of us want to see an accident happen, right?"

Martin shouted, "I'm not stupid! Get over here in front of me." He began to turn towards Phil to face him.

Phil knew he was out of time and had one chance to react. He quickly tossed his pistol into the entryway to draw Martin's attention to the noise. The gun landed with a loud bang on the wood floor. When Martin turned his head to his left, Phil drove his right hand quickly forward and grabbed the revolver and drove it away from Edith's head, and then lifted it above her head. He held the gun above them and grabbed Martin's hair with his left hand and yanked him backward and spun him down to the floor as fast and hard as he could using his lower leg to trip Martin. Martin let go of both the gun and Edith to grab at the hand that controlled him by his hair. Edith fell to the floor and quickly scooted herself across the floor away from the two men, terrified. The gun fell to the floor harmlessly, and Martin went face down to the floor with Phil landing squarely on top of him.

"Get off of me!" Martin screamed, followed by a line of curses.

Phil took Martin's arm and rammed it up behind his back to hold him there, inflicting as much pain as he could to keep control of the scrawny man. Phil glanced back up the stairs, "It's safe! Do you want me to break his arm?" Bella was already downstairs, consoling Edith, who sat on the floor sobbing.

"No, Angela went to get Matt!" Bella said, more concerned about her three ladies. "Wait for Matt; he'll take care of him."

Matt was out of breath by the time he had run the distance between the Marshal's Office and the dance hall. He entered quickly with his gun drawn and saw Christine sitting at the bar holding a rag filled with ice over her nose. Blood had dripped over the front of her robe. Martin was sitting in a chair being covered by Phil and Dave, who both held a gun on him. Matt went to Christine with concern. "What happened?" he asked with a fierceness growing in his eyes. He lifted the rag carefully to see a swollen and bloody nose.

Bella, who was teary-eyed with rage, said, "Martin hit her! He was trying to kidnap Edith. He hit Helen too. He dragged Edith out of her room with a gun to her head, and Phil stopped him. Thank goodness."

Matt glared at Martin with a cold stare. "Stand him up," Matt ordered.

Phil grabbed him and stood him upright.

Martin raised his hands to calm Matt down. "It didn't happen like that. Edith and I are were having a slight disagreement, and they all overreacted. I didn't mean to…"

"I don't care!" Matt cut him off as he stepped closer and threw a hard-right fist that connected with Martin's nose and broke it as he was driven to the floor by the blow. "That's for hitting Christine!" he glanced at Phil. "Stand him back up!"

Martin was crying from the pain of his nose. It bled profusely through his fingers, and blood dripped heavily onto the dancefloor. Phil grabbed him and forced him to stand back up on his feet. Matt's deputies entered the dance hall also out of breath, and stopped to watch.

Matt grabbed the badge on Martin's shirt and ripped it off his chest. "You never should've had this to begin with!" He drove a hard-right fist upwards into Martin's breadbasket. Martin gasped while choking on his blood and collapsed to the floor, unable to breathe. His blood flowed onto the floor.

Matt said, "Stand him back up."

"Boss," Nate Robertson said carefully. "Do you think he's had enough?"

Truet Davis answered shortly, "Be quiet and stay out of it."

Matt took a deep breath and turned towards Bella. No one said a word as they watched. "Sorry about your floor, Bella, but at the moment, I couldn't care less if he bleeds to death."

Bella shook her head and waved a hand uncaringly. The only sound was Martin's attempts to breathe and the drops of blood hitting the floor, mixed with his occasional sobs.

Tim Wright came dashing inside with his deputy Bob Ewing and saw Martin standing weakly on his two feet, struggling to breathe and bleeding heavily. "What happened?" he asked, horrified.

Matt sneered and threw Martin's badge at him as hard as he could.

"Whoa, Matt!" Tim yelled as he turned to avoid the badge flying through the air and bounced off the wall in the entry.

Matt pointed at him and shouted, "I told you to take his badge! He's your problem, you take him and lock him up! Send him back with your deputies and lock him up! Bella and Dave will tell you what happened. I'm taking Christine to the doctor before he gets to see him."

Christine looked at Matt with the ice on her face. "Matt, I'm not dressed."

His eyes watered just a bit. "Nate, run and get me a buggy as fast you can." He took a deep breath with his eyes on Christine. "You can get dressed if you want to, but I want your nose examined by Doctor Ambrose."

Truet ordered Nate impatiently. "Go now!"

"Matt," Bella asked, "Can you take Helen too. I think she'll need sutures on her lip."

He nodded. "Absolutely."

Tim had his deputies to hold Martin by the arms to control him while he examined his nose. It was sideways with a cut across the middle. Tim looked at Matt and asked shortly, "Did you have to do that to him?"

Matt nodded. "He may have broken Christine's nose and could've killed Edith. Do you think I have any mercy for him?"

Tim shook his head, irritatedly. He spoke to his deputy, Bob Ewing, "Get him to the doctor and then jail for now."

Matt glared at Bob warningly. "Don't you dare take him to the doctor before I get Christine there. Wait an hour."

Bob smirked pleasantly. "It would be my pleasure, Matt. But I don't want to wait an hour with him bleeding everywhere. I'll tell the doc you're bringing two ladies over, and they need to be looked at first."

Matt nodded.

Bob jerked Martin towards the door roughly. "Come on, you little…"

"Edith," Martin said as Bob guided him off the ballroom floor. "Edith," he called out frantically. "I still love you, baby. I'll see you soon. I have to talk to Edith. Where's Edith?" he yelled as Bob walked him towards the door.

"I'm up here," she said bitterly from top of the stairs. There was a bitter scowl on her usually sweet face.

Bob stopped to hear what Edith would say to Martin. Martin grinned slightly as he saw her. "I love you, honey. We'll talk soon."

She hissed, "You can go to hell! We will never speak again. Not ever! I never want to see you again!" She turned away and walked down the hall.

He smiled slightly despite the pain it brought. "She's just mad."

Bob chuckled and rammed Martin's head into the door purposely. "Oops. I better open the door first," he said as Martin cried out in pain.

25

"Matt, this is my friend from medical school, Doctor Mitchell Ryland. He's visiting me for a week and decided to join me at the office to see how we mountain people do it out here in the wild. Mitch, this is the man you were asking me about, the U.S. Marshal Matt Bannister," Doctor Bruce Ambrose said, introducing the two men. They were in the doctor's office in a small room where there were just a few chairs and a cot. The main medical room was where the two doctors were looking over Martin when Matt brought Christine and Helen to the office.

Doctor Mitchell Ryland had a broad grin as he shook Matt's hand. He was a thin, middle-aged man with neatly combed light blonde hair with a touch gray and a mustache and goatee about two inches long. He wore spectacles over his blue eyes and had a long and thin face. "You'll have to forgive me. This is most unprofessional, but I must say it is an honor to meet a real legend of the west. A gunfighter. The people back home aren't going to believe me when I say I shook Matt Bannister's hand." He laughed. "I know I feel like an excited kid, but I've been in the city so long, and I've always wanted to see this wild country before it becomes like Boston. I'm excited to get out here and be a part of it. So here I am on my first day joining up with Bruce, and I get to see a hell of a broken nose given by Matt Bannister." He chuckled. "I love it."

Matt smiled, slightly humored by the man's excitement. "Nice to meet you. This is Christine. I brought her in her to have her nose checked out, and Helen might need some stitches in her lip. These ladies are the cause of that man's broken nose. He hit these two ladies."

"Oh! Well, I can tell you right now, this beautiful young lady's nose is not broken. But let's look it over." Doctor Ryland examined Christine's nose for a moment and then washed the blood off of her face. "Young lady, your nose is going to be sore for a few days, some slight swelling for a day or two maybe, but then it will be as good as new. You'll have a beautiful schnauzer again before you know it," he said with a smile. He moved over to Helen and examined at her lip. He grimaced and held up four fingers. "Four stitches and you'll be as good as new too. If you give me one moment, I'll have you fixed up."

After he finished suturing up Helen's lip, he turned back to Matt. "Now, tell me, have you ever been back east?"

Matt shook his head. "No. I never wanted to. I think the border of Iowa and Missouri is probably the furthest east I've been. And that was only because I was trailing a man in Nebraska. I don't have much of an interest in large cities."

Mitchell Ryland groaned. "I've spent my career in Boston, and I am tired of the city. I always wanted to come west and live near the mountains and hunt wild game and fish. Maybe do a little trapping too. Out here, it isn't so civilized and condensed; a man can breathe. I wanted to experience the wildness while it's still wild, you know. Because someday it isn't going to be, and then all of this will be a part of history."

"And you're moving to Portland?" Matt asked skeptically.

He frowned. "I am. How'd you know that?"

"Doctor Ambrose told me last week. Portland's a city if you ask me. I haven't been there, but that's our biggest city in Oregon. I like it here. It's small, but we're not missing anything. And if you're looking to hunt, fish or trap, where better to do it? My brother goes way up in the mountain's elk hunting every summer, and they stay up there for a week and make jerky from whatever they kill, elk, deer, bear, and wolves. They trap wolves while their up there."

Mitchell stared at him. "That sounds like a dream come true."

"He does it every year. It's too bad you're moving to Portland, or you could get to know my brother and go with him, I'm sure."

"He goes up there for a week to hunt, trap and make jerky, huh? You're tempting me to want to stay here, Matt." He laughed lightly.

"We keep the Doctor Ambrose pretty busy around here, that's for sure. He may not mind some help if you want to talk to him about it."

Doctor Ryland asked curiously, "Is there a lot of roughnecks around here? I mean, I hear about those tough towns like Dodge City, Tombstone, and others, but this doesn't seem like one of those kinds of towns. Is it?"

Matt sighed. "We don't have that reputation, no. We like to think we're a family-friendly community, but we have silver miners, gold miners, lumbermen, timbermen, cowboys, farmers, your generic petty thieves, and outlaws. We have murderers and outlaw gangs and a Chinatown too. Yeah, we're full of roughnecks, and a lot of them don't get along very well with each other at all. There's always fights in the saloons and an occasional stabbing or shooting. If that's what you're looking for, then you're in the right area."

Mitchell pointed to the other room where Martin was. "And bad deputy's too?"

Matt frowned with annoyance. "Yeah, an occasional bad lawman too."

"Excluding yourself, of course."

"Of course. I'm the guy trying to keep it all together. Anyway, nice talking to you, Doctor Ryland, but I need to get these two hurting ladies back home."

"Well, it was sure a pleasure meeting you. And I might get back in touch to meet your brother and see if I can join his hunting trip."

"Welcome to Oregon's wild country, Doctor. Some of us call it home, others, not so hearty, move to Portland," Matt said with a wink and a smile as he walked out of the room with the two ladies.

Mitchell laughed.

26

Rumors spread, and not one made a whole lot of sense. There were Black Widows around, and they came inside where it was warm in the wintertime. But they usually made a web in a corner and remained there. Seldom did they bite, and most folks knew to either kill them or leave them be. The more the rumors spread and the more was known, the more the death of Leroy Haywood sounded like a cruel murder, unless he got so hungry from his wife leaving him, that he stalked spiders for dinner and had a craving for black ones. It was insane to think so, but that's what the coroner and the Marshal's Office wanted the public to believe because there were no answers. There was not one person motivated to harm Leroy, and there was not one person who would be capable of doing what they did to Leroy without causing a hell of a fight. Any one of his neighbors would have heard a fight, but there was nothing except complete silence that night. It was a mystery that made no sense at all to almost everyone, except for Leroy's best friend, Roger Lavigne. Roger knew if anybody had a reason to want to kill Leroy, it would be the Chinese man Wu-Pen because Leroy had spat in his face twice. Wu-Pen was the only reasonable suspect that came to mind. Roger knew how easily Wu-Pen's two guards had controlled Leroy, Tony Rosso, and himself, even when Roger pulled a knife, he was no match to the skill and speed of the guard who could have easily killed Roger with his own knife.

There was no question; those two Chinese guards of Wu-Pen's could easily handle Leroy physically. The Chinese were very different than Americans in just about every way he could imagine. Roger worked with Chinese men at the silver mine and had watched a Chinaman eat grasshoppers for dinner over the Summer. He'd seen them gather together and make bets on insect battles to the death. The Chinese seemed to like insects for one reason or another. He recalled one of the Chineses laborers out at the mine was excited when he had caught a Black Widow to pit against the reigning insect champion, a praying mantis one of the Chinese, kept in a box to pit against other insects for money. In hindsight, it only made sense that it was Wu-Pen and his two guards who murdered Leroy. In a perfect society, they would be arrested and sentenced to death for their crimes against a white man, but they didn't live in an ideal community. The Marshal protected the immigrants more than the hard-working Americans, which explained why Leroy's death remained such a mystery. The killers were the Marshal's Chinese friends, or so Roger reasoned as he sat in Ugly John's Saloon having another drink.

Roger was troubled about losing his friend to unknown circumstances and grew angrier the more he dissected it and came to his conclusion. If the town sheriff or the marshal weren't going to do something about it, then he would. He peered at the empty stool next to him, where Leroy had sat the last time they were in there together. He recalled the last threat Leroy had made about burning the Chinatown down. "Why not?" Roger asked himself and turned to the barkeep and paid his tab. Ugly John's was lit up with oil lanterns hanging from hooks on the ceiling, and when he was sure the barkeep wasn't looking, he unhooked a lantern and walked out of the saloon without a word to anyone. If anyone saw him take the lantern, they didn't say anything. He walked over to Chinatown and walked up the street. It wasn't quite dark, and many of the merchants were getting ready to start closing as the city ordinances stated that all Chinese had to be inside at dusk and remain indoors until sunup unless they were going to work for a white man. He carried the lantern to the building with a red door that Wu-Pen and his men had come out of the last time they met. Roger stood in the middle of the street, staring at the red door. He turned the flame up on high in the lamp and got ready to throw the light at the door but paused as a Chinese man behind him came out of a building onto the street, speaking loudly in Chinese. The man was making a loud commotion as he yelled at Roger.

Wu-Pen and his guards heard the warning and peeked out the window of his office, which was in the connected building beside the temple. The way upstairs was through the temple or a private stairway hidden in the store below his office. The stairway led to the corridor outside of Wu-Pen's office. In case there was ever a need for a fast escape out of the building, there was a one-inch thick pole hidden in a secret closet inside of Wu-Pen's office. Bing Jue and Uang Yang quickly slid down the pole and exited out of a small hidden door behind the door of the store and stepped outside to confront Roger.

Roger saw the two guards of Wu-Pen step outside and separate. One walked towards the red door, and the other approached Roger. Uang Yang pointed at the ground at Roger's feet and spoke coarsely in his native tongue. The eyes of the Chinaman were deadly serious. Roger couldn't understand the words, but he knew exactly what he was saying.

Roger smiled slowly in his intoxicated state of mind. "I have no idea what you're saying, you slit-eyed puke." When Uang shouted more forcefully, Roger shook his head. "It's going to burn," he said as he motioned the lantern back in forth with his hand threatening to throw it against the temple. He froze and nearly dropped the lantern when he saw two men in orange appear on the roof of the temple and aim their longbows at him. They were ready to release their arrows in no time at all.

The red door opened, and Wu-Pen walked out

of the temple. "I would put that down if I was you. This is a sacred temple, and they will protect it with their lives. If you want to live, put it down, and leave now." There was no friendliness in his expressions this time.

Roger set the lamp down. "All right, I'll be going." He said softly. All of the courage and anger he had felt was suddenly turning weak-kneed and cowardice.

"What is your name?" Wu-Pen asked.

"Why?" he asked with a shaking voice, "The sheriff won't arrest me for a joke. I wasn't going to burn it down. I was just playing." Roger didn't like the atmosphere he was feeling.

Wu-Pen smiled. "A good joke, yes. No need for the sheriff, no harm was done. I am Wu-Pen, and you are?" he asked while walking over to shake Roger's hand.

"Roger."

"Roger, nice to meet you. We welcome you any-time as a friend. Please forgive our rude behavior; I'm afraid these men did not see the humor. I will translate." He spoke in Chinese, and all the men, including the ones on the roof, laughed. Wu-Pen turned back to Roger. "You scared us." he laughed. "Have a good evening."

Roger smiled, feeling some relief. "Yeah, you too." He walked away, thanking his lucky stars or num-bers or whatever was working for his saving his life.

Wu-Pen stepped into the temple and turned to face his two guards and spoke in Chinese, "The month of life I gave him ends tonight! He wanted to burn us; we will show him a fire. Prepare!"

27

Sylvia and Barbra Ballenger walked into the Sheriff's Office with Henry Redlin after dinner. They hadn't heard about Martin being in jail until not long before. Sylvia gasped, "Oh my gosh!" She began weeping and wrapped her arms around her daughter, Barbra, for the comfort it brought.

Martin was sitting on the bottom bunk of a bunkbed staring at his mother with no emotion. A thick wad of gauze was covering his nose. A white dressing was wrapped around his head and tied in a knot to keep the wad of gauze on his nose. The bandage covering his nose had red soaking through it from the bleeding. For Sylvia, it did not matter how old her son got, seeing her son in pain broke her heart. Seeing him sitting behind bars was traumatic for her as well.

He smirked lightly. "Don't cry, Mother. I'll be fine," he said with a nasally sound to his voice. "Can you take a letter for Edith to the dance hall for me?"

"Martin, are you all right?" Sylvia asked heart-broken to see her son in such a condition.

"I will be when my nose heals. It's broken. Everything else is just a misunderstanding. Will you take that letter for me when you leave?"

Sylvia frowned with concern, "Sure. Martin, what happened? Is it true that you tried to kidnap that girl?"

He closed his eyes from the throbbing of his nose. "No. Far from it. I wanted to talk to Edith, and everyone started screaming for no reason. I thought Dave was going to kill me, so I drew my gun to protect myself. I wanted to get out of there unharmed, so I kept Edith between Dave and me. He wanted to hurt me. But it's just a big misunderstanding."

Sylvia looked at the deputy on duty, Alan Garrison. "Can I take him home?"

Alan shook his head. "I'm afraid not, Misses Ballenger. Martin is charged with some serious charges. Attempted kidnapping, three or four charges of assault, along with brandishing a weapon, intimidation, and so on. He has a court date tomorrow to see Judge Jacoby. The Judge might set bail, or he may not, I don't know."

"Do you know what time?" she asked.

Alan glanced at a paper on the Sheriff's desk. "No, it doesn't say."

Henry Redlin grabbed one of the bars of the jail and asked Martin, "Was it Dave, who broke your nose?"

Martin shook his head just slightly. "No. It was the Marshal."

"Matt?" Henry asked, surprised. "Matt did that?"

"Yeah, and I was being held by two men. He had no reason to hit me; he just did."

Sylvia's eyes narrowed angrily. "Two men were holding you, and he hit you for no reason?" she asked in a raised voice.

He nodded slowly. "He did, Mother. And he made sure I lost my job too. He ripped the badge off my shirt, ripping my new shirt. And I have to pay twenty-five dollars to the doctor for fixing my nose. It was messed up pretty bad." He placed his hands on his forehead as he leaned forward just a bit and began to weep. "He destroyed me and everything I am..."

Sylvia glared at the deputy Alan Garrison. "Is this how the law works around here? Do you know what gave Matt the right to hit my son while two men were holding him?"

Alan shrugged. "I wasn't there, Ma'am, I have no idea."

"Did he fire my son?" she demanded to know.

Alan answered awkwardly, "Matt's with the U.S. Marshal's Office, he can't fire Martin. But the Sheriff did fire him, yes."

"Why?" she demanded.

Alan shrugged. "Misses Ballenger, I don't have all of the answers, because I wasn't there or know too much about what happened. But from what I heard, Martin broke Matt's friend Christine's nose..."

"Did you hurt her?" Henry asked quickly.

Martin lifted his hands with a slight shrug as he stood up slowly and stepped nearer to the cell bars carrying a folded up piece of paper. "Not intentionally. She bumped into me, and I thought she was the security guard, Phil. I hit her accidentally. She was bleeding a bit."

Henry closed his eyes and sighed. "That's why Matt hit him, then."

"It doesn't matter! He had no right to lay his hands on my son!" Sylvia vented.

Martin handed the letter to his mother. "Please make sure Edith gets this for me tonight. I need to apologize to her."

"I'll make sure it gets to her."

"Misses Ballenger," Alan offered, "I like Martin, and I am sorry any of this took place, but whatever happened had to be pretty serious, because I know the Sheriff liked Martin too. He wouldn't fire him and throw him jail for nothing. I won't argue with Martin, because I don't know, but I suggest coming back tomorrow and talking to the Sheriff yourself. I know he wrote his report and sent it to the courthouse late in the day, that's why there's no court date or time yet. But he's the man you need to talk to for answers, not me."

A few hours later, the office door opened with the sound of laughter as Sam Troyer and Paul Johnson came walking into the Sheriff's Office. "Good evening, Alan. We just came in to visit with Martin for a minute, is that all right?" Sam asked.

Alan shrugged. "That's fine," he said, looking up from a book he was reading.

Paul and Sam stepped over to the jail cell and

laughed when they saw him lying on the bed with his face covered with a bloody bandage. He glanced over at them and then stared back at the bottom of the top bunk.

Paul shook his head with a smile. "You are the dumbest man I've ever met. Did you really think we would talk to Bella and tell her it was our fault that you're an idiot? Are you really stupid enough to believe what you're told, when you have a gun on someone? Maybe you should've asked Edith to marry you when you held a gun to her head." He laughed.

"She still would've said no," Sam spoke seriously. "I hear she didn't want to talk to you at all today. That must be tough because you went through all that trouble to see her. How many women did you hit to get to her? I think you're a piece of dung, Martin. A low-down yellow spined piece of dung. And when you get out of here, and your nose heals, I'm going to break it again for hitting Helen. I can't kiss her for a few days. Instead, I have to watch Paul kissing Edith, and that's tough to do." He smiled as Martin glanced irritably at him. "Oh yeah, Bella gave Edith the night off, and Paul was comforting her. I told you they'd get back together."

Martin stared upwards again as he said, "Edith and I will be married, just wait and see." He turned his head to look at them. "And I don't care what you think of me. We're not friends."

Sam laughed. "No, we're not!"

Paul had a small inquisitive smile. "Martin, how are you going to marry Edith, when she's already promised to marry me? Can you answer that?" he chuckled.

"She's not marrying you. We kissed, remember? Her love belongs to me."

Paul laughed. "You're an idiot. Listen, in all seriousness; you need to leave her alone. Enough is enough, and she has no interest in you. She'll never talk to you again."

Martin looked evenly at Paul. "She will. She's just mad at me right now. You're not courting her anymore, I am."

Paul narrowed his eyes. "Listen, Edith came over to the house to tell…"

"I know!" Martin's eyes hardened as he shouted. He covered the reddened bandage on his face with his hand in pain. "I kissed her on the way to your house."

Paul asked irritably, "Do you know why she was coming over, Martin? Do you know that too?"

"Helen asked her too. But she promised me she wouldn't go back to you. Edith wouldn't lie to me about that," he said, sounding unsure of himself now that he thought about it. She had lied about kissing him after all.

Paul scoffed lightly. "Sure, she would. Let me tell you why Edith came over. She had just found out she is pregnant. We're going to have a baby her and me. She came over to tell me that. We talked, and now we're getting married. So, I guess you can keep thinking you're going to marry her, but there's a little piece of me growing inside of her just so you know. Now realistically, who do you think she's going marry, the father of her baby, or the freak that put a gun to her head?"

Martin's jaw clenched as a rage grew within him.

228

He stood up quickly and pointed at Paul. "I'll kill you for even saying that about her!" he shouted. "Edith isn't pregnant! Take it back! She will never be your wife or anyone else's except mine! I am her soul mate, and you'll never change that! I don't believe you! She's not having a baby, and if she were, it would be my baby! She wouldn't lay down for you anyway!"

Paul grimaced and shook his head. "Are you crazy or just stupid? You just threatened to kill me in front of a deputy sheriff." He chuckled. "We're getting married on Valentine's Day, Martin. You'll still be in jail probably. I think you have bigger problems than Edith. By the way, here's your letter back from Edith. She wrote a little message for you on it." He pulled a folded piece of paper out of his pocket and tossed it to Martin. "She doesn't love you; she doesn't even like you, and I know you like to brag about it, but she won't ever kiss you again." He smiled. "But she'll be kissing me every day for the next forty years or so. Good luck in prison, Martin. Hey, maybe you can find some fella in there to kiss on for the next twenty years or so."

Sam laughed at him and turned to leave the jail.

Fury filled Martin's eyes as he shouted, "I'm not going to prison! I won't let her go. Not ever!" he yelled as they two men walked outside. He sat down on the bed and opened the letter his mother had delivered to Bella's Dance Hall for him. All across his most sincere love letter were the three words written by Edith's own hand. "Go to hell!"

28

Once again, Matt Bannister was called out to the Slater's Mile early in the morning to investigate a death. This time it was the body of Roger Lavigne who had died in a cabin fire. The fire started inside the cabin, and flames fully engulfed it by the time the neighbors noticed it at three o'clock in the morning. Neighbors tried to douse the fire with buckets of water, but it was of no use. The priority of the residents was to save the cottages next to Roger's using buckets of water from the nearby creek and community well. Roger's cabin had burned out and was smoking as some men threw buckets of water on the coals to cool it down. The cabin was nothing more than a few fragile, but still standing blackened walls that were as hazardous as a widow maker in a weak tree limb. Matt stood in the cold morning air waiting for the floor to cool down so he and his uncle Solomon could go in and pull out the remains of Roger and try to determine how the fire started.

Once inside, they found the body of Roger on what remained of his bed. He held an empty whiskey bottle in his hand. His body was in bad shape, but Matt and his uncle Solomon wrapped his body in a blanket and carried it to Solomon's wagon. It was a dirty job and one that Truet Davis couldn't stomach as he ran out of the ashes to vomit beside the building. Once Solomon left to take the body to his funeral parlor, Matt and Truet began the work of removing the ceiling boards and cedar tiles to reach the floor and start looking for a cause. It didn't take too long to find the explanation. The wood stove door was left open, and there were multiple articles of burned clothing, trash, and other easily flammable materials spread out across the floor. It was easy to conclude that a spark might have flown out of the opened stove door and ignited anything from newspapers to clothing saturated in oil from the stamp mill. If it smoldered for some length of time, smoke inhalation might have explained why he didn't wake up, but so did the bottle in his hand, which was a pretty good indication of why. The stove pipe rising to the ceiling was forcefully disconnected and pulled back towards the wall separating the seam, but that could have been caused by the roof collapsing. There weren't any signs of foul play or anything that stood out as unexplainable to Matt and Truet's eyes. It was a sad situation, and if there were a cause, it would be alcohol-induced negligence.

Oscar Belding approached Matt as he and Truet were leaving. "Marshal Bannister, can I ask you something? Leroy died of very suspicious circumstances, and I don't know if it's true, but people are saying it was the Chinese. There's a rumor that it was that one Chinese man who did it. That's what Roger thought, anyway. And now Roger's dead too. That's two people who I was with when they killed those Chinese men. " Oscar was nervous. "Do you think this fire was in any way started by those Chinese? I'll be honest; I'm afraid for my family and me."

Matt shook his head. "First of all, there is no evidence at all that ties Leroy's death to anyone, including the Chinese. I investigated his cottage and the doctor examined his body, and there was no evidence of that. As Doctor Ambrose wrote on Leroy's death certificate, it was asphyxiation from Black Widow bites. He actually wrote the scientific names of the spider and all those technical terms that I probably couldn't pronounce right anyway. I agree, it's strange that it was more than one spider, but there's no evidence that it was a murder. And this," he motioned at the burnt-out cabin. "Roger was holding an empty whiskey bottle in his hand on his bed, and the stove door was open. It appears he passed out, and a spark lit the clutter on the floor. I don't have any reason to suspect anything more than that or anyone, including the Chinese. It was accidental or as I would say carelessness that caused his death. I believe your safe, Oscar."

As they were leaving, Slater's Mile, Truet spoke, "Leroy, Roger, and Oscar threw two Chinese men over the rim of the quarry pit and scourged Ah See to near death. They were acquitted of any crime even though we all know they did it. Now Leroy and

Roger are dead. I think Oscar may have something to worry about, or it's a very eerie coincidence."

Matt nodded. "Yeah, I was thinking the same thing."

"And what do we do if Oscar is next for some unexplainable reason?"

Matt chuckled slightly. "It may be just a coincidence. Leroy was murdered, that we do know, but this looks to be simple carelessness to me. But we might be thinking along the same lines. Do you think Wu-Pen has anything to do with Roger's death?"

"I do. Do you?"

Matt nodded. "I overheard one the mine employees ask his friend why Roger would drink a bottle of whiskey knowing he had to work this morning. That question makes me wonder if it wasn't typical for him. I say we see Wu-Pen a bit later on today and let him know we're suspicious anyway. What do you think?"

Truet nodded. "I'm all for it. Let me get cleaned up first so I can head out of town when we're done and go to Willow Falls and help Annie with some fence building."

Matt and Truet walked into the prep room of his uncle's funeral parlor and saw Doctor Ambrose and Mitchell Ryland looking over the charred body of Roger Lavigne, which they had opened up. Doctor Ambrose glanced over at Matt and said, "Good morning. This is becoming a common occurrence. What have you got going on out there at Slater's Mile?"

Matt sat down in a chair. "I don't know yet. This

man was found in his bed, holding an empty bottle of whiskey. His woodstove door was open with quite a bit of burnt clutter on the floor. I reason it was a spark that started the fire, and he was too drunk to notice."

Bruce Ambrose nodded. "Well, he's been through a fire."

Truet shook his head in disgust and left the room.

Matt smiled. "The smell gets to him."

Mitchell Ryland looked at Matt strangely. "He died of smoke inhalation. That's the first thing we checked, and he did. You said the bottle of whiskey was empty and, in his hand, right?"

"I did."

Doctor Ryland nodded. "He might've been drunk, but the contents of that bottle was still in his stomach. No food, just whiskey. One could die of alcohol poisoning if they digested it, but the fact is it wasn't digested, it wasn't in his system yet. That leads me to believe that someone either poured it down his throat after he was dead or just before he died."

Matt frowned. "Don't tell me it's another suspicious death."

Doctor Ryland shrugged. "I don't know. What I do know is he did not digest that bottle of whiskey. Maybe you could bring me that bottle, and we'll fill it back up with what I got out of his stomach. I'll bet it's a full bottle or very close to it. He was dead or very close to it when it went into his system."

Matt sighed. "So, it was a murder?"

Bruce Ambrose spoke, "It seems like it. Just like last time, I believe a gag was put into his mouth to keep him quiet because the nasal passages contain traces of smoke and soot, none was in the mouth."

Matt said thoughtfully, "Really? Well, that's what I needed to know. Again, put the cause of death as smoke inhalation since that's what killed him, and you can add pending investigation. For now, I'd like to keep the murder part of it quiet if I can. Does that sound all right?"

Doctor Ambrose nodded. "It'll work for now, but pending investigations need to be closed at some point," he said pointedly.

Doctor Mitchell Ryland peered at Matt quizzically. "Do you have any suspects?"

Matt nodded. "I do. But I won't name him yet. Well, I'll talk to you, men later. I need to go talk to my suspected murderer."

Wu-Pen was surprised to see Matt and Truet enter his office, escorted by one of the priests in an orange robe. "Marshal Bannister and Truet, I am most happy to see you. Welcome. Have a seat." He invited as he stood up behind his desk with a friendly smile while pointing at the two chairs in front of his desk, invitingly. "Please, what can I get you, food, drinks?"

"No, thank you," Matt said, sitting down.

"I'm surprised to see you. I hope all is well. Is there something I can do for you, or is this a casual meeting of friends?" Wu-Pen asked with a smile as he sat down after shaking both men's hands.

Matt shook his head. "Unfortunately, not. I'm

afraid I must tell you that Roger Lavigne was killed last night in a house fire. He apparently got drunk and passed out and left his cookstove burning with the door open."

"Oh." Wu-Pen frowned. "I wish I could offer my sympathy, but under the circumstances, I cannot."

"So, you know who he is?" Matt asked.

Wu-Pen smiled and put his hands together on his desk. "Yes. He and his friends killed two of my people."

Matt's eyes scanned the two faces of Uang Yang and Bing Jue, who stood in their places behind the seated Wu-Pen. They may not have understood English, but they watched everything Matt and Truet did like hawks. "It wasn't an accident, Wu-Pen. It was another murder."

Wu-Pen's eyes widened, just a touch in surprise. "I hope you don't think it was my people or me."

Matt sighed. "It's circumstantially looking like it. I can't prove anything right now, but if anything happens to the third man the courts failed to convict, Oscar Belding, I will come back here and make an arrest. And if any of your people try to stop me, I will shoot them," Matt said, darting quick glances at the two guards to make a point.

A quick flash of hostility flickered in Wu-Pen's facial expression. And then he smiled calmly. "Marshal Bannister, we are friends, yes?"

Matt eyed him carefully. "I'd like to be."

"Yes, me too. I will tell you that we are not involved in any murders. We have killed no one. If I recall from our last talk, it was spiders and now smoke that has killed those men. My people and I have nothing to do with that. Though I wish I could be more sympathetic, I cannot. They hurt my people. Karma has taken her revenge. Yes?"

Matt met his eyes evenly. "I said Roger died in a house fire, not by smoke. But in fact, he did die by smoke inhalation, you're right. And then someone poured a bottle of whiskey down his throat and put the bottle in his hand before starting the fire. That doesn't sound like karma to me; it sounds like a very un-American way to kill someone. Again, it's just not what people around here do."

"Matt, I assure you we are innocent of any crimes."

Matt stared at the table, considering if he should continue or not. He bit his bottom lip and spoke, "I'm going to guess Roger was tied to a chair, gagged and helpless while someone broke the stove pipe and let the smoke fill the room until he was dead. Maybe even threw in some of his oily clothes or something else to increase the smoke toxicity, and later went in and put him to bed and poured the whiskey down his throat. Am I about right?" Matt put up his hands to stop him from answering. "That's my guess. Who did it? I can't say yet, but I will warn you right now, if anything happens to Oscar, I'll know exactly where to come. They killed two of your men; I think you killed two of those men. End it there. If I'm wrong, forgive me. But from where I'm standing, it looks like you and those two men behind you are guilty to me. As I said, I can't prove it right now. But if it is you, end it now," Matt said pointedly with his eyes burning into Wu-Pen.

It took a moment for Wu-Pen to form his friendly smile. "I do not know who is doing that, but if it is any Chinese, I will make it known to stop now or face Chinese penalties. I will work with you on this, yes?"

"No. Just end it here." Matt stood up. "Listen, Wu-Pen, I don't want any trouble, and there's already a whole community out there suspecting something. Roger thought it was you, and so do others. I don't want any more Americans or Chinese killed. So, if it is you, stop it and if it's not, find out who it is and make them stop. Are we in agreement?"

Wu-Pen smiled as he stood up. "I just said I would work with you, yes? I did. It will end. But so that you know, my men and I are innocent of their blood."

"I hope you have nothing to do with this Wu-Pen because I like you and your men. I respect all of you. But right now, I do think it was you and your men. Yes."

"No...not us. Thank you for stopping by Marshal Bannister and Mister Truet. It's always a pleasure visiting with you."

When Matt and Truet left, Uang Yang asked in Chinese, "Is Everything acceptable, Uncle?"

Wu-Pen hesitated to calm a flame of anger that passed through him. He then pulled out the set of keys to Matt's house and stared at them quietly.

Bing Jue asked, "Do you want him dead too?"

Wu-Pen shook his head. "No. The Marshal is very smart. He knows we did it and how. We could kill him now, but let's see what happens when Oscar Belding is dead. We will wait a month, but his family must not be harmed. They've done us no harm. Then, the Marshal will die too if he causes us any trouble."

29

Sylvia Ballenger had been told by Sheriff Wright early that morning that Martin's court hearing would be at ten o'clock that morning. She left work and went to the courthouse to be at his preliminary hearing. Henry Redlin was most supportive of her leaving work to be there for her son, but he stayed at the butcher shop to keep it open and fill an order from one of the restaurants in town.

It was evident that Sylvia had been crying when she entered the shop and stared at Henry behind the counter with quivering tight lips.

He frowned noticeably. "What's wrong?" he asked while walking around the counter quickly to give Sylvia a supportive hug.

"He pleaded not guilty, but they're not letting him come home." She began crying and wrapped her arms around Henry. He held her affectionately and let her cry on his shoulder. She pulled away from him and wiped her tears. "Martin said he was sorry, and the Judge said he didn't believe him. The Judge wouldn't let Martin come home. He set the bail up so high I can't afford to get Martin out of jail. He needs to come home; he's hurt." She looked at Henry curiously. "Henry, I hate to ask, but do you have a hundred dollars I could borrow to get him out?"

He answered, "Ten percent of that is ten dollars, that's not so bad to get him out of jail. But you know, I'm of the mindset of if someone breaks the law, then they should pay the consequences of their actions. Martin seems to have an excuse for everything he did, and it's not adding up."

"Like what?" she asked, sounding defensive.

"Like hitting Christine and another lady in the face. Like putting a gun to a woman's head. If he was afraid of Dave, then why wouldn't he point the gun at Dave instead of trying to take that young lady out of there by force? It makes no sense, Sylvia. I think he needs to stay in jail to cool down after what he did to you and Barbra too. But if you want to, we can pay the bond to get him out. It isn't going to break us to pay ten dollars."

She smiled slightly with gratefulness and hugged him again. "Thank you, Henry. I know he's been a bit angry lately, but that woman just keeps playing hot and cold with him and then to lie to him as she did. He was confused, and it got to him. By the way, it's not ten dollars. It'll take a hundred dollars to get him out. That judge put his bail at one thousand dollars. Can you believe that? It's disgraceful! I don't even know how I'm going to pay my rent next week, and he set the bail that high? How could I possibly ever get him out?"

Henry frowned with a furrowed brow. "Sylvia, I thought you said it was a hundred-dollar bail?"

"I did. That's what it's going to cost to get Martin out of jail."

"When's his trial?"

"In two weeks. He already told the judge he wasn't guilty, and it was a misunderstanding. He apologized for everything and promised to behave. And that judge still wouldn't let him come home."

Henry grimaced hesitantly. "Sylvia, I'd help you in any way I could, because you're important to me, but I'm not going to pay a hundred dollars to get him out of jail when I really don't think he deserves to be."

She gasped as her jaw dropped in surprise. "You said you would."

"When I thought it was ten dollars, yes. I was willing to pay that even though I don't think he deserves to be out of jail. But I'm not paying a hundred dollars."

Sylvia rolled her eyes in frustration. "What am I supposed to do then?"

He put a hand on her shoulder. "Sylvia, you're an amazing lady, but Martin's a grown man and has been for a long time. He's not a child, and you need to stop treating him like one. You need to quit rescuing him and let him sink or swim."

She brushed his massive paw off her shoulder. "He's my son," she spoke angrily. "I can't just let him sit in jail. What do you expect me to do, Henry? Let him go to prison?"

He spoke sincerely with a soft voice. "Sweetheart, there's nothing you can do. Martin's choices put him there, and if he goes to prison, it'll be his actions that put him there too. There's not a darn thing you can do about that. I am sorry you have to go through this, but it's Martin's own doing."

Moisture gathered in her eyes as she bit her lip brewing in hostility. She shouted, "And you probably think he deserved to have Matt break his nose too, don't you? You probably think it's okay that two men held him there for your Marshal friend to hit him, don't you?"

Henry shook his head. "That's Martin's version of the story. I heard another, and Martin wasn't being held."

"Martin's a lot smaller than the Marshal! He didn't have any right to hit him that hard!"

"Sylvia," Henry said, growing frustrated. "Martin hit Matt's lady. It wasn't an accident, as Martin said. I would've hit Martin too if your face was covered in blood because he hit you. That's what men do; men don't hit women! No, I don't blame Matt for hitting him. You're son's lying, and I'm not going to reward him for it. He can stay in jail where he belongs. I have no empathy for woman beaters, and that's what your son is."

"He could go to prison! Doesn't that matter to you?" she asked sharply while glaring at him.

Henry nodded slowly. "Yeah, he could." He wanted to add, 'and he should,' but decided against it. "But bailing him out isn't going to change that one bit. That's for the court to decide and if he does, it's by his own doing. There is no one else to blame but himself."

She was agitated. She glared at him for a moment

longer and then turned towards the counter. "Well, I have work to do, and so do you. If you wouldn't mind leaving me alone for a while, please," she sounded like she was going to cry.

Henry watched her compassionately. "I do not mean to upset you, but it's just how I feel about it."

"It's fine."

"No, it's not fine. It's a horrible and tragic thing."

She glanced at him irritably. "Henry. It's fine! I'm just upset right now."

His lips opened as he breathed through them. "Are we still good?" he asked anxiously.

She nodded. "Yes, we are fine."

He smiled and stepped forward to hug her. "I'm sorry, Sylvia. I'm sorry about the whole situation."

When he went into the back to cut the meat for his orders, Sylvia said she needed to use the privy out back and went into Henry's house next door instead. She knew Henry didn't trust banks fully and split his earnings each week between his bank and a tin box in his bedroom. Sylvia had never been in his bedroom, but she found his room, and the tin box was under his bed. She opened up the tin box where he kept his money and counted out one-hundred dollars and stuffed the paper bills into her pocket, and left his house.

An hour later, she leaned on the door jamb and watched him for a moment as he sliced up some rib-eye steaks. "Henry, I just to say I'm sorry. I probably shouldn't have even asked you for that kind of money. I want you to know there are no hard feelings."

He gave her a soft smile. "I'm glad to hear that. I want you to know you can ask me anything and I'll do what I can to help you."

She lowered her head sadly. "I know. I'm going to lunch, Henry. I need to go walk around and do some thinking, praying and just calm down."

He nodded. "Okay. I'll see you after lunch then." He paused as she stared down at the floor. "Are you all right?"

She nodded sadly. "Yeah. I'll be back later."

30

"Edith, let's walk down to the Monarch Restaurant and have lunch, shall we?" Bella had asked.

The question sent a chill down Edith's spine. Bella had never asked her or anyone else to have lunch at a restaurant by themselves before. She knew her time at the dance hall was limited by her pregnancy, but after yesterday's terrorizing ordeal of Martin's coming inside and hurting Christine and Helen, Edith was scared this was her last day to have a home in the dance hall. They were three ladies short the previous night, with Christine's nose swollen, Helen's fattened and split lip, and the traumatic state that Edith was in as well. It had been a tough night, and Edith hadn't slept well. The inconvenience Martin caused Bella and Dave, had cost the dance hall financially with lost dances and lost drinks. Bella usually never complained about missing a night or two of work when someone was sick, but nothing like what had happened had ever taken place before.

Edith dressed warmly to endure the cold walk to the Monarch Hotel and went downstairs to face the music, whatever it would be. She expected the worst. She found Bella talking with her husband, Dave, at one of the tables near the bar.

"Bella, I'm ready to go anytime you are," Edith said anxiously. She added quickly, "But if you're taking me to lunch to tell me you're letting me go and I need to leave, you can do that here. I can start packing and talk to Paul this afternoon about moving in with him."

Bella watched her compassionately. She smiled warmly as she stood up to hug Edith. "Sweetheart, no." She wrapped her arms around her. She continued as she pulled away from her, "We're not letting you go or asking you to move out. After yesterday I'm just glad to have you with us still and wanted to ask you to join me for lunch just to talk and make sure you're okay in there." She touched Edith's head with her finger.

"Oh," Edith gasped with relief. "I thought you were going to ask me to leave."

"No," Bella laughed. "Let me grab my coat, and we'll leave. It's going to be a bit of a walk though, because I want to go to the Second Street Market to pick up a little something, I got you. They're engraving it for me, but it should be done by now."

Edith took a deep breath. "What if we run into Martin? Should Dave or Phil come with us, just in case?" Her anxiety about running into him on the street was high.

Bella smiled comfortingly. "I told you I went

to his preliminary hearing this morning and that puke is never getting out until he serves prison time. Judge Jacoby set his bail so high no one is going to pay for his bond. He's in jail, sweetheart. You have nothing to fear."

Edith nodded. "Good."

Sheriff Tim Wright unlocked the jail cell and pulled open the door. "Martin, you're a free man for now."

Martin smiled slightly from the pain in his nose. It was far more sore now than it was the night before. Both of his eyes were swollen and black as well. "For now? I'll be free from here on out. Once the jury understands it was self-defense, I'll be let go. Thank you, Mother," he said, turning to her with as much of a smile as he could bear.

Tim closed the cell door. "I have a paper for you sign understanding you have a court date and promising to be there. If you're not, Matt will come looking for you, and I won't try to stop him."

"He'll be there," Sylvia said shortly. "My son has nothing to run from."

"We'll see what the jury says about that," Tim replied shortly in reply. "Come, sign this, Martin."

Martin went to Tim's desk and signed the promissory note. He glanced up, and out of the window, he saw Bella and Edith walking up Main Street. Martin froze and was overcome with temptation to run after them. He wanted to talk some sense into Edith and tell her he loved her.

"You're free to go," Tim said unhappily, not noticing the women walking across the street.

Martin paused. "Am I going to get my job back? I didn't do anything wrong."

Tim sat down behind his desk. "No. I'm pretty laid back and let a lot of stuff go, but I saw what you did to the girls, and I won't allow any of my deputies to act like that. I'm not giving you your job back, and the draw you took out, we'll consider that your pay. Now you're free to go."

"What draw?" Sylvia asked heatedly.

Tim answered, "Martin took a ten-dollar draw out the other day. That equals half a month's pay, and you've only been hired for two weeks. We're even."

Sylvia glared at her son. "Where's the money, Martin? We have rent to pay next week, and we need more food. How much do you have left?"

He shook his head. "None."

"Where it go?" she shouted.

"This shirt the Marshal ripped and these pants. The rest went to the dance hall."

Sylvia exhaled forcefully. "You told me the Sheriff bought you those clothes as part of your uniform!"

Tim shook his head with disgust. "No, Ma'am. All these lies are going to come up in court, Martin."

Martin grew aggravated. "My gun belt." He pointed at his gun belt, sitting on a shelf near the sheriff's desk.

Tim tossed it to him. "Goodbye," he hinted.

"Nice working for you. You're making a mistake letting me go. I'm the best deputy you have!"

Tim nodded. "You deliver mail well."

"Yeah, and you can kiss that dinner with Rose goodbye. When you see Edith and me having dinner, you think about what you could have had," Martin spoke heatedly.

Tim laughed lightly. "Get out of my office."

Outside, he scanned up Main Street and saw the two ladies two blocks down the street. "Mother, I have to go find a job so I can pay our rent. Thank you for getting me out."

"You'll have to pay Henry back too. We need money, Martin, but you need to heal up before you can work."

"I haven't got time, Mother. I heard the stamp mills hiring, so I'm going to inquire about that. I love you, and thank you," he said hurriedly, already stepping away from Sylvia.

"Oh, okay. I must get back to work anyway. I love you too, Son."

Martin walked south on Main Street while Sylvia walked North. Martin followed Bella and Edith at a distance and watched as the two women went into the Monarch Hotel. His chest was filling with the pressure of a growing animosity. Martin's thoughts wouldn't leave him as he wondered if Edith was going to the hotel with Bella to meet a high paying customer. He stood on the corner until he was too cold to wait outside any longer. Martin went into a store and pretended to be looking at various items as he watched the hotel door through the window. It seemed to be taking an eternity. He observed the clock on the wall and knew it had been over an hour when they finally came out of the hotel. Edith was looking at a necklace that was around her neck as they left the hotel. She seemed delighted with it. Martin snarled and left the store in a hurry as he walked purposely across the street towards them.

He shouted angrily at Bella when he got close enough behind them, "What did you do, whore her out?" His eyes burned into Bella.

She and Edith both spun around petrified to see Martin coming at them viciously. They didn't have time to respond as Martin pushed Bella as hard as he could, and she flew backward down onto the boardwalk, she hit her head as she landed. Bella held her head painfully with both hands. Martin began kicking her in the stomach and ribs repeatedly while shouting, "Leave her alone, you old hag! She's my woman now. You don't own her!"

Edith was horrified. She watched in terror until she came to her sense and stepped in and pulled on the back of Martin's coat, trying to pull him away from Bella.

Martin spun around with a wildness in his eyes and slapped Edith across the face as hard as he could. "Don't touch me!" he screamed. "Now come on, you're coming with me! I'm tired of you playing these games!" He grabbed her wrist and began to pull her towards the street.

She tried to jerk her hand away, but his grasp was too firm. "Martin, stop! I'm not going with you! Stop!" she screamed.

"What?" he shouted in her face as he turned back towards her. His expression was wild, and his fist was clenched and ready to strike. "You're coming with me, Edith! We're going to have that baby taken out of you, and then we're leaving town. So, let's go!"

Fear had taken over, and Edith began sobbing over her high pitched desperate words, "I'm not going anywhere with you!" She was terrified and strenuously tried to pull away from him. "Help!" she cried out loudly. "Someone help me!"

He turned and slapped her again with a stinging right. He drew close to her face and threatened in a lowered voice so no one on the street could hear, "You're causing a scene! Stop it! You're coming with me, or I'll kill you! You don't have a choice. You're my woman, and I won't let you go! Now come along, or you're going to get somebody killed. Look around. You're causing a scene, don't piss me off, Edith! I'm warning you. Now come on."

"You're scaring me," she began to sob loudly.

He screamed, "We're just going to talk, okay? I'm not going to hurt you!"

"Yes, you are! It's my baby," she sobbed.

His eyes narrowed demonically. "It's not our baby! It's coming out if I have to cut it out of there myself. Do you hear me?" he raised his voice.

"No," she whimpered while sobbing. "Let me go!" she yelled. "Help! Jesus, help me!"

Martin's fear of being confronted on the street was realized when he heard a grave voice order loudly, "Let her go, right now!"

Martin glanced up and seen the long curly blonde-haired security guard from the Monarch Hotel, William Fasana, stepping quickly towards him. William's coat was tucked behind his two revolvers and appeared unfriendly at best as he stepped near. Martin was tempted to draw his gun and threaten William, but Martin knew if he did, he would be killed just that quickly. He was about to release Edith's wrist when Edith rammed the palm of her hand, forcefully into his already broken nose. The pain was severe, and he let go and stumbled out into the street and dropped down to his knees as he cried out in pain. He was able to glance up to see her running up the boardwalk towards the Marshal's Office through his watering eyes. It took all the control he had not to draw his revolver and shoot her in the back; if William Fasana wasn't there, Martin would've.

Martin could hear William laughing at him while he helped Bella up. She was telling William to restrain Martin. Upon hearing those words, Martin began to run. He ran block after block without looking back. He had no idea if William chased after him or not. Martin ran into the east side of town and collapsed down behind a private privy behind someone's home. He tried to catch his breath and wept from the throbbing pain of his nose being broken again. He could feel the blood running down his face under the bandages. He couldn't breathe well through his nose, so he breathed through his mouth. He knew both the Sheriff and the Marshal, and their deputies would be looking for him for hurting Bella and trying to talk to Edith again. He couldn't go back to the doctor to get his nose fixed again or to his home, because he was sure to be found at either one. His options were few, but then he had a thought and got back to his feet and made his way to the Sheriff Tim Wright's house. Martin went around to the back door that was never locked, and he went inside, knowing Tim wouldn't be home. In the two weeks that Martin had known him, Tim had never come home until the day was over. Martin welcomed himself to grab a clean cloth and washed the blood off his face with a pitcher of water. He sat down and ate the last piece of pie left in a pie box and had a drink or two of a half-full bottle of whiskey of good quality. Martin grabbed the blankets and pillow off Tim's bed and went back out the back door and climbed under Tim's back porch and curled up on the ground with the blankets and pillow. The covered sides of the porch kept the cold breeze at bay, and with the wool blankets, pillow and bottle of whiskey, he was finally able to warm up a bit.

It hurt to lay his head down, but he laid there trying to relax. Edith had hit him where it hurt the most, and it wasn't his nose. She was refusing him, rejecting him, and carrying another man's baby. He had planned to get rid of the other man's baby and replace it with his own. They could've lived happily ever after as a family. It was the perfect plan and the right thing to do. He loved her, and she loved him too. He knew she did. They belonged together.

31

Christine stomped in the frozen snow in a straight line for about a hundred feet and then made a sharp right turn and stomped for another hundred feet and made a sharp right and repeated to create a large square in the snow. She never explained what she was doing; she only told Matt to wait and stay where he was.

"What are you doing?" Matt called out with a joy-filled smile. He loved seeing her playing in the snow with childlike excitement.

"Shhh." She traced her tracks around the square and held her long dress up and leaped into the square and began to carefully stomp heel to toe in the snow in carefully planned steps. She needed to focus on where to place her feet next. Patience was a virtue that Matt was just going to have to learn. She needed to concentrate.

Matt was watching from a distance because he wasn't supposed to come in any closer until she called him over. It was clear she was writing something in the snow with her careful steps and leaps from one letter to the next, but he couldn't tell what she was writing in the fresh snow. Christine had asked him to take her back up to the top of the hill north of town, where she could see the view of the valley and mountains again since it had snowed overnight. She had dressed to be warm and was in high spirits as she stomped something in the snow. She held her dress up near the top of her boots so the hem wouldn't touch the fresh snow and smear her labors. Finally, she hopped, leaped, and carefully worked her way out of her large square and walked over to him with a face that shined with excitement and happiness.

"Close your eyes," she said with elevated breathing.

"Close my eyes?" Matt asked, looking at her adoringly in her knitted hat, fur-lined ear muffs, and a knitted scarf wrapped around her neck.

"Yep," she said with a wide grin and a sparkle in her eyes.

Matt closed his eyes. She grabbed his hand and led him quickly towards where she had created something. She stopped him and continued forward without him. "Okay, open your eyes."

Matt opened his eyes and saw Christine standing in the middle of the square with her arms extended out to her sides. She had stomped in the snow the words; I love U. And under it were the words, Our home.

She explained quickly, "This is where I want our house. Please let me invite you inside. The front door will be right here, with a big deck that goes all around the house. Big windows facing South and North, the kitchen will be over here, a family room here." She moved around the square, leaping into the words written in the snow. "A den over here, and stairs that go upstairs where the bedrooms are. Three of them, because I want to have children with you. A lot of them. We'll need a big house. And I want a deck outside of our bedroom." She paused to take a breath. "This is where I want our house, and I know how I want it. I haven't stopped thinking about it since you brought me up here for that picnic. What do you think?"

He laughed lightly and stared at her with a grin. "I think it's a beautiful plan. A lot of children, though?"

She looked at him with her light-hearted smile. "Do you see those words that say I love you? I'm not a seventeen-year-old girl with an infatuation. I love you, Matthew Bannister. I want to spend the rest of my life with you, and this is my dream home. But even if it never happens, and we have to live in a shack somewhere, I'll still want to spend my life with you, and I'll still want to have as many children as God will bless us with. I know you love children, so I don't think you'd mind that, either."

A strange warmth moistened Matt's eyes. He was overcome with an emotion he wasn't expecting. He couldn't identify it immediately, overwhelmed with a sense of acceptance, perhaps. Gratitude, hopefulness, adoration, and love, maybe it was a mix of them all that filled his chest with warmth and excitement. All he knew was that he was happy.

She smiled slightly. "Your eyes are watering."

He shook his head emotionally. "No one's ever said that to me before."

She leaped her way out of the square and stepped over to him and put her arms on his shoulders. "I'm blessed no one has, because they wouldn't have meant it as much as I do. I love you, Matt." She kissed him. "Now, can you imagine having a passel of children living up here at this time of year? We could get a big sled and go sledding down that hill and hope we don't die," she laughed joking about the steepness of the hill.

He laughed and looked around from the hilltop. The view was magnificent, as always, no matter what season of the year it was. "What kind of a house? A big log cabin or one like Lee's?"

She shook her head. "I've never been to Lee's house. I don't even know where he lives, so I have no idea what kind of house he has."

Matt answered, "Oh, he has a big Victorian home. His place pretty much takes up a city block with the yard, carriage house, and stuff like that."

She wrinkled her nose. "No, our home doesn't have to be fancy, just big enough to raise a family and for us grow old in."

He watched her fondly as she gazed out at the snow-covered mountains in awe."It sounds wonderful. Not to change the subject, but speaking of family, I got a telegraph from Aunt Mary, and she wants to know if you're coming to the Christmas dinner this year?"

She turned to him with her eyebrows raised with doubt. "Matt, what if she doesn't like me?"

He laughed. "She likes you already. You have nothing to worry about."

"Then, of course, I'll go. I do look forward to meeting her and your Uncle Charlie."

"Good. I'll let Aunt Mary know that you're coming. You'll love my family, and they'll love you too."

She spoke with a touch of sadness in her eyes, "You know I was an only child, and so was my mother, so I don't have any family anymore. I always wanted to be a part of a big family, so you have no idea what it would mean to me if we were married, and your family accepted me as one of their own. It's something I've always wanted, but have never known."

"Once you're in, you're in for good. Trust me; once you get out there to the ranch, you won't even want to talk to me because they'll keep you entertained."

She smiled. "I'm looking forward to it," she said and noticed Matt staring at her. "What?"

He took a deep breath and exhaled. "I was just thinking about the first time I ever saw you, and how you took my breath away. I just want you to know you still do. You always will."

She smiled. "I love you, Matt. And I always will."

32

Sylvia Ballenger was working at the front counter of Redlin Meats when Deputy Marshal's Jed Clark and Nate Robertson walked into the butcher shop.

"Hello, Gentlemen, can I help you?" she asked with a friendly smile.

Jed wasn't smiling. "Ma'am, are you Sylvia Ballenger?"

"I am." She continued with concern showing on her face. "Why? Is something wrong?"

Jed nodded slowly. "Yeah, have you seen your son? We're looking for him."

"For what?" she asked loudly as her mother's heart for her son began to race with panic.

Jed watched her without an ounce of emotion in his eyes. "Assaulting two women on the street."

"What!" she gasped. "Who? There must be a mistake."

"I'm afraid not, Ma'am. He attacked them without cause, and there were plenty of witnesses to confess to that. Do you know where he is?"

Henry walked in from the back of the store, drying his hands on his apron. "Gentlemen, hello. Martin's in the city jail. He's been there since yesterday."

Nate Robertson offered, "Not anymore. He assaulted two women in front of the Monarch Hotel about an hour ago. We went by Missis Ballenger's place and searched her house, your daughter let us in," he explained. "And now we're here. You folks haven't seen Martin?"

"No," Henry said with a confused expression. "I thought he was in jail."

"Not anymore. Martin was bailed out by Miss is Ballenger shortly before he assaulted the women."

"What?" Henry asked in a raised voice. He gave a harsh look at Sylvia.

Sylvia asked the deputies quickly, "Who did he assault?"

Nate answered, "Bella, I don't know her last name, but the owner of Bella's Dance Hall and the same lady he tried taking yesterday, Miss Edith Williams. She got away by punching him in the nose."

"Oh, my gosh," she gasped, knowing how bad it must've hurt him. "Is he okay?"

Jed answered with a scowl, "We don't know. We can't find him."

Nate added, "William Fasana came out of the hotel and scared Martin away. Edith came to our office, screaming for help. She was terrified. Martin threatened to kill her this time, and we're not taking any chances. So, we need to find him."

Sylvia began crying. She threw a towel down on

the counter and covered her face with her hands. She stared up at the two lawmen, "What did she say to him to make him do that?"

Jed shook his head slowly. "Nothing. She wanted nothing to do with him, and that's why. There were plenty of witnesses that agreed to that. We went by the sheriff's, and his men are looking for him too. If you see your son, you might want to tell him he'll be safer if he turns himself in right away. William said it appeared to him like Martin thought about pulling his gun. He's lucky he didn't, or we'd be here to tell you Martin was dead. William's not a man to test your speed or willingness with a gun."

Henry's eyes hardened, revealing his anger, but he waited patiently for the two men to leave. When they did, he turned to Sylvia and spoke calmly, "Sylvia, did you bail him out of jail?"

She nodded as she wept bitterly and picked up the towel to cover her face.

"Did you?" he asked pointedly.

She turned towards Henry answered through her tears, "I had to. I know you said no, but Henry, he's my son. What was I supposed to do, leave him there in jail in pain? I couldn't do it." She covered her face back up and wept.

His eyes narrowed a touch angrier. "Where'd you get the money to do so?"

She refused to answer and kept her face covered.

"Sylvia, where did you get the money?" he asked softly.

Her head lowered. "From you."

"I never gave you any money. So, you stole money from me?" Henry asked, breathing a bit heavier through his opened lips.

She nodded quickly with her hands holding the rag over her face. She closed her eyes tightly, and her shoulders began to jerk as she sobbed.

Henry took a deep breath and exhaled slowly. He spoke softly, "Sylvia, I'm very disappointed. I wanted to trust you and believe we could have an honest relationship. You stole from me even after I explained why I wasn't willing to pay that. Is that how it's always going to be?"

She was taken off guard by his soft and calm voice. It wasn't what she was expecting, and it took her a moment to look at him. She was surprised that he was so calm. "Aren't you mad?" she asked, lowering the rag.

He nodded. "I am. But I'm more disappointed. I was hoping we were on an honest path with each other and not one of deceit. I had made myself pretty clear, I thought. It wasn't about the money, and it wasn't because I didn't want to help you. It was because I thought Martin needed to stay in jail, and now he's hurt someone else. He's got something going on in him that's making him dangerous. That's why I said no. I'm not mad about the money; I've got plenty. It's the point of it. You went against my wishes and stole my money to do so." He appeared heartbroken.

She could see his disappointment. She'd rather be hit with a raging fist than to ever see that expression of disappointment because of her, on his face again. Her voice trembled with emotion, "Henry, I'm sorry. I knew it was wrong, and I shouldn't have, but I was desperate to help my son. He's my son, I love him, Henry. And I'm scared of what's going to happen to him. I was afraid he was going to prison, and I wanted to spend time with my son before he went. I never imagined he'd get in trouble again. I don't know what he's doing." Another tear slid down her cheek as she couldn't control her tears any longer.

Henry put his big arms around her and held her. He spoke softly, "Sylvia, I said I have attentions of marrying you, and I do, but don't do that again, please. I want to trust you, and if I can't, then I won't marry you."

She looked into his eyes. "I swear, I'll never do anything like that again."

He smiled softly. "Alright. Maybe we should close the shop and go look for your boy before the deputies find him."

"What about the restaurant orders?"

"I can finish those tonight. Let's go find Martin and take him back to the Sheriff's Office."

She peered at him awkwardly. "Why are you so nice to me?"

"I'm nice to everyone, but I'm falling in love with you. Let's close up and go find your boy."

33

Christine Knapp took Edith by the hand and led her down the hallway to Helen Monroe's room, which was on the north side of the dance hall's second story.

"What are we doing?" Edith asked with a short laugh. The ordeal with Martin on Main Street had scared her a great deal, but extra precautions were being arranged to assure she would be kept safe until Martin was found and put back in jail. Phil Mears was guarding the door, and Dave was nearby with a revolver in a shoulder holster as well. Sheriff Tim Wright had promised to keep his best deputy Bob Ewing in the dance hall until Martin was back in custody. Matt vowed to stay in the dance hall as well during their working hours and a few hours afterward to visit with Christine. The extra protection lifted her spirits and helped to settle her anxiety knowing they all would be watching out for her. She feared Martin, and she feared for her baby, but she was reassured that there was no way he would be coming into the dance hall tonight, and she would not be unprotected until Martin was back in jail. Matt and Tim both assigned a deputy to stay all night at the dance hall after Matt, and Bob Ewing went home to quiet her fears.

"I want to show you where we're going to have dinners and get-togethers in the years ahead." Christine knocked on Helen's door and went inside uninvited when Helen opened it.

"Hi," Helen said as they passed by her to go look out her window. "What's outside?"

Christine opened her curtain and pointed out over the town to a hill in the distance. She glanced back at Helen with an excited grin. "Do you girls see that hill way out there? Matt and I are going to build a house on top of that hill someday. And we three will all get together there for dinners and parties. I already told Matt I wanted a big house with a wrap-around porch, and that's what we're going to do. So that, ladies, is where I'll be living." She grinned at her two friends. "We're all engaged now. Can you believe it?"

Edith smiled and shook her hands with excitement. "Did Matt ask you to marry him?" she shouted expectedly.

Helen's eyes widened as she grabbed Christine's arm. "Did he?"

"No, but we're courting, right?"

Helen exhaled heavily. "He didn't ask you?"

"No. But he will when he's ready. But I told Matt I wanted a house up there big enough to raise a passel of children..."

"And he ran away?" Helen asked quickly.

She frowned at Helen skeptically. "No, he got teary-eyed and agreed to build it for me someday."

"How sweet!" Edith said sincerely. "I'm so happy for you, Christine. I'm happy for all three of us. Who knew when we moved over here that we would find such gentlemen to marry us within a year of being here? I know Paul and I have had some issues, but it's all good now. He's excited about the baby, and I am too, actually."

Helen smiled slowly. "Me too. It's going to be a different world when none of us are dancing anymore and become housewives. We'll be living here in town with our sawmill husbands, and Christine will be living in a mansion on the hill."

"No," Christine spoke, "I already told Matt I don't care what the house looks like, it just has to be big enough to raise a family. Matt's not particularly wealthy, and even if he was, I doubt he'd act like it or want to show it. He won't have a mansion, just a house. The view is what I love from up there. It's amazing!"

Edith spoke, "I bet! Life will be different, though. Have either of you wondered what you're going to do with all your dresses? I doubt any of us will need to dress as we do here to cook meals, wash our husband's dirty laundry, and chase the baby around. We'll just be housewives day after day."

Christine laughed slightly. "We have danced for going on four years together, and all we've ever wanted was to find a man we could love and be loved by and get married. And now that you have, you make the future sound so unexciting."

Edith grinned. "I don't mean to, but I'm going to miss this place. I'm going to miss having our own rooms and those midnight talks in the hallway, and the fun and excitement of living in the dance hall." She shrugged. "Dancing is our life, but we may never dance again once we leave here. I have to leave here because I'm having a baby, but I'm going to miss the life we've all known. I'm going to miss you two the most, though."

Helen shook her head. "No, you won't because we'll be over all the time."

Christine smiled sadly. "I know what you mean. I wasn't at all excited about dancing when I started, but it's become my life, and I'll miss it too. But you know, Edith, it's just a season in life. Season's change, and we must move on. None of us can do this forever. We'll all age and lose our appeal to younger men and lose our job eventually. We have become good friends, and I'm thankful for that. The Lord couldn't have put me in a better place when Richard died, nor given me better friends to remain friends with for the rest of our lives. And we're all going to live right here in town. We'll always have each other now."

"That's right," Helen agreed. "And you know what that means, right? It means when you two leave the dance hall, Rose will become the top lady, and what does that say about the dance hall?"

Christine shook her head. "No, I think Angela will. She has a quieter spirit, and that is an important quality that will be hard for the men to resist. Rose is loud and crude, Angela is like a dove. That's going to put her far above Rose in popularity and pay."

Edith shrugged. "I think you're both wrong. I think Meredith will be the one stealing hearts when we're all gone."

"She certainly could," Christine agreed. "Anyway, I'm going to take a bath and get ready for tonight. I want to feel clean when I dance with my love tonight."

34

Darkness came upon Branson, and Martin slid out from under Tim's porch and wrapped a blanket around his head and shoulders before leaving Tim's back yard. It was cold and threatening to snow more with clouds overhead and a few flakes falling slowly. But aside from trying to stay warm with the blanket, he wanted to keep his face hidden from view. He knew he was going back to jail and wouldn't be getting out until he served his time. It was a conspiracy against him, and now he was sure Bella would press charges against him too for pushing her down. He hadn't even pushed her that hard, she tripped over her own feet and fell. And Edith, acted like she didn't even know him, and hit him in the nose. His nose still throbbed. She had no right to hurt him the way she had, not just physically, but his heart was in despair, and he was desperate just to make her see that he was the one for her. They could raise a family, and his life would be complete and fulfilled as would hers, because he would make sure of it.

He walked down to the dance hall and stood outside of it. He knew the dancing hadn't started yet, because it was still early, and the girls didn't come downstairs for another fifteen minutes or so. A line of men walked through the open door and hung up their coats, hats, and guns if they had them. He was hoping to sneak in and find Edith, but he could see Phil standing just inside the door. There was no way Phil would allow him inside. Martin's teeth clenched, and his eyes hardened when he saw Sam Troyer and Paul Johnson walk up the few stairs to enter the dance hall. He watched as Paul pulled his coat off and stepped to the right to hang it on a hook and then stepped back into view to shake Phil's hand and chit chat for a moment. Martin stepped back into the shadows between two buildings and pulled the blanket over the white bandage covering his nose and head. He didn't want to be spotted by anyone. He watched Paul move to the bottom of the stairs, Phil guarded.

Paul hesitated at the bottom of the stairs and hollered up them, "Hey, beautiful, I'm here. I'll be at the bar." He then moved into the dance hall.

Martin could feel his heart pounding with outrage, and he wanted to beat Paul senseless. Shortly the band began to play, and Martin found himself walking towards the door like a cobra swaying to the sound of music. He watched Rose and a young lady named Meredith descend the stairs looking beautiful as ever in their colorful dresses. They stepped down the stairs side by side, as they always did when the dancers entered the ballroom where the men would get their first look at the ladies. Angela and Ruth came down the stairs next, followed by June and Sally Mae; by the time they reached the bottom of the stairs, the next two were stepping down the top steps to keep the pace consistent. Catherine and Mary followed them, then Susan and Jenny, Loretta and Bonnie, Lisa and Heather, Claire and Nancy all came downstairs. Martin was beginning to wonder if Edith was working tonight. And then he saw Edith walking down the stairs with Hannah.

Martin knew he was unwelcome, and Phil was in his way of getting to Edith. Martin didn't think about it; he simply drew his revolver and rushed up the steps. He aimed at the back of Phil's head and pulled the trigger. The percussion sounded, and Phil dropped to the floor dead.

He made eye contact with Edith near the bottom of the stairs. She stopped and stared in sudden terror and pushed Hannah forward, causing her to fall to the floor off the stairs. The look of horror in her eyes infuriated Martin all the more. The thought of another man's baby in her belly sent a fire through him that he couldn't control. He had been led to believe she would be his lady, and all along, she knew another man's baby grew inside of her. "You whore!" he yelled and raised his revolver and pulled the trigger. The bullet ripped into her stomach. She hit the wall behind her in horror and grabbed her belly. She stared up at Martin in shock.

"My baby," she said softly with a tear slipped out of her eyes.

271

Martin aiming, fired again, the bullet drove into her chest. She fell three steps down to the floor and rolled to her back, trying to breathe while staring at him. She shook her head with a desperate pleading in her eyes as a tear slid out and rolled down her face. Martin ignored the chaos that erupting around him and pulled the hammer back, and aiming at her head, pulled the trigger.

What seemed to have taken minutes, had taken seconds. At the top of the stairs, Christine screamed and came quickly down the stairs crying out for Edith. Martin heard the voice of Matt Bannister telling someone to get the hell out of his way as he fought through the crowd of men who stood like hypnotized sheep standing in the ballroom doorway, shocked and dumbfounded. Bob Ewing as well, was heard cursing men for not getting out of his way. To stop Matt from getting to him, Martin swung his revolver and quickly aimed at Christine and pulled the trigger. The bullet hit Christine in the gut. She grabbed her stomach and tumbled the rest of the way down the stairs landing on the floor near the body of Edith.

Martin glanced at the men who stood like wide-eyed sheep and yelled, "Don't move!" He saw Matt appear shoving a man down to get past him. Martin didn't say another word; he ran out of the building and up the street as fast he could.

Matt burst through the wall of men that had crowded the ballroom doorway by the stairs. He saw Christine lying on the floor in a pool of blood and dropped to his knees beside her. His anguish was visible on his face when he saw that she had been gut shot. "Oh, Lord, no," he said in a petrified voice as he helped her out of the growing pool of blood that was mostly, Edith's. He sat her up on the second stair and ran his hand over her back and found no trace of the blood of an exit wound.

Paul Johnson and Sam Troyer pushed a couple of men out of their way and got to the body of Edith. Edith was already gone, and Paul knelt in the pool of blood and picked up her head into his arms and began to cry out in agony.

"Matt," Christine said softly as in a trance, "I got shot."

Matt's body jerked as tears flooded his eyes thickly. He couldn't speak for a moment as chaos and screaming began erupting all around him. Matt glanced at Sam Troyer, who stood there, staring at the three-shot bodies in shock. Matt pointed at the door and yelled at Sam, "Sam, follow him!" he demanded. Sam hesitated only for a moment for the words to sink in and then ran outside.

Matt seemed to come alive as well as he stood up and grabbed the first young man that he could catch. Matt yanked the young man close, speaking into his face above the screaming and crying of Bella and the other ladies and the chaos in the dance hall. "Go tell Doctor Ambrose I'm bringing Christine to his office right now. Tell him he better hurry! Go now!" he threw the man towards the door.

"Matt!" Bob Ewing shouted above the crying, "We need to go get Martin! These guys can take care of Christine."

Matt glared at him, infuriated by the statement. "She's my priority! Martin can wait, Christine can't! If you don't find him, I will later. Go get him, Bob!" Matt waved towards the door. Bob nodded and ran outside.

Matt kneeled and scooped Christine up in his arms and screamed for people to get out of his way as he carried her outside. Matt's eyes filled with water, and it was hard for him to see as he walked briskly while carrying her in his arms. His lips tightened together, and his chest surged with contractions that he forced away, trying to control himself. She put her arms around his neck to hang on as they left the chaos of the dance hall.

"Who's carrying Edith?" Christine asked in shock.

Matt clenched his jaw tightly and blinked to get control of the hot tears that burned his eyes. "Paul. She's in good hands, my love. You just stay with me, okay? Do you hear me, Christine, you just relax and stay with me. Don't you die on me!"

She smiled slightly. "He killed Phil. Is Edith alive?"

He knew well by the placing of the shots Edith wasn't. But he debated if he should be completely honest as she was in danger herself. "I don't know," he lied.

She closed her eyes as a tear slipped out and ran down her face. "It hurts, Matt. It hurts so much." The pain of the bullet's damage was beginning to be felt now that the initial shock was over.

Matt's bottom lip quivered as he fought from allowing the tears to fall. His voice shook despite his fight to control his body, "I know. You have to bear it until we get to the doctor's okay? I can't put you down, and I can't stop. Because if I do, I'm going to..." he stopped talking as his emotions were taking over. Breaking down and sobbing like a little girl was only moments away. The woman he loved had been shot in the gut, and he knew all too well how fatal those kinds of wounds were. He was carrying a dead woman, and that was all he could think of at the moment. He had to try, though. He had to get her to the doctor and pray that he could save her. "You're going to be okay, Christine. You're going to have to be because if you give up, I don't know what I'd do without you," he said with a cracking voice. He squeezed his lips tightly as he walked. He had seven blocks of walking to do, and it seemed to be taking forever even though he walked as fast as he could. "Don't you die in my arms."

She watched the anguish revealed on his face. "Matt."

"What hon?" he asked, focusing on the board-walk in front of him.

"Matt," she said, wanting him to look at her. When he did, she could see his worry, and it was tearing him up like the gunshot to her gut had her. "If I die, you'll live." She smiled slightly. "And I want you to live well."

He shook his head as a determined tear slipped out of his flooded eyes. "How about you don't die, and we'll be fine, okay?" he clenched his jaw tight-ly. "We have a house to build with a wrap-around porch that we can dance on around the whole house without stopping. A house big enough to raise our children in and a hill to slide down. A house where we can watch our first baby take its first steps, and laugh together." He stopped to catch his breath and stared at her with tears streaming down his face. His lips twitched uncontrollably. "Christine, you can't give me dreams to strive for and then take them away. You can't do that; you can't do that to me." He began walking again.

She touched his face softly as her tears slipped out of her eyes. The love she had for him showed in her eyes. "Matt, I love you. But we both know I'm in the lord's hands."

He had two sudden bursts of short and painful jerks of his chest as he fought from sobbing. His breathing was quick and labored. "You're going to be fine." His voice was higher pitched than she'd ever it heard before.

"He shot me to stop you," she said softly.

Matt's brows furrowed downward, not understanding. "What?"

"He heard you coming, so he shot me. I saw his face. I knew it was coming." Her breathing was becoming labored.

Matt walked as fast as he could. There were horses he could have borrowed to get her to the doctor's office quicker, but not knowing where the bullet was inside of her or how much damage it caused made him wary of putting her on a horse. If the bullet was lodged against her spine or vital organ, it could cause far more damage if there was any jarring to her body. Matt chose to carry her to keep her body as still and comfortable as he could. "I'm sorry," he said, biting his lip.

"I love you," she nearly whispered. She grimaced in pain.

"I know," he said with determination to get her to the doctor's office. "I love you, Christine."

Through her grimaces and labored breathing, she said, "Tell your aunt that I won't make it to Christmas dinner after all."

Matt nearly smiled and nearly wept at the same time. "She'll understand." His chest convulsed again as a new wave of moisture rolled through his eyes like an ocean current.

The noise in the streets became louder as the news of the shooting alarmed the town of something tragic that had happened. People came outside trying to figure out what was going on and why there was so much noise coming from Rose Street.

He glanced at Christine; she was staring straight up with a peaceful expression on her face. "We don't have much further to go, so hang on."

"They're beautiful," she said softly.

"What is?" he asked, quickly alarmed by the statement.

"The snowflakes." She was staring straight up as snowflakes fell in the streetlamp lights.

Matt sighed with relief that she wasn't talking about seeing Angels at the moment. He stepped in front of the Doctor's Office. There was no light inside, and the door was locked. Matt grimaced and kicked the door open ferociously. She cried out in pain as it jolted her body, and she began crying as he carried her inside and took her back to the doctor's procedure room and laid her carefully on the table.

"Where's the doctor!" he shouted angrily. "I'm sorry, Christine. I didn't mean for that to hurt you." He couldn't control the tears that fell down his face as he searched for a lantern. "Where's a lantern?" he shouted, feeling the fear and pressure of his lady dying. He was angry that the doctor wasn't there.

Christine pointed with one hand while holding her stomach with the other. "There," she whispered.

Matt grabbed the lantern and turned up the gas with shaking hands. He set it down and looked at Christine. Her pain-filled eyes maintained a sense of calm, and it soothed him for a second.

"I'm cold," she said with shivering lips. It was the first time he had even considered how cold she might be having been carried that far without a coat on. Matt grabbed two blankets out of a cabinet and covered her to warm her up. He sat on the edge of the table and held her hand lovingly. There were snowflakes still in her hair. "You are beautiful," he said softly.

She stared at him affectionately and then reached up to touch his face. "It's okay."

He shook his head as the tears clouded his eyes and slipped out and down his face. "No, it's not. I can't lose you, Christine."

She grimaced in pain and said, "You'll always be my hero. Don't let the soot build up again. Keep that beautiful man I know soot-free." Her face twitched, and her lips tightened emotionally as a tear slid down the side of her face. "If I go to Heaven tonight, promise me you'll let me go without blaming yourself or God. Promise me you'll move on and live a good life."

Matt allowed his tears to fall freely. He shook his head. "No talking like that. We have a home to build...together," his voice was soft and weak.

"Promise me, Matt. I know how bad it is. I can see it in your face."

It felt like the oxygen had been sucked out of the room, and it became hard to breathe. He watched her, sorrowfully. "I promise I'll try."

She smiled slightly as a tear slipped out of her eyes. Matt wiped it away and kissed her softly on the lips. "We have too much for you live for, so no more talking like that."

"Okay," she said and stared into his eyes.

The voice of Bruce Ambrose was heard at the door, "It looks like Matt's here," he said as he came through the broken door. He walked into the procedure room and saw Matt sitting on the edge of the table beside Christine. "Tell me what happened," he said as he took off his coat and began preparing the room for the items he would need to look at Christine. He was followed in by Doctor Mitchell Ryland.

Matt explained as the two men removed the blanket and examined the entry wound and felt around her abdomen cavity, taking notice where she winced and cried out in pain.

Doctor Ryland spoke, "She's wearing a high-quality silk dress, that's good. The entry wound looks like a smaller caliber, most likely a .32, that's good. Hmm, entering in an upward angle, that's not good." He glanced at Bruce Ambrose. "We need to start operating now."

Doctor Ambrose spoke, "Matt, you're going to have to leave, and no one's allowed to bother us while we're in here tonight. Since the door's lock is broke, I need someone out there to guard this office. We need to begin surgery right now, and I can't predict how long it will take us or how successful we'll be. So you have a minute to say what you need to say, but we have to begin."

Matt could see Christine's eyes were more afraid than they were earlier, but even so, there was a strength and peace in her eyes. He squeezed his lips together tightly. "I have to go, but they know what they're doing. I'll be praying." He pointed a shaking finger at her while his abdominal muscles tightened in short spasms as he fought from sobbing. He knew it might be the last time he saw her alive. His eyes grew thick with water again. "I'll see you soon. I love you, Christine."

She smiled tightly. "I love you. Do me a favor."

He nodded. "Anything."

"Find Martin before he hurts someone else. He killed my friend, didn't he?"

Matt sighed sadly and nodded.

She closed her eyes. "Find him because I want to ask him why?"

"I'll find him. You know, I will. I'll be here when you wake up."

Doctor Ryland walked out of the room with Matt and closed the procedure door behind him. He appeared quite concerned. "Matt, I wanted to let you know, she has a severe wound. There's a lot of things that can be damaged in there, and a lot of things that can go wrong. You know how fatal these kinds of injuries can be. It depends on how much damage has been done, where that bullet is and if the injuries can be repaired or not. I can't promise you she'll survive the surgery, but the one thing I can promise you is Doctor Ambrose, and I will do our very best to save her."

"What about infection?" Matt asked. He knew gunshots often resulted in life-ending infections. He had just been notified that the Prairieville Sheriff, Chuck Dielschneider, had died of an infection from a bullet wound to his back."

Doctor Ryland shook his head. "We'll talk about that when it becomes a point of concern. Right now, we have surgery to do. Let's get through that first before we worry about anything else. I suggest you pray because that's the best thing you can do."

Matt walked out into the doctor's front waiting room and sat down in a chair and wept. He was a broken man.

35

Sam Troyer ran out of the dance hall and saw Martin running down Rose Street and took off after him as fast as he could. Matt had told him to follow Martin, but Sam wanted to catch Martin and hurt him for what he had done. He ran as fast as he could and was gaining on Martin, who was running out of steam it appeared, as his running was slowing down a bit.

As Martin was getting closer to the corner of the next block, Sam saw Joe and Ritchie Thorn walking around the corner with a few of their friends coming onto Rose Street. Sam yelled, "Stop him, Joe!"

Martin turned around slowing as he stepped backward and raised his revolver and pulled the trigger. His five-shot Remington clicked on an already spent cartridge. Cursing, Martin turned around to start running again but ran into the crook of a hard-swinging arm thrown by Joe Thorn. It connected squarely on Martin's nose, and he fell to the ground hitting the back of his head first on the frozen ground. He curled up in a ball and held his nose in severe pain. He began to cry out in pain.

Ritchie Thorn and his friends laughed. "Good hit, Joe!"

Joe smiled. "Yeah, it was! That looks like it hurts," Joe said, leaning over Martin with a proud grin. He watched Sam as he came to a running stop. "Sam, did this guy steal your drink or something? Why was he shooting at you?"

Sam kicked Martin in the back and then stomped on the side of his head. "No, he shot up the dance hall! Phil and two of the girls are dead!"

Joe's face went blank. "What?"

Sam kicked Martin again. He glanced at Joe severely. "You heard me. He killed two of the dancers and Phil! Just now!"

"What girls?" one of the men named Bobby Alper asked nervously.

"Edith and Christine!"

"What?" Bobby shouted. "He killed them?"

"Yes! Right now, he was running away."

"Hell no, let's get him back there!" Joe said, watching Bob Ewing jogging towards them.

Bobby Alper began kicking Martin, too, with a flurry of curses. The others started kicking him also.

Deputy Bob Ewing came to a running stop and bent over as he was out of breath. "Stop it!" he ordered as he stepped into the group of men and tossed down a pair of wrist shackles. "Put those on him, if you want to do something," he said and exhaled heavily.

Sam had the great pleasure of yanking Martin's arms behind his back and shackling his wrists as tight as he could get them. He stomped on the back of Martin's head, driving his face into the road. Martin began sobbing loudly from the excruciating pain of already broken and now deformed nose that was bleeding heavily again. A group of about fifty men walked hurriedly towards them, and others came out of the saloons wondering what was going on and then joined the others in a growing number of angry men loudly demanding justice for the shootings.

"Someone go get a rope!" One man cried out, and five or six men ran off in different directions.

"You're not taking him to jail!" one of the men in the lead shouted at Bob. The man appeared to be a lumberman who had wanted to dance. There were no other alternatives that would persuade them from their justice.

Bob yanked Martin up to his feet harshly. His hands were helplessly shackled behind his back. Bob looked at the bloody face of Martin. "Give me one good reason to save you."

Martin looked up at Bob, confused. He was trying to get his senses back after being kicked and stomped on multiple times. His nose ached severely, and now there was a large group of angry men shouting at him and each other. He was scared of the anger growing more hostile in the crowd of men. He had trouble hearing over the shouts and just wanted Bob to take him back to the doctor then to jail. He peered at Bob, seemingly incoherent. "What?"

Bob shook his head. "That's not a reason." He pushed Martin into the crowd of men. "Take him and do what you will."

The logger grabbed him and spun him around harshly, and then pushed him into the crowd of men. "Let's hang him! Find a rope!" the man yelled.

"Get a rope!"

"There's no trees!"

"Shoot him!"

"Let me hit him!" one man said and hit Martin in the face. Martin would've fallen if he wasn't being held up.

"He murdered a woman!"

"He murdered four women. He shot Bella!"

"What? Kill him!" A man said from the boardwalk.

"Gut him right here and now!"

"Find a tree!"

"They cut all the trees down!"

"Just cut his throat and be done with him!"

"Take him to jail."

"Shut up! He's not going to jail!"

"Where's the Marshal?"

"He killed the Marshal's woman!"

"Kill him!" The saloons, bordellos, Bella's Dance Hall, hotels, and other buildings emptied onto the street and joined the growing crowd that pushed, carried, and drug Martin towards a pending doom.

"I know, hang him from the balcony of the Shady Ben's Hotel!"

"No, the old oak on Seventh!"

"No," the logger yelled as he led Martin down Rose Street. "We're hanging him on the Rose Street headgate. Anyone have a rope yet?"

"Where?" someone asked.

"The headgate on Rose and Third Street. Hurry up and let everyone know. He's going to hang!"

"Willis went to get a rope. He'll be right there."

Martin was being pulled closer to his home, which was on Second and Dogwood Streets. The headgate to the Rose Street red-light district was on Third and Rose Streets, one block up and over from Martin's home. The first two blocks of Rose Street were homes, and a few small bunkhouses rented out like hotels for men who came to town for a weekend. The Rose Street headgate was made out of three logs, two standing upright twenty feet tall, and a log running over the road and secured onto the two supporting logs. A Sign hung by a short chain on both sides that read, 'Rose Street – Gentlemen welcome.'

Martin saw the headgate and wanted to run home to the safety of his mother. "I gotta go home," he said frightenedly. "I have to go see my mother. Please," he begged.

A fist connected to his already bloody face. "You're going up by your neck, that's the only place you're going!"

"This is what happens when you shoot women!" another voice exclaimed unmercifully.

"Where's that rope?"

"It's coming!"

"Willis has the rope!"

"Tie a noose!"

Sylvia Ballenger had been told of the crowd of men bringing Martin to the headgate by a neighbor and ran as fast as she could the short distance. She could hear the anger and wrath of the crowd, but it didn't hinder her efforts to save her son. She ran into the group that was circling Martin. She arrived just as they threw the noose up and over the log running over the street. She cried out desperately, "Let him go! You can't do this to my son! Please, take him to jail."

She was pushed backward by one of the men, and she fell onto the street. She climbed back up to her feet as she heard Martin's voice.

"Mother! Oh, lord, please. Mother! Don't let them do this. Please..." Martin began to cry out desperately.

"Martin! I'm here!" she answered with her eyes on her son. She shouted louder, "I'm here, Martin!" She peered around quickly and saw Deputy Bob Ewing standing just outside of the circle of men watching with a slight smile. She ran to him in desperation. "Please, make them stop! Please, take him to jail. You can't let them do this! Please," she pleaded.

Bob shrugged uncaringly. "I'm outnumbered. I can't do anything."

They put the noose around his neck and tightened it.

"Mother! Help me. Stop! Lord, help me!" Martin yelled desperately.

"Stop it! Let my son go!" Sylvia cried out as only a mother could as she tried to run through the men to save her son. She reached out to grab Martin and barely touched his shirt. "I'm here, baby," she said. An unknown man grabbed her and pulled her out of the group of men; he threw her face down in the street like a bag of trash.

A gunshot drew everyone's attention as Deputy Marshal Jed Clark fired in the air. He yelled, "Let him go! I'm telling you all right now, get that noose off him, or I'll hold you all here until the Marshal arrives. And you can try to explain this to him!"

"This man killed Matt's woman! He isn't going to care!"

Jed was unmoved. "You heard me, let him go!"

Sylvia ran to Jed, thanking him with a stream of tears pouring out of her eyes. She was joined by Barbra, who was pleading for the men to spare Martin's life as well.

One of the men in the crowd circled behind Jed and rammed the stock of his rifle into the back of Jed's head. Jed collapsed, and the man struck Jed again to knock him unconscious.

Sylvia screamed.

The man holding the rifle shouted, "String him up!"

"Mother!" Martin cried out in terror.

"Martin," Sylvia cried out as she fell to her knees, reaching out to him. She wailed loudly as Martin was lifted into the air one foot after the other until he was hanging ten feet in the air. The men tied the rope to a wagon's wheel. Sylvia couldn't stand to watch Martin struggle and wrapped her arms around Barbra as they both wailed in horror while the large crowd of men laughed and congratulated themselves on a job well done.

Behind the crowd of men, a teary-eyed Bella stood with a satisfied sneer as she watched Martin's struggling come to a cease.

"Let him hang there for a few days as a warning to any other would-be women killers." One of the men said.

Fifteen minutes later, Matt Bannister walked down Rose Street and stared at Martin hanging motionless with his hands secured by shackles behind his back. There was still a large crowd of men watching Martin and inquiring about a photographer to take their picture. Some made a bonfire in the street for more lighting and warmth to continue to celebrate with. The men all quieted when Matt stepped in front of them and looked up at Martin with a dangerous sneer on his lips. There was a part of him that wanted to kill Martin himself, but he could hear the heart-shattering cries of Sylvia and her daughter Barbra. He took a deep breath and fought the tears that wanted to flow again. Matt lowered his head and shook it slowly in disgust. He breathed through his mouth to gain control of his emotions.

"Someone shut those women up!" one of the men snapped, trying to be respectful of Matt's mourning his woman.

A man walked over towards Sylvia and Barbra with nothing but aggression on his face. Matt pointed at him, "Leave them be," Matt said to the man with hardened eyes. He went to Sylvia and Barbra and knelt with them. "Let's get you home, Sylvia."

She gazed up at him helplessly. "Where were

you? You could have saved him," she began sobbing. "They hung my son."

Matt took a deep breath and put his arms around her as she held him sobbing into his shoulder. "I'm sorry."

One of the men in the crowd said, "That's what happens when you raise a woman killer! Good riddance!"

Matt glanced over to see who said it. "You!" he shouted with a pointed finger. "Say another word, I dare you!" he waited for a moment. "I thought not." He turned his attention back to Sylvia. "Let's get you and Barbra home. It's not going to do you any good to stay here." He helped her to stand. "Barbra," he said and hugged her. She wept loudly in his arms.

He saw at his deputy Jed Clark standing up from being knocked out for a bit. He was holding the back of his head where a good-sized cut bled heavily. "What happened to you?"

"Someone hit me when I tried to stop this."

Matt walked over to Deputy Bob Ewing, who held a small bottle of liquor. "Who hit my friend?"

"Sorry to hear about your woman, Matt," he said in reply.

"Who hit my friend?" he demanded louder.

"I don't know," Bob said. "It was all a bit chaotic, you know?" Others in the crowd shrugged their shoulders and refused to say who hit Jed.

Matt turned his attention back to Jed. "Jed, I know you're hurt, but will you walk over and let Henry Redlin know what happened so he can be with Sylvia and Barbra, please? I don't want them left alone. I'm going to walk them home."

Sylvia whimpered, "Why? Why did they do this to my son? What did he do, Matt? Please, don't let them leave him there all night. Please!" she begged as Matt helped her stand.

Matt answered softly, "They'll take him down right now, and I promise you that. Let's get you home."

Matt looked around and sighed. "Bob, this isn't good. Get him down before I get back. I want him taken him to the funeral parlor and not set up somewhere around town to look at."

Matt held Sylvia upright as he walked her home. Once inside, she sat down in her chair and wiped her eyes dry. "What did he do?" she asked, not understanding why a bunch of men hung Martin. "Who did he kill?"

Matt pulled a kitchen chair in front of Sylvia and Barbra, who sat in the two cushioned chairs. Matt's eyes watered as he spoke softly, "Martin shot a killed Phil Mears who was the security guard at the dance hall. He shot and killed Edith Williams with three bullets, and he shot Christine." He took a breath. "She's alive at the moment. The doctor has her in surgery right now, but it's a gutshot. She may not survive," he said sadly. "That's why they hung him like that."

"Why would he do that?" Sylvia gasped, overwhelmed by the horror she just heard.

Matt shrugged. "I don't know. I was there; he just started shooting."

"You didn't stop him?" she asked with a grimace.

Matt raised his eyebrows. "No, I couldn't. He'd be lying dead in the dance hall if I could've. I'm sorry for your loss, I really am, but Martin destroyed more lives than his own tonight." Matt wanted to say more. He wanted to say Martin would have been hung anyway, but he resisted. "I need to go, but Henry will be here soon. My condolences to you both."

"You would've shot my son?" she asked, sounding surprised.

Matt nodded. "If I could've stopped him, I would have. I wish I was out front and not in the ballroom. I might've been able to save all of their lives if I had been."

36

It had been hours, and Matt waited in the doctor's office for any news of how the surgery was going. The medical room door opened, and Doctor Bruce Ambrose walked out to the kitchen area of his office and washed the blood off his hands in a bucket of water. He was exhausted and dried his hands on a towel, before pouring himself a cup of coffee and sitting down with Matt.

"How is she?" Matt asked. He was drinking a cup of coffee himself.

Doctor Ambrose shook his head. "Not good. The bullet did a lot of damage inside of her. We had to remove one ovary already, which is beyond my expertise, Matt. Doctor Ryland is trying to repair some intestinal damage right now. The bullet was successfully removed, but the damage like I said was extensive." He spoke to Matt empathetically. "If she survives the night, there is still a risk of infection, and I don't need to tell you how dangerous that is. Doctor Ryland's a gifted surgeon with years of practice, but we're working in my office and not a big city hospital like he's used to. I don't have a lot of things he uses or needs. So imagine, trying to frame a bed without a hammer. That's what it's like in there. Matt. I don't want to lie to you; it doesn't look good. I don't want to say it's unlikely she'll live through this, but you might want to prepare yourself for the worse. She could recover, but it's a very slippery slope on a slim chance."

Matt closed his eyes for a moment and then stared at his friend. "But she could, Bruce?"

"There's a possibility, yeah. If Christine was in his surgical room back in Boston, the chances would be a lot better. He's the expert, and he's doing his best, which is beyond my capabilities. Even with Mitchell's skill and knowledge, her chances of survival and going without an infection somewhere in there are slim. It wasn't a straight forward shot, Matt. The bullet entered Christine from a downward angle and went across her abdominal cavity. As I told you, we had to remove one of her ovaries, and there is intestinal damage that Mitchell's trying to repair now. I wish I had better news for you." He paused and then added, "I have to get some coffee and get back in there. We should be done in another hour or two."

Matt felt numb as he walked out into the cold. It was three in the morning, but the snow on the ground and falling out of the sky made it much lighter and quieter than usual. He walked through the street down to the livery stable and saddled his horse and rode out of town. He rode five miles out of town to the large hill and then up it's side to the top. He dismounted and walked over to where he could see the large square Christine had made that day outlining their future home. In the heart of the outline of their future home were the words she had stomped into the snow, I love U and under that the words, Our home.

Matt stepped into the square and sighed emotionally. He scanned the horizons from the top of the hill and could make out the mountain ranges all covered in snow. Even at three in the morning, the view was spectacular and dead silent as well. He knelt to his knees in the snow and stared upward at the gray clouds that sputtered fresh snow downwards.

"Father, I ask your forgiveness for my sins. I try to do what's right, but I still fail. This community's hurting tonight in so many ways. I don't know if Phil believed in you or not, but I hope so. I know Edith did, and I hope she's with you in Heaven. And Martin, Lord, there's so much death today. I don't know where any of them stood with you, but I hope they all accepted you as their savior at some point. I hope they're all in Heaven with you. I pray that you'll bring healing and peace to the hearts of Sylvia and Barbra. And to the ladies and all the people at the dance hall.

"What I do know, Lord, is if Christine doesn't survive this, she will be with you. And I'm very grateful for that. Jesus, I haven't always been the perfect Christian, and as I said, I fail you every day. But I am up here tonight to ask you to spare

Christine. I ask you to put your blessing upon the surgeon's hands and let his work help mend my friend. I'm scared." His abdominal muscles clenched tightly as his eyes filled with tears and emptied over his cheeks. "I'm afraid I'm going to lose the most important person in my life . Jesus, please don't call her home." He took a deep breath, "I've never been one to get too attached to anyone, but you brought her into my life, and she's changed it. She's changed me and become my best friend. I love her, Lord. Right now, she's laying on a table cut open and bleeding. There's so much going wrong, and I know you are already present and in control. I just ask that you'll spare her so we can enjoy the love we have and the life we would like to make together. So, we can dream and strive to create a home right up here. She made these tracks just today, Lord. Please don't take her from me. I'm asking you to touch her body and let her heal without any infections, and without anything coming undone inside of her. I don't know what all is hurt, but you do. She is your child, and Lord, I ask you to heal her. I pray that you'll hear this prayer and work on her behalf to bring her through this horrible time. Jesus, my Lord, I love her. Will you please spare her and bring her back to good health? All I can do is ask you and trust in your answer whether you save her or not. I will serve you no matter what happens. But Lord, I hope you'll save her, because I'm in love with her. In the powerful name of Jesus, I ask that you'll spare my friend and help her to heal. Amen."

Matt put his hands in her footprints and wept.

37

Christine opened her eyes and blinked a few times, trying to understand where she was. She was feeling lost in an unfamiliar room. A large covered window faintly lit it. It was a tall room with ten-foot ceilings, with bookshelves full of books lined the walls and a desk near the window. She turned her head and seen a single bed near hers separated by a small table with her Bible on it. There was another Bible near it, but there was nothing that explained where she was. Her abdomen hurt, and she wasn't feeling too well, but she was a bit disoriented and frightened, not knowing where she was.

The tall wooden door with fancy paneling opened casting in a ray of light, and she could hear the voices of a group of people in another room. A short, robust woman walked in. She had a round friendly face and appeared surprised to see Christine awake. The older woman had long black with some gray hair tied in a long braided ponytail. She came to Christine's side with a warm smile. "Hi, it's nice of you to join us. How are you feeling?" Her eyes shined with joy and sincere caring.

Christine frowned and licked her dry lips. "Okay." She peered at the woman strangely. It hurt a little to speak.

The older woman who appeared to be part Indian smiled comfortingly. "You're probably wondering where you are, huh? Maybe even wondering who I am, am I right?"

Christine nodded.

The woman smiled as she pulled a chair between the two beds and sat down. She grabbed Christine's hand and held it. "Well, since you refused to come over to my place for Christmas, the whole family came here to spend Christmas with you. I'm Aunt Mary." She explained when Christine seemed slow to understand. "Matt's Aunt Mary. It's nice to meet you finally, Christine."

Christine's eyes opened wider. "Oh. Matt's Aunt Mary. Hi," she said softly, staring at her awkwardly. "Where am I?"

Mary gave a gentle laugh. "You're at Lee and Regina's house. It was the only house large enough and quiet enough for you to rest. The doctor comes every day to check on you. It's also the only house big enough for the whole family to come here and have Christmas with you and Matt."

Christine furrowed her brow curiously. "Oh. Who's sleeping there, you?" she asked, motioning to the other bed.

Mary shook her head. "Matt. He hasn't left your side, Christine. I'm afraid that boy loves you."

Christine smiled slightly. "I love him. Is he here?"

"He had to leave momentarily. The doctor has kept you heavily drugged until today. Matt will be back soon, though. Would you like a drink of water?"

Christine nodded. "I'd love a drink of water, yes," she said softly. "How long have I been here?" she asked.

"A week. The doctor made sure you were heavily drugged to keep you from feeling the worst of the pain. And to keep you from moving around too much."

"I feel it," Christine said of her pain level.

"I'm sure you do. I came here as soon as I heard you had been shot. I have been praying at your side since they brought you here six days ago. Thankfully, it looks like the good Lord heard our prayers, and you're going to make it just fine. Are you still tired?"

Christine nodded and closed her heavy eyes and fell back to sleep.

When Christine woke up, Matt was sitting beside her holding her hand with a smile. He looked tired and worn down from worry, but relieved to see her open her eyes. The corners of her lips lifted when she realized he was holding her hand.

"Good morning, beautiful," he said.

"Morning. Is it morning?"

"No. It's about eight at night. But it's good to see awake again."

"Matt," she said with a frown. "What happened to Edith? Was she killed?"

Matt frowned. "She was."

Christine closed her eyes and started crying silently. "And Phil was, I remember. Anyone else?"

"No. No one else was hurt at all."

"Did you catch Martin?" She glanced at him firmly as a tear slipped down her cheek.

Matt frowned. "He was caught and hung by the men of the dance hall before I got back there. I didn't arrest any of them."

She moved her head to look forward again. Her voice was soft, "The doctor came in earlier today. He said he had to remove one of my ovaries and the other one's tilted a little bit. He said I might never be able to have children." Another tear fell down her cheek. "I won't be able to raise a bunch of children, after all."

Matt kissed her hand softly. "He told me. But it's a miracle to me that you're alive. And right now, that's all I care about."

She smiled sadly as she squeezed his hand. "I met your Aunt Mary. She's very nice."

"Since you couldn't go to the Big Z for Christmas, everyone came here. That was Aunt Mary's idea. She wanted to take care of you. This is the first time any Holiday has ever been anywhere except the Big Z Ranch. That makes you kind of special, I think. And there's a whole herd of family out there wanting to meet you. Aunt Mary won't let anyone come in here, though, not until you're feeling well enough to meet them all."

She smiled slightly. "I must look frightening and smell horrendous by now."

Matt chuckled slightly. "You look more beautiful than I've ever seen you look."

"You must be lying."

"No. This has been the longest week of my life, not knowing if you were going to survive or not. I didn't want to leave you, so I slept here. If there is anything this week has taught me, it's that I don't want to be without you again. I realized what you mean to me, and I want to spend the rest of my life with you. So," he paused and lifted her left hand and slid a ring onto her finger. It was a silver band with a diamond. "Christine, will you give me the honor of having you as my wife? Will you marry me?"

She stared at Matt with a dumbfounded expression. "Yes. I would love to." A tear fell down her cheek

He stood up and kissed her slowly. "You just made me a very happy man."

She smiled. "I'm a very happy girl."

"Would it be okay if I invited everyone in here and shared the news with them?"

"I look horrible, Matt, I have to look horrible."

He shook his head. "You are beautiful, my lady. If you don't want anyone in here, though, I understand. It can wait."

She shook her head. "No, if they came here for me, then bring them in. I better get to know them when I'm looking my worst anyway."

Matt stepped out of the room for a moment and then came back with a large group of people. Some she knew like Regina and Mellissa, others she didn't know from any other strangers on the street. Matt held her hand up in the air. "Everyone, this is Christine, and I want you all to know that... she said, 'yes.' We're getting married!"

"What? Oh my! Congratulations!" Aunt Mary exclaimed and hugged Christine lightly. "Welcome to the family, young lady!"

"Thank you," Christine said.

"Christine, this my husband, Charlie Ziegler."

Charlie shook her hand with a cheerful grin. "Glad to meet you, Christine. I'll hug you when you're up and moving around, how's that?"

"That's fine. I've heard a lot about you both. It's an honor to meet you."

Steven Bannister and his family stepped up to Christine's bedside to introduce themselves. When they had and shook her hand, Steven said, "Matt always told me he wanted his wife either barefoot in the kitchen or barefoot in bed, one or the other. I just didn't know it would start before he got married!" He grinned as Nora, his wife, slapped his shoulder and apologized to Christine. "I'm sorry. He's incorrigible. You just have to get used to him and his bad jokes."

Christine grimaced, trying not to laugh. "It's fine. I like him already."

William Fasana's laughter was loud as usual as he followed Steven's family. He bent over gently and kissed her softly on the forehead. "Welcome to the family, Christine. I always knew you two would get married. Get well."

"Thank you, William."

William grinned at Matt. "Now I can tell everyone I kissed Christine. And I'm going to every time someone mentions her name; I'm going to say 'Yeah, Matt's not the only one that's kissed her, I kissed her even after they were engaged.'"

"Great, start some rumors, William," Matt chuckled.

"Oh, I am!" he laughed loudly.

"Get out of the way," Annie said, pushing William aside. Annie shook her head as she peered down at Christine. "You know why he asked you to marry him here and now, don't you?"

Christine raised her eyebrows questionably. "Because he realized how much I meant to him," she answered though it sounded more like a question than a statement.

Annie grimaced. "No! It's because if you said no, he was going to tell you to get up out of that bed and walk your butt back home! Good thing you said yes!" She smiled and hugged her. "There's always room for a new sister! And I better be a bridesmaid, or the doctor's going to have to fix your eye. You hear me?" she threatened.

Christine held her abdomen and grimaced. "Don't make me laugh…" she winced.

Steven's jaw dropped dramatically as he looked at Annie. "I don't think she's scared of you yet. You're not going to be a bridesmaid."

Annie groaned. "I'll beat her up when she's feeling better. I'll be a bridesmaid, or I'll hit you in the eye too!"

Christine grinned as she watched Annie and Steven. She was quickly wrapped by the arms of one tearful Tiffany Foster, who wept bitterly. "I'm so thankful you're okay! We've been praying for you since we heard. That makes you my aunt, doesn't it?" she asked.

"I suppose it does, yes."

"I love you, Aunt Christine."

Christine smiled warmly as her eyes filled with moisture. "I love you too, Tiffany. When I get better, how about we go shopping again?"

"I'd love to."

Steven frowned. "Wait, I need to go shopping. I'll bring Tiffany into town."

Christine smiled warmly. "Matt told me you wanted to go shopping. When I'm healed, bring Tiffany, and we'll go."

Adam Bannister touched Steven's belly. "Nora's dresses aren't fitting you anymore, huh?" he laughed.

"I don't wear dresses! We're going shopping for... tools," Steven answered with an uncomfortable shrug. He had wanted to buy a dress for his wife, Nora, but it was supposed to be a secret.

Charlie Ziegler stood at the foot of Christine's bed with a smirk on his face as he glanced down and saw the bare foot of Christine's sticking out of the sheet.

Annie frowned curiously. "Uncle Charlie, what are you smirking about? What are you up to?"

He asked Lee. "Do you have any wood match sticks?"

Lee nodded. "Yeah, there should be some on the desk over there. Why?"

Charlie stepped over and grabbed two match sticks out of a bronze holder, and came back to the foot of the bed. He explained as he lowered a matchstick towards her foot, "The doctor said she needs to start moving around a bit, and she might be a little slow to start. So I figured I'd put a match stick between her toes and light it. We'll see how quick she starts moving then."

Christine's slight smile from Steven's terrible lying ability suddenly fell to a stern expression of concern.

Mary pointed at Charlie. "Charles, don't you dare do that to her!"

He laughed heartedly. "I'm just teasing."

Mary explained, "It might take some getting used to being around this family. There's a lot of terrible teasing and bad jokes, but you won't find a bigger bunch of loving people. I think you'll fit right in."

Adam Bannister introduced himself and his family to Christine, followed by Uncle Luther and Billy Jo Fasana. Darius and Rory Jackson, Mellissa Bannister, gave her an affectionate hug, as did Albert. Lee and Regina were the last ones to congratulate her.

"Thank you for letting me stay here," Christine said sincerely.

Lee nodded. "We wouldn't want it any other way. Welcome to the family, Christine."

Regina hugged her. "You're one of us now. And all of this is just part of your new family."

Christine watched Matt as he sat down beside her. "I've always wanted a big family."

Annie sputtered, "Oh, sister, you've got a family!" She turned to Rory Jackson, "She may not like us for long, but she has a new family now."

Rory nodded agreeably. "Right."

Aunt Mary chuckled. "Did Christine get to meet everyone here? Tomorrow there will be more here to introduce you too. We have a large family. Don't we, Matthew?"

Matt took Christine's hand in his and said softly,

"Yeah, now you have aunts, uncles, brothers, sisters, nephews, nieces, cousins, even a father-in-law, and stepmother over in Portland. We're going to need a big space for a wedding reception because there is going to be a lot of family there. And I fear you're going to drain our savings doing Christmas and Birthday shopping every year."

She looked around at the large family with a bunch of children she couldn't wait to get to know. She smiled, and then her face deformed as she fought the individual trail of tears that slowly raced down both sides of her cheeks unexpectedly.

"What's wrong, sweetie?" Mary asked with concern.

"I just want to thank you all for being here. I've never had siblings, aunts or uncles, cousins or anything. So thank you for being here and caring about me."

Charlie Ziegler spoke from the foot of her bed, "That's what we do; we're family."

"Thank you," she said. "You don't know how blessed you are to have a family." She wiped her eyes dry with an embarrassed smile.

Mary Fasana touched Christine's leg softly to get her attention. "Yes, we do. And so are you. We are your family now, Christine. Every one of us."

38

The Reverend Eli Painter had gone to the home of Sylvia Ballenger as soon as he heard what had happened on Rose Street. He sat with her and Barbra for most of the night, along with Henry Redlin. It was hard to offer any consolation under such horrific circumstances, but he let them know he cared about them, and he let them know the church would cover her rent and would be bringing them dinners for the next week. It was the least the church could do for one of their own new believers. He could think of nothing more unbearable than a parent having to witness what Sylvia had to endure. The sheer agony she felt would indeed shake her faith to the very core of her being, and it was important for her to know that the church stood with her and would support her. As surely as the seed of faith hits the ground, it is not surprising for trouble to come and try to steal the joys of salvation away. Jesus warned of it. As a Reverend, Eli Painter did his best to make sure the seeds of faith in Jesus, landed on good soil and took root and grew. It did no good to reach a new believer and then let them slip away with the troubles and tangles of the world or to be sprout quickly and wilt at the first sign of trouble. It did no good to let the seeds of hope remain isolated in the burning sun and wilt away because no one was there to water the roots. For Eli, as the shepherd of his flock, it was his duty to guide, rescue, and be there for his hurting congregation. Sylvia and Barbra were brand new Christians and would probably never face a harder moment in their lifetimes than the one they were facing when Martin committed such unspeakable crimes and was then strung up by cruel vigilantes in front of them. The Reverend would have liked to have seen his congregation flock around them in support. It was his prayer that they would.

But there had been a bit of discord after Martin Ballenger had murdered two individuals and shot the church's own Christine Knapp. Phil Mears had never been to the church, and few people knew him. Edith Williams had attended church occasionally and knew some people, including the Reverend. The murders themselves didn't cause the discord among the congregation. The issue was the presence of Martin's mother and sister being in the church. Sylvia Ballenger had missed two weeks of church mourning her son, who had not only been killed by vigilantes but also became the most hated name in the community. Being his mother, brought a lot of blame and pointed fingers, some even saying it was her fault for raising a murderer. Branson had turned on the Ballenger's, and even young Barbra was harassed on the street. Threats, harassment, and fear added to their time of mourning for Martin. Redlin Meats suffered in sales for a while as someone started a rumor that Sylvia was a witch and poisoning the meat to punish the city for their treatment of her son. However, when the church itself turned against them by refusing to acknowledge them and listening to horrible rumors, Reverend Painter stepped in and put a stern end to the nonsense. Martin's actions should have no bearing on his family or darken their reputation for one family member's offense, no matter how horrible it was.

Martin was responsible for his actions, not his mother or sister. It disgusted the Reverend how many people were quick to believe the nonsense and judge all too quickly the most innocent of people. The unimaginable heartache Sylvia and Barbra endured knowing what their loved one did without a reason was horrible enough. To lose him to half-drunk men beating and hanging him on the street without a fair trial was punishing enough. For Sylvia and Barbra to be ostracised, harassed, and blamed for Martin's actions, it was a nightmare. The blaming had to come to an end, and that's when the Reverend wrote an article for the local paper and addressed his church quite boldly about the subject. The gossip would not be tolerated anymore, and if anyone had an issue with the presence of Sylvia or Barbra, then those folks would be asked to leave the congregation. Sylvia and Barbra were both new believers in Jesus Christ, and they were being treated like lepers for no fault of their own by the church members. That was not the way Christians should treat anyone, including lepers. Gossip was a severe sin that could destroy people's lives, not just spiritually but physically as well. It would be interesting to know someday in heaven, just how many people ended their lives because of gossip in the church. After what happened recently, Reverend Painter supposed it would be a lot. He had gone to the Ballenger home and asked them to come back to church. As the shepherd of his flock, it was his obligation to go after the wandering sheep, and when the congregation began bullying weaker sheep, the shepherd must step in and correct the flock.

Today, Sylvia reemerged with her daughter and sat with Henry Redlin in the back pew. Sylvia appeared uncomfortable, but so far had not been ostracised by those in the congregation.

Near the front of the pews sat Christine Knapp. It was her first time back to church since she had been wounded by Martin three weeks before. She was still quite tender and moved slowly, but came to church with Matt Bannister. She was as beautiful as ever, but not quite back to her normal self yet. She read her Bible as always as she followed along in the service. It was good to see her moving around and trying to get back to normal.

For Reverend Painter, it was a little uncomfortable not knowing how Christine and Matt would react to Sylvia, or Sylvia would react to them. There was a cloud hanging over the church since the senseless murders, and despite the Reverend's best efforts to calm the waters, there was still a lingering threat of a brewing storm if the victim, Christine, couldn't accept Sylvia and Barbra in the church. There was no way the Reverend was going to ask Sylvia and Barbra to leave. They had done nothing wrong and were made victims of the aftermath as well.

Reverend Painter stood behind his podium and closed his Bible. "Before we leave today, I want to point out that Christine Knapp is back with us today." There was an applause. Glancing over, the Reverend saw Sylvia and Barbra were applauding softly.

He continued, "I want to let you know, Christine, that we have been praying for you since that night. And we are so grateful to our Heavenly Father for keeping you with us. We love to hear stories about miracle healings. They still happen today and will until the Lord comes back. But sometimes, the Lord does a miracle, and we don't see it right away. For those who don't know, Doctor Mitchell Ryland is a renowned surgeon in Boston, Massachusetts. He's one of the best in the nation, and he was here for one week before he was going to Portland to look for a house to buy. That one week, while he was here, was when Christine was shot in the stomach. The wounds were severe, and in our own Doctor Ambrose's words, he would not have been able to save her. Doctor Ryland worked on Christine all night and then kept her unconscious for almost a week to heal internally. The bullet was removed, her injuries repaired, and here she is today sitting with us. Praise God!"

He took a deep breath and added, "She would not have survived if God had not placed Doctor Ryland here for that one week. If he had come on any of the other fifty-one weeks of the year, she would have died. I call that the providence of God, or, in other words, the foresight of God working on Christine's behalf. Ours too, because she's our friend. God works all things for the good for those who love him. And through his providence is how he does it. Let us not ever overlook these miracles as well. Our God is awesome! And one last thing, Doctor Ryland is staying here! He's not moving to Portland. Now we have two great doctors in our city, and I am thrilled about that. Folks, welcome Mitchell Ryland to our community, and welcome Christine back. May the Lord bless you all this week."

Matt and Christine slowly made their way through the church. The congregation gathered around her to hug and welcome her back. As they left the building, they saw Henry Redlin, Sylvia, and Barbra Ballenger standing by themselves off to the side, waiting for them to step outside.

It was Sylvia who stepped forward to approach Christine. "Christine, I am so happy you recovered from this. I don't know what to say; I'm just sorry." Sylvia began crying and turned away shamefully.

"Sylvia," Christine called quickly and reached out for her shoulder. Sylvia appeared to have aged ten years in just a few weeks. When Sylvia turned back towards her, Christine continued, "Thank you. You know it's not your fault, and you have nothing to be sorry for. Friends?" she asked, extending her hand.

Sylvia couldn't quit weeping as she nodded and weakly shook Christine's hand.

Christine let her hand go and hugged Sylvia. Sylvia began to sob. "It's not your fault. I don't blame you. No one can blame you. You hold your head up, and I hope to see you and Barbra smiling again soon. Mourn for your son, but don't hide your face from me or anyone else. Stand strong and tall. You have every reason to."

Sylvia broke the hug slowly. "Thank you."

"Do you and your family want to have lunch with Matt and me this week?"

She nodded. A slight smile of gratitude came to her lips before she said, " I'd like that."

"Great, because Matt and I were just going to the Monarch Restaurant for some lunch. Why don't you, Henry and Barbra, join us? Our treat."

Sylvia smiled with a great sense of relief. "Henry, are you wanting to do that?"

He chuckled. "Sweetheart, look at me, do you think I got this big by turning away free meals? Of course, I want to go."

Matt smiled as he put his arm around Christine. "Then let's go get ourselves a table, my friends, and have some lunch."

Reverend Painter stood on the steps of his church, watching Christine and Sylvia. He smiled warmly and glanced upwards towards the gray cloudy sky. "Thank you, Jesus. I think we're going to be okay."

Take a look at
A Winding Trail to Justice by Reg Quist

AWARD WINNING AUTHOR OF THE MAC'S WAY INTRODUCES BOOK TWO OF A NEW WHOLESOME WESTERN SERIES!

Zac Trimbell has found himself in Las Vegas, New Mexico where a troubled lady, Claire Maddison, arrives at his ranch seeking help. Claire's sister and brother-in-law are missing, and all their cattle has been stolen. The sheriff advised Claire that if Zac can't help, no one can. Trig Mason pushes his way into the search and together the three set out to solve the mystery and return the cattle.

The sister and her husband are located wounded and weary. They are taken back to the ranch while Zac and the others look for the lost cattle. A long ride following the churned up, grassy trail takes them back to the gold country of Colorado.

While Zac continues to struggle with his post-Civil War PTSD, he makes it his mission to help where he is needed and see that justice is done.

Now it's time for the age-old question, "Is it still well with your soul?"

AVAILABLE NOW

About the Author

Ken Pratt and his wife, Cathy, have been married for 22 years and are blessed with five children and six grandchildren. They live on the Oregon Coast where they are raising the youngest of their children. Ken Pratt grew up in the small farming community of Dayton, Oregon.

Ken worked to make a living, but his passion has always been writing. Having a busy family, the only "free" time he had to write was late at night getting no more than five hours of sleep a night. He has penned several novels that are being published along with several children stories as well.

READ MORE ABOUT KEN PRATT AT
http://christiankindlenews.com

Made in United States
Orlando, FL
18 January 2022

13638177R00200